Frederick B. Hofman

The Trouble of Living Alone

A novel

Frederick B. Hofman

The Trouble of Living Alone
A novel

ISBN/EAN: 9783337045463

Printed in Europe, USA, Canada, Australia, Japan

Cover: Foto ©Andreas Hilbeck / pixelio.de

More available books at **www.hansebooks.com**

THE TROUBLE

OF

LIVING ALONE.

A Novel.

BY

F. B. HOFMAN.

All the deliciousness of the purer parts of my life comes back to me, when contemplating what is right.

BOSTON
ARENA PUBLISHING COMPANY
COPLEY SQUARE
1894

INTRODUCTION.

Up prance the mighty hordes
Of fears, pretensions, sections, callous creeds
And drivel wisdom
Set with selfish tears.
As rolls the mighty deep its roaring waves
O'er landscapes hidden from inquiring eyes
Down, deep, bedaggled, with such weighty gloom
False ideas rage submerging where the fair
Might range with pleasing air.
There reptiles grovel — so are cares infest!
Down, deep, there lurks suspicion, serpent-like,
And preys on hiding foes;
It lives not by its nourishment
But on its self-wrought woes!
Kind creatures, heed the lesson of the hour!
If glittering gold no human eyes perceive
And silver's shimmer be enwrapped in gloom
Would you be dazzled by the thought thereof?
Intrinsic value ranges with its creed —
Oft when the hour of need is sorely pressed
That merits solely that has not abscessed.
Then onwards falls the onslaught —
Amidst the din and terrors of the battle-cries
The tumult rising, swaying to and fro,
Anon a vantage, e'er the warfares' fates,
The blistering, torrid thought comes home,
"It is a war —

Would I were safe where cooling springs lave fevered
brow,
And arms of love entwine espoused their lord
And cooing words!"
No sigh that heaves such as the weary one,
Meet is for anguish, frenzy, brings despair;
List! hearkening soul,
The battle wages, hot!
At night the birdlings seek their tenored rest,
One flutter and a pipe ere they sink low —
Gloom brings them peace
Or such security as suits them best, the lift from care.

THE TROUBLE OF LIVING ALONE.

CHAPTER I.

BORN AND REARED.

I was born within the cheerful confines of the old Buckeye state, where I played, studied, dreamed and labored, until in early manhood a spirit of roving took me away from the serene hills and peaceful valleys of my native home, whose picturesqueness was thereafter to linger for me solely in my fondly indulged remembrance of its love.

Not altogether of a light nor for that matter either of a morose temperament, I possessed a spirit more turbulent and refractory than placid. I roved and wandered always — if not in fact, then with my fancies, and in the latter as well many real moments of delight were spent in localities where all the delicious luxury of color and sound rapt the senses in ecstasies of pleasure.

> I could portray joy's glorious peace,
> I could discover truth and rest;
> I could disport where pleased me best.

Some at least of the vagaries of my enterprising fancy were to be realized — some exceeded. These things need

not startle us, did we but employ our natural wisdom; in
their innovations on anything my mind had yet conceived
or knowledge comprehended, I realized how nature in the
appreciable constructions of the Great Creator excels our
conjectures, and proves, in the most homely way, that ourselves cannot contrive as well as has already been done for
us—ourselves only a part of the great structure.   I
learned, more and more, to have faith in the sublimity
of things; to apprehend, that in the bosom and in the
mind there might awaken in the plainest manner the
strongest confidence in and consciousness of a higher
Power and that Power through its consistent and persist-
ent invocation reduce the resistance to our earnest desires
to the smallest part.   Proceeding, in trepidation, it was
with anguish and fearful concern, that I attempted to
sound the depths, immeasurable, inscrutable; to grasp the
illimitable; to comprehend the indivisible; to plunge into
the darkness, with the pulsations of the heart almost
stilled by apprehension—only to be buoyed and guided,
in protection all the more grateful and colossal, in that
its succoring might contrived through a mysterious and
unforeknown force and influence—the simple potency of
faith.   Why should I contrive: casting upwards, for
power to survey the whole from off the commanding
heights, I need but trust, to find the elevating spirit to
give elucidation to my troubled brain.

> If inspiration comes unto the wicked's score
> And gilds his phantoms of a beauteous store,
> Because persistence merits its fair lore,
> Then may not *well* obtain the higher cause,
> As this receiving start where oth'r must pause
> And then soar upwards, by the same curt laws ?

CHAPTER II.

I START.

It was a glorious morning; the sun rose in all its splendor, and the outlook for my journey to be regarded as auspicious; on the other hand, there lay in this brightness and joyousness of nature not the least suggestion of tears or regret at my departure. Indeed, there was no one particularly interested in this event, at least to my knowledge; though what tender, maidenly heart may have pulsated, or lips slightly quivered upon reading of my departure in the morning paper, I shall never know. Suffice it to say, that the severance of my social and commercial relations with my native place was devoid of the usual pain of such partings. With a trifling incumbrance of baggage and a purse which held no inducement to indolence or reckless extravagance, I proceeded to the depot — but not without a little shade or gloom falling upon me as I in passing looked more closely at each familiar object. I was not quite as indifferent as I appeared, or as my cheery greetings or responses to the few astir at the early hour before the business-world had resumed its humdrum, tended to show. And if I passed through a street whose directness could not have recommended it to me (I had taken the precaution to start early) can you question the feeling that led me past the abode of one whose sweet innocent eyes were yet closed in slumber, the fair one, glorious in my imagination and to my eyes, utterly unconscious of me, unless, indeed, at such moments some angel may whisper in caressing dream, that the incense of

devotion is nigh?   Nor knows she, that one whose distant
admiration was the sole advance he dared—that, too,
without recompense from her, then and there silently
poured out the soft anguish of his sufferings; and if perhaps a subtle uneasiness caused her to start from her
repose, she will never indict for she knew me not,
unless her glorious eyes may have rested a moment on
mine, and the delicate fabric of her memory been
imprinted by the ardor of my gaze at that time.

Thus, my last devotion completed; and my memory
hastened back to other maidenly charms, whose possessors'
smiles I had unworthily enjoyed, with a touch of
regret. The trees, the shrubbery, the grass; the hills,
near and in the distance; the limpid stream, which
had often given me refreshment and sport; the church-
spires; the court-house, whose clock-bell was then pealing
the few strokes of the hour; the houses; at length to
them all *farewell.*

> I thought so callous and austere had grown my heart,
> That I could leave these scenes with ne'er a sigh,
> But, yet, my spirit-heart effulges to my eye.

I was perfectly agreed with myself to lean back in the
soft cushioned seat of the railway coach, to close my eyes,
to forget; to hear, see, comprehend nothing—nothing,
until away from those familiar scenes; and as, after
awhile, a drowsiness stole over me, the ensuing slumber
and consequent oblivion was an agreeable curtain to the
last hour.

CHAPTER III.

I BEGIN TO WANDER.

WHEN I again realized my surroundings, I was far enough from my boyhood haunts to become at once aroused, and interested in what met my view. Youth is not compatible with prolonged grief and channels, by which a succession of thoughts at that time of life may course, are even easily deviated by every new object in the way. Strangely enough to one inexperienced, the people who came in sight, as we passed, resembled so closely, in some or many features, well-known friends or acquaintances at home, that I was almost inclined to accost them with familiar greetings—and my close gaze directed to some was at times undoubtedly disconcerting to them.

The world becomes more circumscribed and the relationship between its inmates less diversified as one wanders farther and remains longer from home. These sensations are unique and peculiar to the traveler; and, after a certain distance, his whole native state is composed of "friends" and "relations." Anyone he may meet therefrom, and, subsequently, anyone from his whole native country becomes kindred to him.

Upon reaching the mountains, their acclivities and declivities at places on the two sides of the railroad presented a rather startling effect to the verdant mind in prime condition for the first impressions of the wonders of creation, art and science, as exhibited elsewhere. I wondered at habitations hung on bleak sides, or placed in lonely hollows; that beings like myself should exist and move there. Con-

jectured whether they felt just or similarly as I did or not.
I noted the girls and boys old enough to comprehend, perhaps dreaming of the day, when they too might break through this stillness and monotony into that strangely imagined world beyond — perhaps, too, thereafter, only some day to wander back to that peaceful shelter for a solace from that same glittering outside turmoil and tumult with its attendant shocks. I contemplated the silent majesty of those straight forest constituents whose multitude is yielding to the axman's strokes and prowess for man's fantastical and fanciful manipulations and pastime of this earthly career, perforce, to become a source and subject of quarrels, dissensions and wrangles more tangled than the brush, that impedes the ready view and way, and yet from an origin so plain and simple and not yet nor need be exhausted; the indigenous flowers, those bright little luminaries, that cheer the aching or wearily home-sick heart by recalling recollections of their little kindred at home; the wild rushing brooks, refreshing to the eye in the dust and smoke of the train.

On this mysterious propulsion bore us — perhaps to our imminent destruction, perhaps to pleasure — this presently united concourse never to be identically together again. The stops for refreshment and other incidents in the train-service varied the monotony; but to my eager, excited mind and alert feelings nothing had become irksome; every sight made its impression as yet, nothing seemed a repetition — a devotion to nature which, by the way, forms a marked element in my disposition! Passing what hours of night and repose intervened, to the latter of which a young, vigorous nature willingly accedes, there occurred nothing of note, to my knowledge, excepting the novelty of my situation.

> Shall this wild freak yet take me further on?
> Have I not trembled when perused ere late

Or at my father's knee the tale was told
Of wily tongues that could of fortunes prate
And sirens coyly such sweet bliss unfold?
How have I heard this is the cruel share
The wretch abandoned scarcely dares to prog,
While starving mites first weeting curse their lots;
And I had plenty on the fatted hog
And my demands were honored on the spots.
Then I was innocent and gay and free —
Although the fantasy of what is not
Distorted through my wild, conceited brain;
That life were joy where every trail is hot;
That in the tumult surely there be gain.
What fond, deluded wretch not, now grown sore,
Might whisper word to friv'lous youth, beware!
Might turn the tide, where well it were to stem,
Could that young blood esteem the wisdom there
Learned by hard fate enclosed by ripless hem.
Where well is meed it to thy pleasant part —
This life too short to stir the bitter dregs.
There still remain, by fortune's fickle throw,
Those who *must* strive (and this your pity begs)
All innate genius learns this lot to know.
For peace and joy reign where the mind is still
From whirls and wild, disturbed, weird desire,
A reach, a searching after things, which chill
When even found; thus any genius' fire
But must at length still smoulder to the fate
That naught of worldly can all blasts endure,
So much of toil that moves in any state
That glances oft seek furtively death's door.

How one would feel in walking in the air or on clouds,
I do not know; but when I stepped from the train at
Washington, I heeded not nor felt the ground, for my head
was in a whirl between apprehension and confusion. The
pushing, piling, rushing, crowding throng; the babel of
voices; escaping and puffing steam, and smoke; the cries
of hackmen and hotel-runners, certainly fulfilled my ideas

and desires of 'bustle and excitement—what country-boy
but has pictured to himself the importance he might attain
if he could only reach this plane of existence. Checking
my baggage I sallied forth with all the nonchalance I
could muster. To the invitations of hotel-runners I tried
very knowingly to shake my head, having predetermined
to reconnoiter before selecting my hostelry, and to base
my selection on what my observation and inquiry might
discover. I carry my ordinary quantity of shrewdness
about me with the purpose of putting it in use; and if I
could not entirely conceal my verdancy from experienced
eyes, I still hoped to convey a sufficient impression of solid-
ity to remain unmolested. Direction was of no immediate concern to me, nor time to prosecute it in, so that by
following the body of the crowd I could in no event go
much afoul. The buildings, private and public, began to
loom up, and the streets and cross-streets and their pedes-
trians and vehicles, to and fro, bent on some mission incidental to this jamboree of life, paraded themselves before
me. I soon began to look at everybody, which caused
everybody to survey me, and I presume our admiration was
mutual for I began to think a somewhat contemptuous look
the proper thing in a large city. Once or twice, true, some
insignificant bootblack or newsboy indulged in some
humorous remark or other, addressed to me, but, I regarded
such indifferently. I advanced without forcible opposition.

In due course and circuitous order I visited the notable
objects of interest, and found interest in many other
objects, and passed the massive residences, with their
outer show and inner speculation.

Resting on a seat on one occasion, in one of the shady
park-retreats, the quiet and freshness of the old Buckeye
farm with the flowers and purling brooks and sweet
repose of nature wafted themselves forcibly on my mem-

ory, as the incessancy of passers-by, men, women and children, hurried on the fretful courses, the look of peace nowhere portrayed. Was I impressed at the sight of the government great buildings? Of course; though, when I entered with awe, veneration and even superstitious dread the stately halls where wise men are supposed to assemble, and surveyed the statesmen, their attitudes and conduct, I lost some of my pristine aspirations. Soon I became absorbed in the architectural and designed intricacies of the building; and could not help ruminating on the expected modern perpetuation of the principles depicted in those noble and gorgeous historical paintings. And if the White House and its occupants became less the objects of my excitement, it was because of their mere humanity controlling and composing their existence, less appreciated at a distance, and by the ordinary, popular delusion in the instruments of government; it began to dawn upon me that to find anything removed from the frailties of these worldly affairs man's art and construction must not be sought, and that, after the physical and mental wants are supplied that enter naturally in due course into our regimen, the remainder — the gloss and glitter — may only more glaringly disclose weaknesses and can never apotheosize. I could conceive of a house, in the midst of acres of majestic forest presided over by the stately oak, brightened and refreshed by a capacious stream with a dashing cataract by way of variation, even in the loneliness and the fresh flowers and grasses, as a much more beautiful and inspiring situation than the White House presented, and the former's attendant pastimes be preferable. Yet, art has there done much to make tolerable the slavery of constrained existence, the loss of nature's glory of freedom; although, when trained to this life, it becomes unnaturally feasible, as stimulants may seem to revive a lost vitality.

And continuing with a reflection on the petulancies that
enter into the so-called delights of the closer and refined
sociabilities with our fellowman and woman and purveyed
on the positions of rank and dominance, I could see so little but decidedly inferior to the conditions of naturally
moving graces and adaptations without the inquisitive,
inquisitorial decrees and curiosities of our fellowman.

I soon encountered some adventures, too. An elegant
young man, who addressed me with the familiarity of an
old acquaintance, invited me to take a walk with him —
but, his proposed direction being contrary to mine, I
declined. A little later, a most delicious being, superbly
attired, smiled benignantly and lingeringly at me; I had
never beheld the like before — a female angel sprung into
being, and so gracious, too. Yet I felt abashed, knowing
that so resplendent a creature would find little in me to
interest her, my qualifications extending not even to the
intelligent discussion of the prospective corn-crop. I possessed nothing to offer her, except a restless mind — she
accustomed to ambrosial delectations, no doubt; hence,
my consideration forbade me cruelly to inflict myself upon
her, in which forbearance I was well fortified by a strong
shyness and diffidence. But the apparition continued to
haunt me for several minutes thereafter. And I have
pondered on the importance of our personal adornments in
respect to our material welfare.

I proceeded thence to Baltimore, Philadelphia, New
York — not as briefly but in the order named. I spent
some time at different respectable employments, though
often indifferently remunerated — still, ample in the respect that life and outward appearance were decently
maintained and my small purse kept intact. I even on one
or two occasions had enough surplus to indulge in a parlor-
chair car in my transit from one place to the other — in

fact, never worried, being convinced of the Divine intercession in the sparrow's faithful behalf.

> Hustling, bustling, toiling, whirling,
> Tumbling, tossing, seething, boiling,
> Teasing, tearing, trembling, scaring,
> Well-nigh fainting, all ill-faring,
> None but merits pity's sharing,
> And the crash, that knows no sparing,
> Ceaseless turmoil, headlong plunging,
> Cruel shift and crafty lunging; —
> Ever, on the downward bearing,
> Climbing, mounting, yet, despairing,
> Naught for rest but wrecks comparing:
> Fleeting quicksands make no stairing.

I received the impression, that about all the body of the great mass of people was doing for elevation and progress, was to climb over and on each other, in the delusion that despite the crushing weight at the expense of others they might be enabled to reach something higher; when happiness is, all the time, in and about and around us, and not in dazzling heights, and requiring but our reach of realization. This, then, was the life I had sighed for — which my innocent rural surroundings and the vociferous announcements of the morning-cock had not suggested. Well, I had no reason to complain of ungratified desire in that regard, and had better not confess chagrin to sustain my pride.

How has it come to pass that those massive structures — so much admired and representing an aggregate of skillful endeavor, yet after all not so wonderful from another standpoint — so generally are but monuments of deceit and conceit? When I contemplated the amount of oppression and polished hypocrisy, that thrived as the fundament of and within those walls, I shuddered at the existing, prevailing agony, clearly perceptible, yet tolerated. It is hard to believe, that in this must inevitably ensue or transpire the affairs of this world despite any human efforts or precautions. Perhaps it is true; but sad in every phase and aspect! Lax morals make loose principles; and to this touchstone much of our bitterness may be traced. The unheard voice, impotent in its silence, when its truthful courageous utterances might serve or save a fellow-human, because of its unknown sentiments is reckoned as endorsing these pernicious practices, and so in effect does, conducing furthermore to these conditions and allowing the management by unworthy servitors. While ease and rest are desirable, it is yet better that all good men and women exert themselves with the industry, alertness and carefully acquired knowledge, which those who are injuring our whole fabric persist in — abstractly considered, so creditably. The success, merited by every industrious effort, is evidence of what may be accomplished by care and watchfulness, knowing no night of slumber, keeping vigil ever — for the success of evil must depend largely upon the slumbering of right.

After a period, during which I added considerably to my meagre knowledge and experience, I began to consider the advisability as well as possibility, of yielding to an ardent desire I had long felt to make an ocean trip; and as among other pleasant and to me, in different ways, very helpful people I had met the captain of a sea-going vessel, who had begun to entertain for me a certain kindly interest, I broached the subject to him, and his response was favorable and cordial. So I was to bid good-by to firm soil for a period and in the sequel farewell to my native land.

CHAPTER IV.

I ESSAY THE DEEP.

For the purpose of this narrative it will suffice to say that the vessel on which I shipped was one of the largest, newest and best equipped of its kind, and indeed a veritable little palace on the briny, trackless expanse. My duties, owing to the especial contrivance of my friend, were not arduous, more in the nature of a companionship to my adjutor, and I was thus constantly enabled to experience the inspiration of the occasion.

It is not without emotion, that I recall many incidents. With the kind hearts on board, with the excellent provisions and cuisine, the pleasant sports and jollity, the monotony, which is engendered by the daily view of almost unbroken identity, was scarcely irksome, and for many moods became almost blissful. Day after day passed, and the little band grew closer and closer together, intercourse becoming less strained and real esteem more marked, so that some were beginning to proconceive the pain of separation, that should soon take place, and others to devise some plan for future meeting with some select one or company.

The last day on which it was my good fortune to enjoy their company, found an assemblage that could not be excelled anywhere for the good cheer, happy hopes and kindly disposition toward one another, which seemed to move and stimulate each individual. If any forebodings were harbored, or some spirit of evil presaged in the bosom of anyone the impending calamity, there was no

indication, not the slightest external ripple of it; and I
felt no cross-grain in the flights of my gaiety. Toward
noon and after the meal, flecks of clouds became noticeable, and as the atmospheric conditions changed the
weather-beaten countenances of the old experienced captain and some of the other seamen seemed, even to us, to
take on a more serious aspect; and before long even the
quiet orders aroused somewhat our apprehensions. But
nothing particular was said, and no great amount of alarm
became prevalent, the gayer ones even growing more bois-
terous. Still, we were evidently approaching a storm, and
probably a very violent one, as the captain toward evening admitted to me. I was not much frightened and in
due time sought my bunk, and was, ere many minutes, in
the realm where no disturbance pained my ear or grief my
heart. What little additional commotion had by this
time arisen, and the swaying of the ship, but calmed and
soothed me as I slept.

CHAPTER V.

STARTLING!

WHEN I awoke, what was my astonishment to find myself lying on the floor of the cabin, with a very sore aching head and sickly sensations throughout my body. I
listened; all was silent, save the splash of the waves. A
queer, fearful sensation, in the deathlike silence excited my
alarm, and feeling that something was wrong, I started
up only to be attracted to myself by the pain my movement called forth; then, putting my hand to my head, I
felt that it had been bruised as though by a heavy fall or

hard blow; my position on the floor would indicate the
former.

The sun was shining brightly as the light through the
port-hole glass indicated, and I imagined that the day was
well-advanced. I again started up, my misgivings increasing with every moment, unlocked and opened the door and
went out into the corridor. The door of the opposite cabin
stood open, the room was deserted and everything in confusion. I took it in at a glance, but did not dwell on the
spectacle. I was wild to get out beyond, to assure or
reassure myself of something, I knew not, could not conjecture what. I went on. Not a person, but an ominous
stillness was there, and I was soon groping in darkness,
for all the openings admitting light to the part I now had
reached were closed, which alarmed me beyond measure
and seemed to fulfill my worst forebodings. I found the
stairs leading to the deck, which I rapidly ascended, and
found the covering to this hatchway fortunately unfastened.
I stepped on deck — nobody in sight; I ran all around the
deck, at a breathless speed, and shouted and called — all
in vain. Everywhere were the evidences of a fearfully
devastating storm or hurricane, and — could it be true —
the ship had been abandoned, and I was left behind or
forgotten — I remained here alone! My first impulse was
of terrible bitterness and full of reproach. Then my
reflections staggered me; it was no time for reviling anything, certainly not my late, good friends, when I as yet
knew nothing of them. But I buried my face in my hands
in agony. Again, recollecting myself, I fancied that perhaps my apprehensions were only to be partially realized,
and, again running, I proceeded to investigate all parts of
the ship; I hurried, I stopped, I listened; after a little
while I again called, and — more and more it forced itself
upon my convictions, that my first dreadful belief was true.

Reaching the side of the vessel, other than the one to
which I had ascended and for the first time looking beyond
the confines of it, I, to my overwhelming surprise, beheld
rocks and land—saw that we had run on the rocks.   I
felt like laughing, then wept. So thus after all, although
deserted, I was not lost—for, surely, I should find them
on shore, or, discovering my absence, they would return
or send back for me.   I believed nothing else than that
they had all gone on land; had I reasoned, I might have
concluded all would not have left, if not before the vessel
grounded.   The only supposition then I could have
reached, would have been that they had gone ashore in
the boats; but excitement does not reason.   And I began
to feel easy, and to examine more critically the direful
change which a fearful night must have wrought, and to
experience the novelty of a *wrecked ship*.   (I will add
here, that my expectations of seeing again my fellow-
passengers were never realized; and to me their fates are
unknown — whether the merciless, briny deep engulfed
them or their bleached bones lie scattered upon some burning beach; or whether happy homes and friends again
welcomed any of them.   But I suspect that I am the only
one left to relate this unhappy occurrence, though whether
it will ever reach other ears, I, at this distance and as
yet shut off from the outside world, cannot say.   Perhaps,
an all-absorbing gloom will forever seal their fate and my
own in oblivion; but I believe an all-abiding God will
make the disclosure. God bless their memories!)   Still
nervous, however, I glanced about.   Every evidence betokened a heart-rending time which the kind indulgence of
Providence had spared me.   The masts had been splint-
ered off, and that heavy seas had washed and drenched
every portion of the surface, there was plenty of indication.   And upon further investigation it seemed to me

that the departure must have occurred precipitately, at
any rate all the boats and almost every means of escape
had been employed or removed (which, alone, had my
reasoning faculties just then accompanied my observations,
must have determined when they had abandoned the ship),
though from all appearances I never could discover that
much in the way of victualing was taken along. From
this I reason that they delayed until a moment when
perhaps in a panic they must have been in the worst state
of demoralization, from which one can easily picture the
saddest of results. The fact that all the openings to the
flooding sea below had been closed shows that every
precaution had been taken and hope indulged, until a fatal
moment probably sent the hundreds of souls into eternity,
abandoning what would have been safety. Tributes to
their memories!

Beginning to feel hungry (I was at that time buoyed by
the expectation of finding them on this shore, all the fore-
going reasoning being the later calm deliberation of which
I was not capable then) I first opened the " water opposers,"
so that light might again be shed on the inner recesses;
for it was now a beautiful, warm, bright day, the sun
beaming and the sky serene as though not upon and over
a scene of recent desolation. I proceeded below, first
looking into the dining-room, where I saw nothing in the
way of eatables, but some confusion of broken glass, etc.;
then to the kitchen and cooking department. Here there
was no fire, but every evidence that the supper (or
dinner) of the evening before was the last meal that had
emanated from this department. A time-piece, that registered as well the date, marked ten minutes of four o'clock
and June 20; so that my last recollection of date being
the 19th, I was aware that but one night had elapsed since
I had last retired to sleep and unconsciousness.

Painful was the realization, that I was alone; and even though a hope still lingered to beguile my belief in a speedy reunion with my friends, I must confess that I had a foreboding or presentiment that they would never meet my gaze again.

> Have you yet known the deep solicitude,
> That yearns the being for its species, kind?
> The silence grows oppressive with each hour
> As glow the stars o'er shaded sun still lower.

CHAPTER VI.

YET ALONE.

> No gentle lips dispose to welcome sounds
> Or give disclosure to a yearned presence near
> To troll the mind within its happy sphere.
> The voice is raucous for the want of such dear use
> To give in utterance the sweetly searching tones,
> That need a sympathy to draw them forth
> And, weeting, lingeringly permit them thus to course
> Until their ardors grow to beauty's rounds.
> Calm vision is dispelled, when naught is seen
> Save nature in its true, benignant grace —
> The charm still lacking of the fascinating human face.

Whether alone in the multitude, or away from any human habitation or companionship, the drift of life stays not; and ever the idea lingers, that it will not always be thus.

I could not withstand the demands of a young, vigorous nature, and, despite the burden that weighed upon me, my hunger demanded appeasement; for which purpose I had redescended, shuddering a little, for I half-dreaded some

ghastly or ghostly apparition out of the stillness and
imminent despair, some stalking spirit of a late friend (as
though even if it should appear, such would harm me).
But I gulped down the growing lump in my throat, and
repaired to a well-supplied larder, where, without particular choice or preparation of food and with a generous libation of wine, I revived my fagging strength. Hastily I
retraced my course to the deck; and now began a more
thorough and systematic survey of my surroundings and
position. The ship had landed or rested high and dry,
and to all appearances was not much damaged; it must
have been an unusually powerful billow and gale which
had placed the vessel so far up and almost out of future
danger, except from similar phenomena. I later saw in
this a provision of Providence. My immediate view toward
land was cut off by a high, rocky shore; and after climbing
over the side of the ship and descending by means of a rope-
ladder which I found conveniently and had fastened and
adjusted for the purpose, not without anxious misgivings
I stepped on the rocks, and slowly, cautiously, as quietly
as possible, clambered up. Reaching the top, I looked
upon a beautiful stretch of country, expanding far out and
away in natural stately grove and charming meadow, and
in the distance the blue outline or maze seemed to indicate mountains. There were exquisite flowers, in variety,
and I saw and heard birds, and some insects — but nothing to denote the presence of man in this locality. The
ocean spread out grandly behind me and at the side a
charming beach extended itself, glistening and sparkling
from the waves' spray and wash, on this gloriously sunlit
day, azure canopied with the barest specks of fleecy cloud-
lets interspersed. I could not suppress a feeling of admiration, and a blissful calm momentarily came over, seized
me. "Monarch of all I surveyed," with a laden ship

behind and an immeasured, inviting tract before me, I proceeded farther, always with the utmost caution and cir-
cumspection, with frequent quisitorial glances about me.
Everything indicated a fertile soil for a fructiferous
vegetation, and the scenery, after I had penetrated
some distance from the shore, carefully noting all
the while any evidences by which I might retrace my
steps, possessed a charm of uncultivated verdure than
which I had never beheld a greater, aided or unaided by
the science or art of man; but, nowhere did I find a trace
of that creature, and as the glooms of evening began to be
manifest, I bethought myself of my return, feeling that
the only friend and companion now left was one of man's
handiwork — thus the human being ever turns to his species, or in the absence thereof, seeks comfort in something
that remains of its touch. On remounting the deck and
nervously pacing thereon, I sighed, "What a night!"

I sat on deck long into the night, comfortably ensconced
with a preparation for ready vision both to the ocean and
land. Often I leaned backwards, resting my head on a
coil of rope behind me, watching the stars burst into brilliant darts and points, just as they did at home; and the
moon arose, half full, to cast serenity, beauty and efful-
gence upon the benign scene. Yet I contrasted this unfa-
vorably with the preceding evenings, with a sad comment
on the suddenness of sorrow. With turbulence in my
heart I began to think upon and plan my future conduct,
with no satisfactory solution of the vexed and mooted
question. Fatigued nature gradually asserted itself, and
the balminess of the delightful summer-night began to
yield to the influences of the shades, admonishing me to
seek rest and shelter. Going toward my cabin (I still
occupied my own, although they now all and any stood
open to me) I securely barred every avenue of approach

to me, lastly bolting my cabin-door, and, with a half
smothered sigh and muttered groan, threw myself,
dressed, into my bunk, to sink shortly with sweet welcome into the oblivion of sleep.

I awoke and it was light, and but a moment sufficed for
recollection. The time had come when I must think and
act. Ascending to the deck, as the first duty and precaution, I assured myself that everything remained as I had
found it the day before; the weather was still fine. I
went down again, and after a refreshing and careful ablu-
tion, this time built a fire in the range, and, after a little
skirmishing and furbishing, prepared a generous repast.
I had now cleared for action. I descried nothing in the
unbroken horizon of my mental vision save the reparation
to self-preservation and of the interstices of my faculties.
I first made a more detailed, though still cursory, inspection of the contents of my abode. Besides pictures,
musical instruments and accoutrements of fancy, taste,
fastidiousness, and the numerous incidentals of ship
furnishings and employments, there was a library, with —
as it proved, fortunately for me—a comprehensive scope.
Besides scientific instruments and appliances, I found farming implements, seeds, some plants, merchandise of nearly
all kinds, and numerous other articles, which I did not
then take time to examine; also there remained (but these
I had already determined not to molest unless the extrem-
ity of affairs demanded or justified) the trunks, and other
baggage and personal belongings of the late ill-fated
passengers and crew. And the kitchen stores, supplemented by the excellent butlery and medicine closet,
were well stocked.

I directed a long searching observation over the sea,
using both field-glass and telescope, of which, among an
ample assortment, I selected two magnificent specimens;

but not a speck appeared to give me hope. I next scanned
what portion I could, from this point, of the land, and
perceived nothing human. I then determined, bright
and early, to issue forth upon a reconnoitering tour, to
occupy the whole day if not checked by some circumstance
sooner; and I at once set about preparing therefor. I
took with me food, a double-barreled rifle, revolvers,
ammunition, knife and dagger, a compass and the glasses
referred to, besides seeing that my watch was wound up
and set (and the ship's chronometer left in good running
order) all securely strapped and adjusted to me, save the
rifle, which I carried conveniently in my hands ready for
prompt use. I might have come into collision with the
laws relative to carrying concealed weapons, and so forth,
if there had been any such in force, and anyone inclined to
insist upon their provisions. Again reaching the top of
the bank, I took bearings and noted any conspicuous
objects, by which to guide my return, and proceeding in
the same direction I had previously gone, at first through
the suffrutescence, I soon entered pleasant woods and
delightful glades, and traversed beautiful natural meadow
patches. Although hampered and retarded, here and
there, by brush and luxuriance of vegetation —the undisturbed accumulation, it would seem, of ages, only fallen
trees, and vines, I could not refrain from indulging my
unbounded admiration of untrammeled nature, sparkling in the freshness of the early morning's dewdrops, which glistened in the sunlight, and the
delightful air, odoriferous with the fragrance of exquisite
varicolored and oddly shaped flowers and some blossoms.
It approached indeed my idea of the garden of Eden —
only there lacked a sweet companion for me to complete
the bower of bliss. In this case even a male companionship would have been cheerfully hailed. But I pushed

and worked on. Besides flowers and birds and delightful shrubbery and small streams and sparkling cascades, and some fruits and berries, of which I tasted very charily, I saw nothing but seemingly impenetrable forest, relieved occasionally by bright fertile expanses in great luxuriance, again skirted by huge forest trees and undergrowth. I had all the time carefully observed my bearings and did not consider myself lost. At noon, refreshed by a little cascade from a rock-basined spring where the ground began to be uneven and broken, I rested in comfortable enjoyment, though terribly impressed by the solitude. Never did a person sit down to a repast, more imbued with the alarm and feeling of utter loneliness! So far, birds and insects, besides a respectable-looking snake or two, were the only living objects I had encountered, and these regarded me with varying degrees of indifference, none doing or attempting to do me harm. My discoveries still left me alone, and, what was worse, with no clue for further investigation, with only an interminable depth and mystery around. I concluded to prosecute my inquiries and researches on the morrow, as far as a day's endeavor would carry me, along the coast. Arriving again at my "residence" on the border of the deep, I readily saw that no disturbance had taken place there; and another dreary night set in.

The next day proved equally fruitless, and so the next, and the next, each day's explorations extending in a different direction. Save a little difference in scenery, and one or two glimpses of some larger four-footed, but, to all appearance, yet harmless animals, which fled startled at my approach, I was substantially without progress; certainly in the one cherished desire of finding some human existence besides my own on this enchanting spot, whose very loveliness, however, was beginning to mock my dis-

tress. I believe I could have embraced with joy a canni-
bal, an enemy, the most hideous and endangering wild
man, just to have seen a human being again.

After deliberately cogitating and sunk in reverie awhile
I determined to take an extensive tour, lasting perchance
a month, to satisfy myself as to the presence of any
inhabitants of the place, to ascertain whether or not the
same were an island, and to seek for some means of
escape. I wished to learn, if my life were spared and
escape impossible, under what circumstances I must spend
my remaining days here.

Following the shoreline and making numerous digres-
sions inland, I spent eight weeks, living on fruits and
berries and eatable flesh I captured and cooked, for fish
large and small in sea and in stream, large and small
game and the best of fresh water I found in abundance
and easily acquired, and all of a quality to tempt the
desires and tickle the palate of the epicure; and carrying
enough outfit to make camping practicable, I rested at
night on a blanket spread on the ground in a sheltered
place, lying Indian or Mexican fashion face downward.
The nights were constantly pleasant, as always in this climate at this part of the year; a fire, and a rope encircling
my open couch, warded off animal and reptilian encroachment on my private "apartment," if ever I was threatened therewith; my precautions were, nevertheless, taken
with regular system. And as day after day I still lived
well—in fact, there was no exhausting the supply in
sight—my return was further postponed, in the vain hope
that perhaps one day more would bring the desired joy.
But, no—doomed to disappointment in this, I retraced my
way, going directly and as rapidly as I could, back to the
ship—and to what solace I could find in the reminders of
my former associations. I again found everything undis-

turbed, which was rather a melancholy pleasure than
otherwise, and concluded to settle down, to apply my energies to my own entertainment (I felt no alarm on account
of physical necessities) looking forward to the hour of
deliverance — possibly only that of death.

Thus, the human heart quails and discouragement readily wraps the human being in gloom.

CHAPTER VII.

MY MONOPOLY!

THE next ten days were aimless for me; I ate, slept,
read, yelled, played on the musical instruments — there
were many of them, including an outfit for a brass band —
scampered up and down and over and in and out, exam-
ined everything, minutely, until the inventory of the ship's
contents was at my tongue's end, so to speak. Sometimes
I felt a little hilarious, which was however more than
offset by the settling gloom on my once joyous
temperament.

At the end of that time, this sort of inertia became
gruesome, and I began to consider what I might do to
employ my mind. Impelled by a presage of present useless-
ness I lost sanguineness of discovering anyone and felt convinced of the futility of an effort; not that faith is unnatural
or unproductive, for it is the contrary. If indeed the land
were inhabited at all, unless by some lone individual or
small number cast thereon, somewhat like myself, this
goodly portion would not remain so utterly unexplored
and traceless of human acts and occupation. My mind
was in a terrible conflict, with chasing doubts and conject-

ures to aggravate the evil; why might my companions not have reached the shore here somewhere? Would they not, then, have looked for the wreckage on this beach? Ah! doubts and wishes and desires and despair, how they wring the human heart!

I had the idea, that I was on a very large domain, perhaps a continent itself.

At any rate, I was beginning to consider a pure necessity — and that the greatest of all — the nourishment of the mind, to prevent its decline into actual insanity. I conceived the idea of making (the first food for the mind is regulation of an attachment) a little plantation and erecting an abode on land, and, besides using the seeds of which there was abundance in quantity and variety on board, to employ the indigenous plants and growths both for embellishment and use, and to find cultivation and companionship in these experiments. Nature is always ready to befriend you, and throws itself in your way to attract your attention and distract your sorrows. Land was *cheap*, apparently fertile, and the vagaries of my fancy would be so limited solely by my skill and some natural requirements. I had been here now upward of three months, as the hour and date annotator on board betokened. This I most studiously kept in order and running, during my prolonged absence having kept daily tally in a note-book of the passing days and not allowed my watch to run down. I had also established a sun-dial, by which to test the regularity of my time-pieces; besides astronomical charts, works, instruments etc., amply stowed on ship, aided me. In the meantime however I noted that a change of season was setting in, admonishing me that a fall and winter of some description were to ensue. I had already begun to consider, judging from the kinds of nuts and fruits and grapes, and vegetation generally, that the climatic conditions were very similar to those of my late country. The changed tints of the foliage, the cold rain, the bursting pods, and the fruits reminded me forcibly of the old farm at this time of the year. I began therefore — a kind of instinct, I presume — to gather of the bounty nature had so profusely and delectably provided yet seemed to be wasting, and as time and season progressed together, soon had stowed enough to satisfy a hundred persons; still, this useless surplus employment was the only diversion I could secure.

Oh, nature's store, so much, profusely, yet, all scattered
   o'er
Still famish thousands, who thy bounty ne'er have felt;
There is some fault, before which railings melt.
The crowdings, crushing to some space, as though no other
   fair;
The garnering, gathering over countless space by selfish
   few;
The direful waste; unworthy most, who never seek to
   know,
That Providence has sought for every need to sow.
And many fields, as green, as e'er you've seen,
Await your choice, when you will reap, not glean;
And will spread out all o'er this world's fit range!

The provisions on ship, in salted and canned articles, besides coffee, tea, sugar, spices, and so on, all securely and durably packed, alone would suffice for me for the next five years or more, so that anxiety on the score of food was no part of my troubles.

Soon the wind began to blow and snow to fall, after an exquisitely fine Indian-summer. Thanksgiving day, which I kept with true American devotion, found me of course alone, but at a festive board crowned by a magnificent young wild turkey, with cranberry sauce and oyster-

dressing, a la cook-book, attended by bouillon and fresh
fish, and numerous substantials and delicacies, including a
veritable pudding and a mince-pie — in fact, such a spread
as was not excelled by any of former years. A toast, in a
glass of genuine *imported* champagne (such as a sea-cap-
tain knows how to have) was drunk, silently, standing;
and, if I could return fervent thanks for my strange preservation in an opportune and bountiful manner, still, I
felt sad at my loneliness, and at the fatality which had
transplanted me hither, ever ready to forget that my own
rashness in desiring foreign sights was primarily its cause.
Yet I enjoyed the feast. (The exercise and fresh air in
round after round of explorations of the possibilities and
contents of my immediate neighborhood, had brought me
health, and my weight and appetite were constantly
increasing.) Under the circumstances even the presence
of a dog would have been a solace — and what a feast the
old fellow would have had on the profuse remnants; or, I
do not know, he might have been a fellow-banqueter with
me! I spent the rest of the day prayerfully, and in reading the Bible.

About the only other consolation I had was a violin,
and hour upon hour, at times, found me pouring out the
anguish of my soul by means of its sympathetic depths of
expression, such as only it, next to the voice, can give.
What a strange sound and melody this must have been to
this primitive region!

Snow covered the ground, and ice began to form, until
at Christmas a finer winter scene and condition could
hardly be conceived in a temperate zone. My Christmas
was both devotional and lonely, and, constrained to
observe old customs by my inclinations even in this solitude, additional luxuries, or specially prepared dishes for
my repast, ceremoniously arranged, and decorations of

green commemorated the occasion. Will you smile, when
I say that I added a Christmas-tree to the festivities?

Game proved plentiful and, as yet, fat and savory;
besides, fish, for which I had a great fondness, were so
easily caught, seeming indeed to rush for the honor, as
to present no sport. All in all, as far as bodily wants
were concerned, connected with the ample supply of all
kinds of apparel on board what mortal could intelligently
and consistently desire more? Could he crave the turmoil
and struggle of this life, in its human associations, especially, after having experienced their bitterness and anxieties? These were the questions I frequently asked and
attempted to rebuke myself for my seeming ingratitude,
when never in my life had I been so free from outside
cares. I recollected that dearth of many things which
existed among the general inhabitants of civilization and
their struggle for bare existence; and I was spared this, or
rather freed from it, and a million other sorrows.

Only, the solitude and monotony were intense, and
therein lay a further use of philosophy. I read and read,
and found hours of abstraction and pleasant companionship thus.

Spring announced its approaches, as of old, and burst
forth into delicious, bright splendor, soon studding the
landscape with gorgeous bloom. I began to bestir myself
for amusement and to while away the tedious time to
planting and sowing, and to experiment with some of
the seeds, of which there were such a variety and
abundance on ship-board; and I soon had the excellent
soil in a state of fine preparation, the incidental labor and
sweating but proving a rest to my mind; and corn, pump-
kins, potatoes, beans, radishes, lettuce and other vege-
tables soon were properly imbedded to impregnate the
virgin earth.

Need I continue with these minutiæ?—let us end by saying, that when I gathered the yield was so manifold, that in a populated land, conducted as my old country was, in the state of civilization in vogue, the profits, relatively to the investment, would have been enormous, and I should soon have become a very wealthy man; but here it proved solely a superabundance—gratifying to the husbandman, but deplorable for the mere waste. I garnered some of the wild tributes of kind nature, as the year before, only to cast the bulk of them to the fishes in the following spring and house-cleaning, which served the purpose at least of attracting and congregating them to the watery vicinity of my abode and thus making them still easier prey.

I constructed an elegant fantastical little abode, where I stayed and slept a part of the time, not very far from the shore, backed and bordered by a beautiful grove which I had cleared around about the dwelling and replaced with a well-trimmed lawn, and near it a fountain of cool, clear, sparkling water; vines and climbing roses picturesquely overran the house, adding their charm of beauty and odor; while flower-beds, and ornamental little trees and shrubbery, transplanted from different spots, and mosses and ferns, besides the successful products of seeds I found in the ship all contrived, with the natural grove as a setting, a very charming park. I had also with the seeds I possessed, planted an orchard to which I had added and pruned, grafted and cultivated of the indigenous kinds, by way of further variety and experiment. If I did not possess a little Eden, that is, the garden thereof, where else could one be found? I had plenty of time to indulge every fancy, acquired or imagined, in the way of decorative or landscape art, or for useful purposes, and, almost, no end of means. Botany was a study to which I became greatly attached; and geology and animal life received considerable attention. I had a respectable laboratory, and made a number of useful, entertaining chemical experiments.

Five years — slow, drawn-out, almost weary — were spent without any particular or marking incidents, than such as I have narrated. As time with gentle drops of water wears through adamant, so the heart becomes accustomed and adapts itself to repetition — the mind is least troubled when the heart is at rest. The days had grown less irksome, since I had in a measure formed acquaintance and friendship with inanimate things. Five years — and I had grown that much older, and how far, how far removed from the time and accomplishments of the world! Accomplishments? Does the world accomplish anything by misery and unhappiness and starvation, mental and physical?

CHAPTER VIII.

ALONENESS.

I HAD now arrived at a period, when, as few could, I was enabled from experience to philosophize on the query, "Is it well for man to be alone?" I had enjoyed, or rather been thrust into Adam's condition, barring special dispensations, before his marriage; and that under not unfavorable conditions. I had well-stocked provisions of the thoughts and contrivances of men for the mental and physical wants; a country solely lacking other inhabitants, human habitations and handicrafts to complete the similarity to the one left.

Perhaps, it may be argued, had I never known man, his kind or contrivances, no solitude would have existed for me at this favored spot; I would have been allied to the feathered and finny and hairy tribes, that animated the locality. That, however, remains within the realms of conjecture. The question still remains, Is it well for each individual to belong exclusively to himself; disregarding any idea of propagation, which is nothing, unless either the innate desire of company, or the natural propulsion of animal life; but considering exclusively individual convenience, solace and comfort? My experience answered: In the sublimest moments of self-abnegation; at the most abstract supposition of total oblivion of any former contact with humanity, is the heart, the soul, are the faculties content? No. An inborn instinct feels craving, demands intercourse of like with like; even condescends to inferiority, to gratify that import. And this union and re-union are susceptible of all refinements.

Alone, then, though possessed of ample and plenty, enjoyable to any degree that human ingenuity can devise outside of the divine spell: and yet all this would be sacrificed and abandoned for less — if that less be accompanied only by the desired and cherished companionship. The love, lesser demonstrations of the principle that abandons palace for cottage; friends for its object; even, honor for its appeasing food! Not that morbidness may not abuse even this principle. The provisions of the Creator cannot hence be so circumvented.

As I lay down, like to Adam, a heavy slumber settled deeply over and upon me, and I awoke to my astonishment.

CHAPTER IX.

" HELLO !"

I HEARD, or thought I heard (I was sleeping that night in the deck-cabin of the ship, it being now again summer), human voices — and I started up in affright. The sunlight was streaming brightly in indication that the day was already well advanced. Now, throughly awake, again that voice-sound broke upon my ear, accompanied, this time, by a dull soft smacking sound, a little shuffling, as of bare feet. Hastily jumping up and throwing on the light apparel which, in that warm weather, I wore, I sallied forth. But a few feet distant on the deck, there were the forms of two well-proportioned men, with their backs toward me, they being seemingly intent upon the observation of some object. They were clad in well-fitting dark seemingly home-spun clothing, with broad-brimmed hats, and were bare-footed.

Imagine the quiver of surprise that shook my whole frame! I was speechless with astonishment, and my first impulse, that instinct of well-grounded suspicion I had retained from my civilized life, was to rush back for a weapon — thus even in the midst of hopeless existence, the instinct for the preservation of life is self-accordant — then, recollecting myself, I calculated instantly that my chances of effectual resistance must be eventually blocked by the number of their probable associates, and I had nothing in jeopardy, anyway. Then the next instant, were they desperadoes or no, I would claim their companionship or find through them some succor or relief — almost anything would be the latter.

All these varying and conflicting reflections passed through my mind in the flash of a moment.

So, not without an exultant throb of joy that I might again use my voice to address a human being, I spoke as calmly as I could: "Good morning, gentlemen!" and felt as though a great load was lifted off me, all at once, by the breaking of the long constrained silence!

A sudden almost ludicrous start passed visibly through the men, who immediately turned toward me their full-bearded ruddy weather-beaten countenances (I had during all this time regularly kept my face shaven) upon which were depicted courage and the hardihood of splendid physical condition, while an open character and kindly expression were apparent in their yet keen, blue eyes. They seemed to have their feelings under better control than I, perhaps because more accustomed to unusual occurrences or surprises, or perhaps each feeling fortified by the other, two to one. Yet, they could not know what hidden dangers lurked behind me, nor that I was alone, and their entire demeanor evinced caution, though not separated from an apparent curiosity, and an emotion which I did not then understand, hardly expecting, certainly not thinking of such a thing as what I afterward realized. Had I then known, that — although matured men, one even past middle life — they had never before seen or heard a stranger, I should have spoken and acted differently, and presumed more for myself; but in no event would my joy have been less.

Recovering from the momentary surprise, the elder of the two responded, in a deep, melodious voice, "Good morrow, my friend." The sound of a human voice again addressed to me! Floods upon floods of recollections and keen sensations passed in that second over me, and trembling I would have sunk to the floor but for the support of the door-post. The suddenness of this surprise out of the depths of hopelessness! "Friends or foes," I almost whispered. Perceiving my agitation they both advanced, and the first speaker in the most kindly voice and manner imaginable, holding out both his hard, labor-encrusted hands to me, spoke again, "Friends, if you will. We extend a cordial greeting, though, encroaching upon your domain and hospitality, we should await the greeting from you." It was the grace of natural culture by which these words were uttered. "Ah! gentlemen," I replied, "pardon me; your manner and speech assure me, and I will recollect myself; I have been so long alone" (they started with astonishment) "dwelling only in memory with my fellow-man, that it surprises me that I recollect or can utter speech at all. I was more overcome by delight than fear; by astonishment than trepidation; but, now, I bid you welcome, most heartily welcome, and, if I shed tears, forgive my weakness. Come, come with me!" I had evidently become more than ever a mystery to them; but, leading the way to the shaded side of the vessel, I rushed into the cabin and soon had lugged out two more deck chairs, which I placed near an accustomed seat of mine, with an invitation to them, that they seat themselves thereon. My request was complied with, and our mutual feelings at this time, when our respective histories, each remarkable, were unknown to one another, can be conjectured in the light of subsequent disclosures.

CHAPTER X.

REVIVED SOCIABILITY.

Constance decks a life devoid of bliss.
Thus blissful throbs run through the fevered veins,
When tickling humors broil their happy frames,
In joyous missives rendered part to part.
As in pulsations wild the heart evolves
And the whole mind suffuses with its surge
Clear vision be restored; though dazzling joy
Makes hard its brilliant depths thus oft to scan;
For all the purer elements of guileless bliss
Are found in realms of inner virtuousness.

"How romantic it would have been if these had been robbers, with wild adventures to our hero, and succor in the nick of time by an angelic and voluptuous maiden, with long flowing golden hair!" But this was not the case, at least at this time; we must take life as it comes.

A little interquestioning, with considerable excited speech and frequent ejaculation, in which the other and younger of the two joined with equal animation, soon disclosed enough of our respective histories to acquaint one another with our relative fortunes or misfortunes. My delightful and delighted visitors were men of physical hardihood and great mental intelligence: they would have proven themselves entertaining anywhere, and notable in any grade or condition of society.

Without relating their circumstances and arrival thereto until later, I will say that their residence in these parts dated from their births, although this identical tract had never been before explored by them (and thus still remained my domain "by right of discovery," which they never disputed). On this occasion, these two bold and hearty adventurers had embarked upon a tour of exploration and investigation, on their own accounts — even among a few of mortality in existence the spirit of ever-restless research and ambition coming to the fore with its strifes and perilous endeavors. Employing a kind of small boat of their own rude, yet clever and serviceable construction, equipped with sailing means and a shelter-coop, without compass or guide for direction or return save as the shore would give them such indications, they had coasted for many days, making devious incursions in-land and subsisting mainly on the result of the chase by trapping and the net and line. They had discovered traces of some of the fires I had built, and thence concluded the existence of humanity somewhere about. The evening before they had run into a little sheltered cove, as was their nightly custom, and in making one of their periodical incursions on this morning had encountered my land habitation and gardens, whence the tracks or path to the ship were easily traceable; and to such hardy undertakers such a clue to something would not be fled from. It can be imagined that they were wonderfully and agreeably surprised, when they beheld my ship, never having seen anything like this before, yet possessing man's instinctive appreciation of skill and beauty. These people in addition, as the sequel will show, possessed a high order of intelligence.

Well, to make an otherwise long chapter short, I dined and wined them — the latter indulgence being entirely new, yet not unpleasant to them — and the toasts and merriment were thick and fast. The festive board groaned under everything the season, including my seasoning and

seizing, could afford, even to a fine Havana cigar apiece.
Unfortunately my visitors' inquiries in regard to the latter
and my instructions in the use of this so-called delectation,
and, thereupon, their insistence, resulted in making us all
sick, including myself, because unaddicted to the use of
and not in love with tobacco.

We talked, laughed and shouted far into that night;
and I even got out the old fiddle and played with fantastical variations, making the instrument fairly speak with
joy and pathos, "Backward, oh, backward," "In the
gloaming," "Her bright smile," "By the sad sea waves,"
"Fishers' hornpipe," "Home, sweet home," and a number
of others—which they considered wonderful, reminding
them, they said, of the portrayed possibilities of the upper,
blissful realms, of which they had read. As a guest
chamber, they occupied the best cabin on ship, with the
costliest sheetings, coverings and hangings within grasp —
unknown and unnecessary luxuries to my new friends, and
like to the fairy-tales and stories of wonderland, of which
they had read. They rather hesitated to touch these fine
things, in their admiration for them.

The happiest night of five years robbed me of slumber!
It had been agreed that I should return with them to their
habitation, and their outward voyage terminated at once
with this "one grand discovery." I appreciated their
enthusiasm in my behalf, which was quite natural under
the circumstances, but assured them that their revelation
was not less grateful and wonderful to me—its timeliness
I alone could realize. So the morrow was busied with
preparations for my departure. Having anchored their
little craft in close proximity to the ship, we proceeded to
load it to its utmost capacity, with the best at my command;
eatables, wearables and drinkables; books and smaller
musical instruments; contrivances for amusement; some

scientific and mechanical devices, such as we could conveniently and safely stow, besides seeds, plants, drugs, chemicals and condiments, making altogether a very respectable peace-offering, still leaving a large and valuable store behind. The astonishment and unflagging interest of the men, as they beheld article after article, was intense.

After as securely as possible, fastening and locking all the avenues that opened into the interior of the vessel, I cast a parting look on my beautiful little gardens, which I was about to desert ruthlessly for the companionship of people, who might not possess any such ease and prosperity; which latter, however, I reckoned as comparatively nothing. Many now yearn for these and their joys who have not felt the burden of solitude, but realize only the cares of ordinary existence and the lack of complete, or even approximate happiness there. Indeed my several haunts had become dear to me despite myself and I felt regret at leaving them; and at the dear old ship I looked long and devotedly, and prayed that I might behold it again, intact.

Still the alternative of remaining without the companionship which I had just found, quickly dispelled all such reflections — and soon briskly sailing on our course, my animation reached its former height.

.

Life soon forgets the dearlings of the Past,
When pleasures new exhilarate its chase.
On, catching at such gleams, that bid a choice
Or chance, that radiant hues lie still beyond;
And still at ease descries each novel fund
As so much new or better, finer bliss.
But when sad aches can have no happy chose
In contemplation of the wrecks of hopes
Wherein bright prospects often were misspent,

Then turns the mind to conjure up the cause,
That gave such ornament to bygone days,
And lingers dearly o'er the happiness sped.
And were't not so would this life be esteemed
A truce, a truce wherein to thrall the cret'sins?

CHAPTER XI.

NEW FACES.

To divide one's attention is like hitching horses, one to each end of a vehicle—and then starting the opposing forces; there is apt to be little progress either way, and certainly much loss of time.

Gaily I viewed the pinnacles of the structures erected by this little isolated colony, to whose abodes I was being conducted, as they first appeared in sight in the distance and were pointed out to me.

I had learned in the meantime that fifty persons constituted this little band, shut out and cut off from the outside world; none of them had seen another face than was embraced in their own little company, until these men saw me. They only knew of an outside world and other existence of humanity from old literature in their possession and, strange as it may sound, by tradition. Accustomed only to hear of the authority of tradition in connection with savage or uncivilized, illiterate people, it is far from our reflections that such a condition might affect our descendants or the living ones of civilized people; but such of course may become, and was here as to the latter proposition, the fact. Behold powerful Babylon, glorious Jerusalem, Tyre, Athens, Rome—their present inhabitants, many of them, perhaps are lineal descendants of their

. once great minds and masters; now among their ruins lingers a largely traditionary or legendary memory of them and their times. So we may sink into traditionary or legendary remembrance, perhaps our descendants decline into barbarism upon the greatness of our ruins.

The people of this little colony could all, excepting the mere children, read and write in their tongue, the English language; a regular course of instruction, inaugurated by those whose mishap had first cast them on these shores, was studiously observed, though the printed literature was restricted to that primarily on hand, and bore evidence of long age and wear, although almost sacredly guarded. Their individual writings and records related in a steady sequence their history and discoveries. The foundation and system of perpetuation for an increasingly enlightened people, were well laid by their first ancestors here, who, coming from the civilized world, foresaw the danger of a benighted existence to their beloved progeny, and assiduously sought to arm them against such a calamity, until a merciful God or saviour should succor this helpless flock. Their standards of educational work, judged even from our standpoint, were high, and exhibited the closest attention on their part to the opportunities at hand — although ravages of time, from the long extent of their traditional civilization, and peculiarities that would naturally ensue from local causes and the absence of the more extended human associations, were apparent.

Why do we not understand more — why are what we call the great discoveries of any age so often the result of accident — why may we not calmly and rationally know these things of our knowledge, and prove their sequence, link upon link? It is because the medium of exchange between us is unsatisfactory. But here were resources equal to those of any country on earth; intelligent, honest people; and yet what discovery elsewhere had already demonstrated as the simplest principles, were here unrealized; the urgent necessities, the numbers and diversity, had not brought mind and spirit to work, had not inspired them to words and deeds. I was thus by these accounts of them, tolerably well acquainted with the rest of my future coadjutors before I beheld them in the flesh.

As we approached, we noticed a small boat hastily put out, and a boy hurriedly jumping into the same and tugging rapidly at a pair of oars, soon came alongside. The strapping, handsome little fellow joyfully greeted one of the men as father. Taken into our boat with his fastened to ours astern, almost beside himself with joy, he announced as well as his gasps and excitement would let him, that all had been and were well, and everything was in a satisfactory condition. Upon being presented to me, having, theretofore, scarcely been conscious of my presence, he was not a little abashed and awkwardly, almost fearfully, met my kindly and cordial greetings — with as much astonishment and wonder depicted on his bright glowing guileless countenance towards me, as though a supernatural being were brought to vision to one of you.

CHAPTER XII.

AN ASTONISHED GROUP.

THE news of our little craft's approach had been industriously and enthusiastically heralded to every part of the abodes and places of occupation of the little colony, and as the sun was going down in gorgeous evening glow, the whole populace congregated on the shore to welcome their

beloved adventurers. Running close to a rocky projection
and casting out the moorlines, which were quickly and
skillfully seized by willing hands and fastened, the two
men sprang ashore and were at once engaged in embracing, kissing and shaking the hands of the dear friends,
from whom they had been several months separated.
This voyage was the longest that had ever occurred among
them and was celebrated as an event, and regarded with
marked attention on that account.

I remained seated; the boy had become interested and
engaged in the cautious inspection of some of the strange
articles we had brought along as my contribution. Presently the elder of the two men of my acquaintance raised
his hands in supplication of silence, and beginning slowly
and calmly, said, "My dearly beloved, we have with us a
sojourner in this land of magnificent distances and silent
contemplation, a true man, who, had we solicited a visitation from heaven, could not have come more unexpectedly
to us, or, almost, more welcome. It is an answer to
our true prayers. He is of our kind, and of our species
and race; but, unlike us, has come directly from that
world beyond, of which even our best imagination, aided
by such information as we still entertain thereof, cannot
portray the wonders, concerning which he has given us,
Victor and me, occasional glimpses in his information and
explanations. He too has been ostracised here for some
time, but not, comparatively, long;" (I winced a little at
that) "thither we have had dreams, and have longingly
talked of what lies beyond those great natural walls of
the horizon, this o'erreaching, intervening watery waste
— and, as I said before, next to a visitor directly from
heaven, this worldly emissary exceeds the fulfillment of
all our other desires — being heaven-sent!"

I had stepped forward during this little homily, and,

advancing smilingly and in a state of suppressed excitement, was met by the other individuals with varying degrees of diffidence; all seemingly were too much astonished, mystified, perhaps even awed, as though a supernatural visitation had in fact come to them, to utter more than a few words, as they timidly extended their hands, which I, each in turn, grasped firmly and heartily shook.

Yet what a happy awakening from the stupor of the last five years!

Under the circumstances I rallied to myself the sooner, and resumed my natural equilibrium, feeling that I was more accustomed to meet people, and especially could feel more at home with strangers than they (of course, because they had never met a stranger before; just think of it!) and was consequently, save my two friends, the most at ease of any. "Friends and fellow-beings," I said: "a fated series of occurrences has thrown us together — from so far off, from such different origins. Some were sent of your number to me, when the years of solitude had settled an almost impenetrable gloom of despondency upon my spirit, under which even my stout heart was beginning to quail — but the faith in a Divine Providence can never err. At length I am made the messenger in answer to your prayers, and am succored in answer to mine; and so it seems now clear to me, all the better for the trials and tribulations into which I had wandered and was made to pass, that I was intended to convey to you tidings from the known world about and to bring you the solace of information without. Our meeting is as auspicious as the beautiful evening-glow, suffusing the heavens with its glorious red and warmth of promise and auguring peace and radiance on the morrow. Receive me, then, brethren," I continued almost passionately, "into your congregation, to which I will bring, diligently and conscientiously,

whatever there is worthy in me!" By the motive, enfran-
chising power of eloquence, "We receive you!" "We
welcome you!" "God bless you!" they broke in, in
diverse and fervent exclamations; seeming, all at once, to
have regained their powers of speech. They crowded
around me, with the whole fervency of their artless
natures aglow, so that there could be no more cordial welcome than was now accorded to me.

Someone spoke of possible hunger on our parts, of
which we had truly not thought ourselves, but now were
forced to acknowledge; and led to seats around a table in
a cosy sheltering arbor we were soon bountifully and excel-
lently regaled. Having since very early that morning
labored incessantly to finish the voyage by evening,
fatigue which even the prevalent excitement could not
entirely subside, soon after readily led us to acquiesce in
the suggestion of retirement. And such clean, plain, yet
luxurious couches never received more grateful or, for the
moment, happier frames, than sunk and rested upon these
in blissful relief that night.

Thus, after five years, I was to spend a night in repose
with human slumberers around within easy call of me.

> Fitful shadows sweep at night,
> As alternating shade and light
> Disturb the peace;
>
> The soul is not in soothing rest,
> In consonance with its behest,
> That all be right,
>
> When strict consistence and accord,
> In weighing every deed and word,
> Find much is lost.
>
> For, useless thoughts are mental dross,
> Which bears its weight with heavy loss;
> For, being bought,

Is paid for at the price and pounds,
In which the dearest sum resounds;
And good's foregone.

Oh, gentle spirit, lead me not
With thoughts of hell, nor, cruelly wrought,
Disturb my rest;

That not the night be full of dread,
Or in wild anguish me o'erspread,
Who need its peace.

———

CHAPTER XIII.

THE TRIALS OF OTHERS.

MORE than half a century ago on a morning as bright serene and balmy, as nature is capable of, one of the finest passenger and freight vessels of that day, well laden and peopled, left an English seaport, as jauntily as the gayest of the many gay spirits on board could wish, and essayed the treacherous waves.

Out of sight of land, that horrible invader of the human gastronomy, sea-sickness, began to manifest itself in divers quarters and in fact, made a sweeping onslaught on the large number of novices present; and, at this period, the tender solicitude, respectively, of three couples, attracted their reciprocal notice one to the other, drawing them together, as by some simple union of one accord — a separate little group of fellow-sufferers and, afterward, fellow-jubilators. So began an acquaintance and attachment between these people, of whose fated endurance and intimacy none then entertained the remotest presage. They all belonged to the English middle class; were of the highest respectability, wealthy, refined and educated; and the several honeymoon couples, hailing from different sections of England were thus thrown together by chance — never, thereafter, to separate until death should dissolve the visible earthly bonds. And as, long after, one after the other of the white, sage heads was laid in the strange far-away soil of their last abode on earth, far from the relatives and friends who had long since been compelled to mourn them dead, those remaining shed tears of regret and loving remembrance over the unostentatious bier. And at length the sole survivor, the last connecting link with the outside world, with words of injunction befitting this finality entered into his rest, mourned and attended by those to whom civilization was only a narrative, the children and descendants of these three couples, who had been snatched from the dawn of humanity that their posterity might fashion out a new path, and perhaps wield an influence on the whole earth, from the morning of bright hopes had sunk to — the night of despondency, gloom, despair? Nay, the elements of cheer and comfort were about them in the existence of their beloved children — hence I will only add to the night of natural regret for the latter. But a brighter dawn revealed itself to these on their own accounts. As though the tombs of venerated Patriarchs, these silent graves by that ocean whence their fates had blown them possessed sanctity and fascination.

But, to continue the original story, our voyagers were soon overtaken by misfortune. Day followed day of violently stormy weather, so that all had to remain below, the hatchways were closed, and gloom reigned within and without. Nor were there in those days the happy provisions of our present day steamers. The highest pitch of apprehension and nervous tension was felt for such a length of time, that, when the fatal climax arrived, it was

paradoxically almost a relief; and, terrible though its few
moments were, swiftly it dissolved the bonds of thraldom!

All deeming the vessel lost, even the veteran calm
experienced captain at last conceding this, the order for
preparing the boats was instantly obeyed and these were
peopled with such precipitation and confusion, to which
the terribly heaving sea added consternation, that any
attempt at order was utterly futile. Our little group, as
usual, was together and a little aloof now under the leadership of the oldest of them—a young man of wonderful
coolness and calculating strength of mind—who from
that time seems tacitly and implicitly to have had their
obedience in everything. He restrained them from entering into the rush, believing and counseling that such conduct would involve all engaged in disaster. And so it
proved; for the launching of the boats, in the dreadfully
violent seas, ended immediately under the very eyes of
these six remaining on board, in the saddest of catastrophes.
The captain, after in vain urging this united group to join
them, had himself left the ship; and the day grew darker,
until the wildest of nights obscured all vision and wailed
a dirge over the unescaped separate but not separable new
watery graves.

Now, without any apparent means of escape, the six
had prepared themselves to die; young wife clasped to hus-
band's bosom, their mutual faithfulness never more to be
tried, there remained to each but the consolation that he or
she was not to be left behind the other, but that they could
die, as they had loved to live, together—so thought they,
bestowing upon each other the last glances of undying
affection, when lo! a resounding crash, that seemed to
shake every portion of the vessel. Then, a comparative
settling of the ship and cessation of its motions, whilst the
waves dashed against and over it, and the wind blew with

awful vehemence — followed by oblivion, for, thrown and scattered violently about, all sank into unconsciousness, either fainting from the new fright and overwrought feelings, or stunned by the fall.

> Oh, might oblivion ever rush to aid
> The moments that so sorely try men's souls —
> Or might this sweet forgetfulness dissolve
> In vapors to but seem the tomb's incense!

They must have lain in this stupor for some time. Their leader was the first to revive, dazed and confused, in utter darkness. The vessel, though evidently grinding on and rubbing against some hard substance, was not moving much, from which he correctly inferred that it had grounded.

He recollected having seen a lantern in a corner of the cabin, to which they had retired after the sad catastrophe related, and, making way thereto over the prostrate forms, was fortunate enough to find it, with the further happy event, that the same contained a candle inserted in its holder, and, therefore, was ready for use. God help the poor man's apprehensions at this time; he knew not how many of these dear companions, and his beloved wife, might also be beyond human aid! The light seemed to work as a restorative, for the other two men opened their eyes, and the wife of the first began to move. By rubbing and chafing, the remaining two ladies were restored to consciousness; and the rejoicing of all was great. Our leader informed them of his belief as to the ship's situation, and the spirits of all became more buoyant. In the fitful glow of the dim light, with hopes revived, or immediate apprehension somewhat stilled, they awaited morning. The storm showed signs of abate-

ment. The hours passed slowly, but at length the dim
dawn appeared. Making their way to the deck, as soon
as there was sufficient light to see there, they beheld a still
turbulent sea; but the wind had subsided and the sky
gave speedy promise of serenity. On the other side they
beheld a rock-bound shore; their badly dilapidated vessel,
foundered on a rough shoal, was wedged in between two
peaks projecting from the rocky bottom beneath the
water, like two rugged, intercepting sentinels — which
proved a happy circumstance for them. Falling on their
knees — they were devout people — they thanked God for
this unexpected deliverance.

The sun arose, and all became bright and gay again in
nature; frivolous, as though its own turmoils and embroil-
ments had not recently darkened many another home, and
brought gloom and despondency to hearts which had often
rebounded at the brilliancy of its bland smiles.

The ladies had speedily prepared a bounteous warm
breakfast which revived the party to a considerable extent;
upon the suggestion of their leader, a small quantity of
liquor stimulant was imbibed by each, to offset the terrible
strain of the last few days' ordeals; and all repaired to
their couches for a few hours rest, now that excitement
was beginning to wane succumbing to fatigue; other
unconsciousness, save that of benign sleep, brings no rest.
There is nothing more to add, save that their experiences upon landing on and exploring these shores, were
similar to mine; for though our respective points of location were widely separated, their topography, climate and
productions varied little.

The vessel did not last long; as soon as they had prepared
sufficient quarters, they removed everything they could, and
as the ship broke up assiduously gathered and saved all
the parts they could transport to land from its wreckage,

subsequently raising also many of the heavier parts that had remained in the water, using these latter for the purposes of their other industries. Of these remnants there still remained some vestiges, as reminders of the toils of some far away skillful race; and true gems of reliques they were.

Convinced that an early deliverance was improbable they devoted themselves to their new life, which opened to be sure but an obscure, narrow vista. They adopted regulations and set resolutely about making themselves as comfortable as possible — not a bad tribute to English character — in which moreover they succeeded admirably.

After awhile their population began to grow; so that, when I arrived, the original persons having all passed away, there were fifty in all, descendants of the first parents now almost one family. To this was added, a few days later, a bright bouncing little fellow, who, in honor of my appearance almost coincident with his, was named "Penrod Hilbuck" before his honorable surname "Mason"; and I became consequently and by choice his principal sponsor, in company with an estimable young lady, Kathleen Bertram. Keep an "eye" on the little "Pen"!

The names of the first arrivals on this lonely but beautiful shore, were John (the leader referred to) and Elvira Bertram, Phelix and Alice Mason and Vernon Gregory and Lucy Marianne Talbot.

CHAPTER XIV.

MY FIRST LECTURE.

I SPENT fully the first week in delicious idleness. Petted and pampered by everyone as never before, and feasted every day, I was the hero of the hour.

They were delightful people. Guile and stealth had not crept into their circle to impose on them a hard, suspicious, hypocritical existence.

I was now thirty years of age. One fascinating stately blonde young lady began from the start to exercise a charm over me. Her large, expressive, deep, gloriously blue eyes, and her purely golden-hued hair, shimmering and glimmering like silken threads as it hung in rippling floods down far below her waist, added to her magnificent person and bearing and noble yet gentle demeanor, reminded me of the idyllic dreams of pure, effulgent, feminine realization.

This little community was conducted in exquisite order. Its founders had inaugurated the best of their old customs at home and had handed the same down to their progeny. Therefore each family resided by itself, in a beautiful home, varying with individual tastes; and, upon marriage, each young couple was equipped in a separate home; each family had its own garden-plot, and raised its own provisions on land exclusively occupied by itself. Thus, individual inclinations could be gratified without infringing upon the rights and time that proportionately might belong to others; and the little castle ever dear to the heart might have its independent existence.

Already trading was introduced, for, this one or that, better skilled and so inclined to produce some useful or ornamental article, found ready assent from the others to his employment, and was excused from the common co-operation in other things, to that extent. One individual engaged his whole attention in teaching the children in a school they had established; led in their devotional exercises, Sunday being religiously observed; and was also their annalist and general secretary, keeper of the archives and library; besides being the scholar of the community by reason of his familiarity and constant contact with the old library — in the matter of scholarship, however, I may add that the others were not much behind him.

This official's bodily necessities had thus to be supplied from the contributions of the rest, who received the benefits from his exclusive endeavors. This is the basis of interchange of values, founded on personal independence and liberty, and must exist in all thriving communities, a mutual division, yielding and receiving. A community absolved from individual efforts robs a person of his consistent freedom and thwarts his intellectual growth.

A community of goods, however, with popular election of the votaries to the several employments, comes nearest to this liberty, where the latter is being abused and requires an equitable adjustment. It is all wrong, that it is so hard for worthy people to get along, in our civilized countries; these affairs must be eased up, somewhere, and there is no excuse for the improper conduct of them, anywhere; it is caused by the imbecility of the people in the main, but they are corrupted by the perniciousness of exclusive rulers.

I found thus here so far an orderly arrangement, studiously observed and fostered.

Their tools and mechanical contrivances consisted of some remaining from the ship, and the rest ingeniously fashioned after these examples; and, incited and directed in a measure by the disclosures of the scientific works in their library, they had made excellent and advantageous experiments and employed many of the agencies with which nature abounds far beyond our present ken. Even art had its commendable and happy votaries.

One evening I was asked to give an account of my native country. I had told them many things, in part and in individual sketches, and had prepared the fruitful soil of their minds for other knowledge; but they wanted a more extended description of the whole. I consented, not without some misgivings, and the following Thursday evening was selected for my debut on the rostrum; which, arriving, I spoke:

"MY COUNTRY AND MEN.

Full many a mile, ay thousands, it lies away,
My country, my native vale, my land of youth!
Its broad expanse one score eight hundred miles
From sea to sea, the mountain-skirt Pacific
And pine-clad range of the Atlantic shore —
Not ocean-washed, these stern acclivous hills,
But, by a coast extending varying miles —
And, sixteen hundred miles, from lakes and Britain's
    land
To gulf and Mexico's wild, woolly stretch.
The sun, refreshed, smiles on united soil,
As, bringing morn, emerges from east's main,
And beams the day on enterprising folk;
Whilst, all along, it passes pleasing scenes —
Fine, rolling land, great, fertile plains,
With shimmering dots, and silvery, sinuous threads,
All speckled with the handicraft of man;
And bids good-eve to sturdy, gem-ribbed cliffs,

To glimmer back from snow-clad crests good-night
And peaceful rest; then, laves its heated face.
When, first, that land did greet the mariners' eyes,
'Twas much entangled o'er with thrifty growth;
But, here and there, a space where man did reign —
A wild or unrestrained tribal kind,
With, yet, of art, that gave him human grace;
And there he roamed as free as nature rank.
The mighty oak was emblem of the soil,
And reared its kingly crest, through storm and age,
Set in the garniture of arbors' bowers
(Of species multiplied by kind, degree,
And fructifying, well as timbers' spoils);
From winter's piny knolls, through brumal winds,
And pitchy realms in semi-tropic air,
To rocky wastes, where tower or cling the trees,
The forest-tracks were acres of deep gloom—
Impressive scene.   Here roved the buck
(And roams poetic fancy in the fane)
And, when the vernal burst gave glory's kiss,
Led roe and doe unto luxuriant plain.
There teemed of animal life and strife.
The savage man trod through in cautious-wise,
Bent to his chase, or cruel retribute,
And, scarcely, noted how the soil bare fruits,
Or limpid streams might bear to precious marts.
The happy songsters trilled their lays, I fain,
On listless ears, that deemed their notes in vain.
The enterprising folk have turned the tide,
In which calm nature steadily progressed,
To so constrain it, somewhat, to their use,
That light has dawned within those forest-glades—
Where pilgrims, seeking that inviting shore,
Found hardy toil, and hewed and wrought,
That, soon, the aspect smiled with cozy cheer,
As danger after danger ceased to lurk;
Now, erstwhiles wilderness has lost its clue.

    From foe without and foe within,
      That hardy band, constrained,
    Weft through its way and woofed the web,
      And was not pent therein.

They've come, those folk, from every foreign shore —
Have rushed into the lurking jaws of death
To flee oppression, which at home they could not
    brook,
That dauntless spirit, which will not enslave;
Have, for a conscience' sake, sought peaceful shores —
Wot peace nought threat'ning but the outward man;
Have sheltered in the balm of freedom's bliss.
Some bold adventurers sought worldly gain;
Some fled for crime, some banished came;
And, yearly, thronged this course of wistful wights,
All bent on profit, to this land of hope.
And faith esteems that, which it makes:
If profit, then, thereto betakes.
Foundations, thus, built profit'bly, sure,
For profit, then, must, still, endure.
A country's, profit, fundament
Must rear it to the firmament.
All certainty lies inherent, its own bliss!
Not long, until, our fellow-men, with jealous eye,
Began to list, with av'rice, toward the setting sun,
And sought to menace with might that range.
Alas! the foe without to augment what
Within had been the years of dire distress!
But, recking not the prowess, that a right imbues,
Our hateful brethren fared the lot of traves.
And never was a freer freedom struck,
When valor, growing wrothy, brigue forsook,
And smote the tyranny of ruthless cant.
With, then, a rest gained after so great trials,
The nation grew, cemented, in its ties
Of noble patriots, whom pain made wise,
In that charmed region, seemingly, God-blessed;
And danger, that had made a common foe,
Had welded consonance to stem the woe.
No wonder, noblest words from lip or pen
Graced many a page and echoed mount and glen:
For, manhood throttled, there, the vice of power!
Apace, then, grew the peaceful arts of life,
As soon bright meadows laughed to grain-crowned
    hills,

And gentle domesticity gained sway.
Small marts, with all the bustle of the trading world,
In sprinkling dots, sprung on the busy scene;
And, as the frontier more and more grew hence,
The reign of peace took on a firmer hold,
And former avocations missed their wilds;
The savage man, and equal savage beast,
But glowered from their lairs with quivering fear,
And noted with what fell, encroaching strides
The march of progress settled on their range.
I left, my auditors, a country borne,
In this our century, on wings of peace
(But, after some hard turbulences quelled)
And glorious progress in the every world;
I saw, about me, spread the arts of life;
I could behold the busy weaver's skill,
His taste of beauty and his choice of will;
The artisan wrought many useful things;
The miller plied his steady, needful grind;
The forge was busy, loud the smithy clanged;
And miners delved the bowels of the earth;
Of kine, and kindred, all the life of farm,
Whose fertile acres pictured Ceres' smile —
I could delect you till your ears grow dull.
They make of clothes and can prepare their food —
From finest stuffs to coarser raiment kind,
Of grains and fruits, that reach, near, all the sorts —
In short, there is but little, that the nation wants.
With sixty million people, scattered shore to shore,
In peaceful homes, well-guarded by their love,
The flight of genius coursed such atmosphere,
And marvels, there, are wrought of nature's help,
Adjusted, in devices, for the deeds,
That have facilitated joyful needs.
Four centuries is but all that's covered now.
Yet, in that time, where naked red-skins roved,
And forest-growth and flowers flourished wild,
And beasts of prey were dang'rous to behold,
A pow'rful nation ranks all other lands!
With farm and mine and forest-tracks supplies;
And grazing meads for herds, and masting swine;

With garden-plants and fruits; the cotton bush and
    vine;
The crop of fleece, and silk-worm's little knot,
Their semi-tropics and their temperate zone
Extend so far, that they could live alone —
That is, if sense and spirit limit to a spot.
But, all the world is the American's home!
Their land could be enbound with metal bands,
And sped thereo'er, their genius has devised,
Long sentry-trains armed with a potent force,
That not an instant be devoid of guard,
And messages, dashed through with lightning gait,
Could course the circle in few minutes' time,
Or call the people to their borders' forts;
And sent'nels, cruising on the mains and lakes,
Could be the watch-dogs of their landing-shores!
But, times, immurements crumble, as they fostered
    past!
But, genius flourished in that land of grace.
Called to its birth by adverse, cruel tides,
It armed its friends with gifts of val'rous minds,
And hence they smote, alway, with bravest deeds;
Then was surmounted what encroached the way,
And laid the basis of a virtuous cause,
Wherein its acts of kindness did not pause;
A policy, urged with a fervor, bent
Upon internal, external, eternal rights,
Was made to emanate from righteous hearts,
Than which no body politic had purer parts.
The conscience free, and homes made more secure,
The groundwork builded shall fore'er endure!
Then, genius nurtured in that land of thrift.
Necessity establ'shing its degree,
The keen alertness, due to healthy man,
Caught on the scent in the prolific air,
That scientists learned some twists of nature's laws,
And, by unrav'ling, struck on many flaws,
By which we had been taught to tread our ways.
No doubt, these laws immutable were thus;
And, too, undoubtedly, were once well-kenned:
But, driv'ling into oblivion, burnished new,

Were like the glorious sun-light to the erstwhile
    blind
And eftsoons giddy; the patient, toiling man
Cleft through the rifts of gloomy mind
And murky faith and mean adversity.
      To suffer, ere the glory won;
      To die, perhaps, when just begun;
      Sometime, to perish, ere it's spun —
      In vain to linger, when 'tis done!
And yet the labor is not one-half done!—
In fact can, scarcely say it has begun;
Though we are wondrous at the marvelous gait,
At which our eyes 've been opened here of late,
I trow, 'tis faith, that will remove the clouds,
Reanimate, where stupor, now, beshrouds!
Thus, genius fled not from the conquest hard.
As oft it strove, impassioned in its zeal,
It sought the world's advance and earthly weal;
It struggled in the gloomy hours, when night
But barely gives an outline of its might,
And, with short glimpses by a glimmering ray,
Devised some means of urgent, ambient way.
Of nature's power to nature is the play:
With mystic force, applied to count'ring sway,
The mean development is genius' lay!
Where multitude requires multous things,
Celerity now caters to such wants.
The fecund soil, on which the settlers trod,
Gave its response, as they adduced their care
With such of skill and tools at their command;
The fur and finny tribes them clad and fed,
So skins and flesh of other beasts, and fowl,
      And vegetable growths and fruitings fair;
And, as the silent monarchs fell at strokes,
They yielded shelter and protection, in their course.
Thus fared the pioneer, to danger heark'ning,
Oft, with a blanched cheek; the stealthy lurking
Of foe, to seek his life-flowing blood,
But gave him cautious front and hardihood.
Of opportun'ty born of ample fold;
Of ingenuity thriving with distress;

Of noble efforts feeling on their way
To circumscribe the peccant finitude:
Born, raised, surmounted plenitude —
O'erstepped the bounds, that threatened it to stop
That furtive adiaphan might chase its way.
An amaranth place for those worthy souls,
Who graved the human cause on honor's rolls!
Swiftly, now, the message bears in missive fire
From nook to nook the tale of early news,
With speed, almost, in which the heart could yearn.
And sounds speed through the space, reft into clefts,
Sewn by wire-threads drawing into inguinal parts.
You may preserve your cherished sounds and words,
And, handing down your phiz, write, lock of hair,
May, too, encase your voice in fav'rite ditty,
Or, with your eloquence, in passionate role,
For devolution to posterity.
With unctuous animation, like a whirl,
To rush trite action to the fleet of time,
You may be carried, whither, to or hence.
To feed the hungry, and the limbs to clothe,
One pair of hands may serve ten thousands, more
If need there be compliance to be pressed,
As, to their guidance, yield a million powers —
And more, if need there be, and will.
And, yet, this sweet, beneficent decree
Is, not at all, beginning to be known.
And, though, one pair, now, caters to the mil,
Each of the thousand caters back again,
In one long ceaseless twirl;
Enlarging, twisting, labyrinthine ways,
Untorn, unending in their joined tours,
Each forming ringlets from a new-born ray,
Bound in a circlet of an endless sway."

They expressed satisfaction at this my effort, but also
regret at its brevity, in that it did not dwell on the contrivances referred to, as to construction and applied adaptability to practical uses, and the manipulations of their
products. Others desired to know more of the political

organization and government of the people, and their principal pursuits and objectives: again, others were concerned with the apprehensions of and provision for a future existence—and the dear ladies wanted to know something of the customs, habits and, though of course slightly hinted, of the means of allurement by the counter sexes.

And divers other sequent items from all, now grown brave and curious; so that I regarded my first effort with a sufficient mixture of alarm and comprehension to assure them, individually, of an intended compliance with their requests in the early future. In the meantime I set my wheels of cogitation and reflection to work.

CHAPTER XV.

WHAT IS LOVE.

The bloom and blossom may delight the eye
And please some sense and may dispense
With many a sigh—but where's the prism
Of sweet and tender, clear and blissful zest?

As before indicated, I had formed a decided feeling of attachment for Kathleen Bertram, the daughter of the elder of my discoverers.

From the moment I saw her, which was very soon after landing, I was inspired of a near and important presence, that sensation of intelligence in the natural and spiritual universe of the mutual fitness of things and conditions.

This veridicalism may not be philosophically realized at the time, but, despite subsequent distresses and strictures on its authenticity, develops and superintends the fitness of the establishment.

Appearing tall, she stood erect, a type of the pure, rosy, golden blonde, in the maturing stages of maiden development. Her abundant tresses, which, when unconfined, as they sometimes were, were sufficient to envelop her in maze or mist to her feet, a silken shimmer of softness, beauty and golden hue almost indescribable in its ravishing effect, were then loosely coiled high at the back of her symmetrical head, whilst loose strands waved naturally in dallying silkiness back from her white and shapely brow.

If at first she noticed me at all, it must have been but incidentally to note the presence of a strange face, and the interest of this novelty was for the moment subdued in the passionate delight of the reunion with her father, which was exhibited with such natural grace. An unbeguiled child of nature in that quiet and undefiled far-off spot, reared in innocence, a delightful embellishment to the beautiful scenery of that paradise! Eagerly transported as I was at the time, to behold humanity again, prepared to hail as magnificent and inspiring the humblest of mankind, and feasting my eyes, as though upon the most beautiful vision of my life, intently, uninterruptedly, persistently on the whole group; yet the spirit itself made a distinction even at that time, and an involuntary thrill coursed through my veins, whenever I caught a glimpse of her. But nothing in her demeanor evinced anything but curiosity with reference to me; although her whole carriage and manner portrayed inherent modesty and naive virtue, that would, I believe, have withstood any onslaught in any society — that is, she possessed and manifested an eminently pure heart and mind. For the strict decorum handed down as rules by the first settlers here, had been so quietly and firmly perpetuated, so understood as a matter of course, that in fact no one had even dreamed of a breach thereof. Her undoubted intellectuality shone from her radiant face; her skin was white, smooth and soft, with a pinkish tincture in her cheeks to give lusciousness to the picture, and that firm, compact, full flesh of youth and complete health.

In the interim of the month, my reanimation, preceding my narrated lecture, I was charmingly engaged in cultivating the acquaintance of these interesting personages, whose physical health, vigor and comeliness were no more remarkable than their mental and intellectual capacities. That their want of actual contact with things of, what we may choose to call the world, frequently disclosed itself to me, was to be expected; but, on that account, as auditors they left nothing to be desired. I sometimes reflected, that their attention resembled what would be our attitude (out in our world) if an accredited agent from heaven were to recount incidents thereof in our midst, but probably, owing to our cultivated conceits and attrite skepticisms, we should show less deference. During these conversations, in the intervals of their labors — for, strange as it may seem, these free and multi-supplied folk were a very busy and industrious set — nearly all, old and young, would be present.

Kathleen was a most attentive listener, quiet, not even venturing a question or remark; and as on opportune occasions I had begun to scan her lovely visage (under whatever arduous labor of discourse, that was all the refreshment I needed) I found her large, beautiful, soulful eyes gazing toward me with wondrous expression, with a greater vision inwardly, in the mental conjectures and adaptations of the reality to the impressions gained by the account, than, apparently, attracted by anything in their normal and nominal range. To have been piqued in my vanity, on that account, would have been useless — much more the silly and unhappy destruction of a charming and elevating spectacle. I loved to draw out my narrative, to dwell with almost breathless abidance, to sip the honey of the beautifully unfolding flower at such rare moments, to view the effects or reproductions in this, one of nature's most brilliant, sensitive, human mirrors — nature reproduces or illustrates every principle in life — for her native innocence, never having been invaded by our overdrawn or perverted culture, suggested no destruction or bare discrimination.

My converse, on these occasions, was desultory and suggested by random remarks and momentary occurrences. My first effort at any formal instruction was my just recounted lecture. This was, also, the occasion leading to my first opportunity at a passage with my beloved.

The following morning I set about an engagement to construct a contrivance, recalled to me by my former experience, which I perceived would be useful here, and, for the purpose of my labors, took up a convenient location, somewhat elevated and on a near cliff, overlooking the ocean and also the plantation on the land-side. What was my surprise and delight when, as I was gazing out to sea and picturing busy scenes way off in Ohio with Kathleen as a central figure, I heard someone approach behind me and turned, to become aware of the sole presence I desired above all others — Kathleen, dazzlingly beautiful. Unabashed, she decorously remarked that she hoped she was not disturbing me; but having finished her immediate task, with a few minutes at her disposal, she had felt a curiosity regarding a matter I had vaguely touched upon in my late public discourse, and hoped that I would not be indisposed to gratify her. I was only too delighted, as you can imagine, and hastily rising, bowed her to my comfortably constructed seat, setting up a

block a few feet distant for mine. She demurely took the
proffered place, with an evident air of total absorption in
whatever was engrossing her reflections. I was overjoyed
with the prospect of even a few minutes alone with her,
and viewed her with admiration beyond any efforts at concealment, which to a maiden of our civilized society would
have been embarrassing, but on this sprig of naivete was
completely lost.

Sat, tall, five-six to measure her neat height;
A linten garment flowing to her form
And girt about her shapely, slender waist;
One foot, clad wooden-soled and linen-up,
Was crossed o'er other likewise e'en so meet;
Her slender hands lay rested on her lap.
In graceful poise, bent with attentive ear,
Her luminous orbs filled with abstracted light
Turned toward the deep, that lay before her view,
As to draw in its depths, as well as yond,
While paling cloudless skies before their hue,
With brightness that might mirror sparkling founts,
In that keen interest of the human soul

That gnaws within the convent of its wist,
Her visage glowed with that pure burst of light
That puzzles whither her perplexing front —
A crown of golden silk above her brow
That dazzled o'er the same a yearned-for bliss;
Yet she so innocent of all desire.
She hearkens for a sound to wake her will,
She listens for the craved, she knows not what
That stirs the animation of God's breath
And rouses in the bosom blest aspire —
Oh, curious innocence, oh, ignorant will!

As mildly as the tremulousness of my voice would permit me I inquired her wish. Without the least agitation,
and frankly turning her eyes toward me, with every illu-

sion of any covertness of gaze dispelled from the most
seeking scrutiny, and with the inkling of an artless, lovely
smile playing about her fascinating lips, she said: "I
wish to know something of the customs and pastime of
the young people of the country you came from. Are
they kind in their intercourse with each other? Do they
romp and are they gay and light-hearted? I have read
something about amusements of the young in different
books we have, but those occurrences are so long ago, that,
although I know those works nearly all by memory, I
have never exactly felt toward the subjects of these narratives as though they were or could become play-fellows.
You, who have passed through the actual experience —
just, to think, actual contact! It seems so marvelous, that
I cannot but connect you, almost, with some existence
beyond or other, than ours — something, that fills me with
ideas of inexplicable mystery." I hung on every word,
sound, that passed her lips!

"I am not surprised," I said, "that you should have
such feelings. Your delightful little society, the very
embodiment of ideal peace and tranquillity on earth, would
know nothing but repose, were it not for this inherent
longing for something beyond; but the human heart
begins to yearn, the mind to crave, the whole keen
insight to grow alert for the measure of circumclusion.

"Think of the trials and tribulations that accompanied
the settlements and aggregations of the different peoples,
reft and sundered and swayed by their jealousies and ani-
mosities and developed greeds, and how the ties of relationships were severed or elasticated until they became
weak and could return no more.

"And contrast therewith the peace which prevails here,
with no disturbing element except the natural ambition
for knowledge.

"Now you would marvel that anyone should entertain regret at leaving such a state of society and could desire to return thereto. Well in stoicism it does appear incongruous; in logical sequence it seems that all thinking persons would hasten to withdraw from such chaos, and, in the solitude of secluded spots, commune with undefiled nature and nature's God for the inspiration in calm repose and aspiration for the spiritual existence. Inherently, does not the human soul long for peace; or is it an element of cherishing warfare?

"Born a part of the conglomerate mass, to seethe and surge with its revolutions — he is but the skeptic, the eccentric, the unprofitable to himself and others, who attempts to withdraw himself; and then only with partial success, when he sinks to the degree of the wild beast, whose companionship in that event he cherishes to supply the attachments of his spiritual nature, unless a higher hope can supplant the present desire. It is unnatural for anything whatever in nature to be alone.

"Fellow-being is as essential, as gratifying, and as intimately interwoven into our constitutions as it is material to our developments; so should its intercourse be as consistently and universally at liberty as prudence and propriety with reference to our shortcomings can permit. But the stronger should first take off the burden of the weaker.

"The active philosopher, the worthy preacher, the honorable man, is he who acts and struggles, not above or below, but with the populace — but neither reserved beyond their pale, nor enveloped in their dross, from which a proper activity will always secure him. An exerted leverage is well, but he must appreciate the resistance to apply the power. Society transmits its powers; it transcends its rights, or rather it abuses its privileges.

"Periodically, a wave of evolution sweeps over it, and

seems to search the very crevices in its cleansing or jar-
ring powers—and affairs take another drift. Watch the
potent little influences—for a time, the sentiments or
linguistry of a book, the exalted similitudes of a
series of dramatic representations; the outpouring of eloquence that springs from periods of great calamity; how
the cogencies thereof overspread into every part of the
community! The centuries have continued their foibles—
references with meagre details to active, somewhat glorious
achievements, the collapse to ruin in or by which the
undying spirit reared in new glory, progress, rebounding
ever as the tide smote the wall of adamant separating this
from the region of perfection. But, nothing exceeds in
destructiveness or value—bringing, on the one hand, these
overwhelming revolutions, on the other, overwhelming the
agencies, that would produce the former—the steady
instruction and development of right, *altogether, equal,* no
king and no pauper, no priest and no peer, but, man's
shoulder to man.

Oh, may we seek to clamber o'er this cast?
With single efforts, then, we must essay to scale —
The impetuous mass but bears us dashing on.
How do the lads and embrace their golden hour?
Born in the moulds that foist them gloomy brows
They seek to shift from earliest dawn till death,
And cry "Immortal, mortal," with expiring breath!

"Our young folks find themselves diversely situated:
some with every golden opportunity, princes and prin-
cesses clothed with their semi-godhead, which a half-credu-
lous or weak community grants them; some with the
flowers of life sweet and luxuriant along their paths,
whose oderiferousness offers to them their only employment; some feel the vigor for an active life, implanted in

them, the equipment and impulse for the necessary strife,
while others drivel and drift, menaced and burdened from
the start, and branded with the scars of doom! The
naturally perverse, or unfortunate beyond the usual degree
attendant upon everyone, we will not consider.

"What then are their sports? From the innocence, that
would make the prattling princess the companion of the
beggar's sprig, they drift through toys and merriment,
and tears and fears, distinguishable only by their several
opportunities.

"Soon there breaks upon their common horizon a line
demarque! The tender sprout, whose tendrils cling to
'upper life,' is held exempt, exalts her imperious head,
and is proud; the wistful mite, of other degree, soon
learns the hard decree! Their sports adapt individual
ingenuity from their means and childish dreams and ambitions produce respective gyrations with various success and
deportment. Clothed and fed by their parents according
to the latter's means their society is gauged thereby and
rearing are the weeds or flowers from the seeds, plot, care
and attention and their gardener. Many an obscure
plantlet, however, has proven the greatest blessing to the
world—in which alone lies the sterling quality of manhood and usefulness of mankind.

"In the higher and more favored circles, the young
approach the period of adolescence with much eager anticipation, in the footsteps of their elders, or, consonantly
with the proffered delights and experiences of others, to
enter upon the established disports and routine of fashion.

"The gilded palaces of their parents and their friends'
parents, glimmer and glitter with all the trappings of
wealth, and call upon the resources and contrivances of the
world for their luxuries and dainties.

"They have horses and carriages, sleighs and coachmen;

and they may spend some of their time, which only awaits
killing, in such locomotion; then, they have books and art
and music; and they have physical exercises and bathing
and boating and skating and games; and they indulge in
balls and suppers and theatres and theatricals, and teas,
picnics, excursions, parties — and, at last (often before),
shed tears and experience spiteful pangs at the 'vicissitudes' of life — attributable only to the inordinacy of
their desires.

"The upper society deems it an unnecessary condescension
to heed the less favored, though not less worthy, below,
unless when moments of a leveling calamity call to their
minds the universal brotherhood of man; then anything that
can soften the rigor of their realizations and fears of the
common lot, are eagerly grasped at.

"As a tribute to the American people it must be added,
my appreciative auditor," (for she sat, as though transfixed
with the interest she manifested; and how I reveled in
the delicious attitude!) "that, in times of great, widespread-
ing distress, their responses to appeals for assistance, even
sometimes before they are uttered, are magnanimous and
make no distinctions, scarcely any restrictions; opportunities that are, unfortunately, often abused. And this
sentiment is growing in readiness, as the facilities are
improving for transmission of intelligence — there is an
appreciable enlightenment and progress in this respect.

"The middle classes are imitative — the happy mean from
choice or compulsion — often mere reflections of the other
highest favored class. They are, unwittingly, the strength
of a nation, because they are forced to blend mere ideas
with the operation thereof. To blend with the higher
class is their individual dream; to reach thereunto measures their joy.

"The lowest class, the proverbial poor, grasp and snap in

any direction, without any well-defined purpose, save that of existence; and their enjoyments depend altogether on the presentations of the moment. Where not a disease, poverty is a crime.

"But usually they all love and are loved in turn."

"What is love?" here interposed Kathleen, for the first time breaking her silence. "What is love?"

"What is love?" I said. "It is so old, or reputed to be, that it would have ripened into unutterable bliss could it change in the course of any time; it would illumine as it does delight the earth. Ah! darling"—I started at myself. "I beg your pardon, Kathleen; this world would be a prickly pear without love."

"Why?" she responded, "I have experienced nothing prickly about it; and I don't think love has come among us—at least, I have never seen it."

"Yes, sweet—excuse me," I stammered; "it is here. You may not have seen it; but, but—I hope you will feel it." (What a blundering fool is a man in love!)

"Will it hurt me?" she said.

"My sweet Kathleen—I beg your pardon," again I stammered (I could not refrain from a certain abstraction of thought, which led me to think aloud my ardent wishes); "a fair young lady, like yourself, in all candor I assure you, would not, should never be grieved by love—pure, virtuous stir of the depths of emotion!"

Kathleen seemed perplexed. It was plain that no feeling akin thereto had yet been awakened in her; she did not understand it. Sentiments and reflections outside her quiet life might then first dawn upon her by reason of my presence and information. Was I, then, a beneficent visitor? Might not her life otherwise have been passed in utter tranquillity and blissful ignorance of the woes of life? Fate, however, placed me here, so that I felt no sense of guilt. Providence had guided my steps, and His inscrutable measures evolve benefits out of the means we may divert from their legitimate channels — as the sequel in this matter will undoubtedly show.

Catching the puzzled, quizzical gaze in Kathleen's soulful eyes, I pitied her in her quandary and evident struggle for light; like the poor sunflower, transplanted to and unfolding its bloom in the Arctic regions, on the day of undying light or unsetting sun.

I felt, that, after all, I was a wretch. But, as she gave no evidence of any pained feeling, I felt reassured and proceeded:

"The day has darkened into night o'er many a lea
And weary plodders have returned, with tired tread,
Unto their sheltering homes; a wistful glance is livened
    by a merry shout
And answered by a welcoming smile of —
It beams and breaks until its warming rays infuse the
    chilly heart.
Then flow despair from off the clouded brow
And momentarily of earth forget the travails of a few
    dark hours,
That must course o'er us ere the light we see!
Then 'tis so said that love bears on the torch
And lights the pathway o'er its rose-hid thorns,
That many a brier may be passed with ease.

"Yet, you do not understand! Nay, not until a Heaven blends two spirits with an instantaneous mutual irradiance may the passion of these souls secure its natural vent. Such feelings need no action of the mind: they are of the heart."

CHAPTER XVI.

SOME HISTORY AS IT MIGHT APPEAR.

A FEW days after my conversation with Kathleen, which was abruptly terminated by a call from her mother, in the closing hours of a heated afternoon the whole of this little colony was picturesquely grouped under the shade of a magnificent oak, while the children were disporting themselves in youthful glee and the yet intense rays of the setting sun were obliquely illuminating the scene. One of the elderly members recalled to us all my promise to discourse farther on the civilization I had left behind.

I arose, and the silence and attention at once accorded me could not have been more flattering or deferential. The curiosity and inquiring solicitude had greatly increased among my auditors, all of whom bore evidences, in their thoughtful, wistful countenances, of having, in the meantime, spent many moments in reflection, no doubt dreaming rosy descriptions of the invisible wonders just beyond the horizon. And the various fancies I have no doubt would have proven a study. I began:

"No romancer ever stated or related a thing, that was not then in existence somewhere: for, the spirit cannot but relate truth. He may separate their parts, but he cannot disunite their principles.

"Our people, referring distinctively to the United States of America, is conglomerate; hence, every other country may claim kinship with us by some distinctive feature. The cruel Tartar mingling, somewhere, his blood with the Moor, or some gentle disciple of mercy and goodness; the

Gentile and Jew, the christian and heathen — the passion of the torrid mingles in the veins of the colder zone; and, as care and abandon, shrewdness and diffidence, cunning, deceit, flattery, vice, course with honor, integrity, sobriety, industry, patience and thrift and honesty — light and gloom — so, the mass, compound of all nationalities, presents an anomaly — behind which there is a power and might, individually invincible and collectively invulnerable by any one other nationality. The result is a cementing, in fact, of the theoretical universal brotherhood — and let the result of extension and universal relationship speak for itself on its fields of unparalleled victories.

"Our country was founded in genius — the genius formed by amalgamation of the divers nations, and the genius consisting of the spark by the friction of the several parts of adversity — hence, the means of swift intelligence, of retentive reproducing motive power — God's meteorite, God's scintillator.

Speak not in softer tone but thunderous acclaim:
Th' United States are reared to mortals free!
Heed not a drivelling cant but speed the sweet sesam',
That mortals shall not bear a tyr'nt's decree.

"One of its first steps was to establish a proper and perpetuating form of government — and upon that shortly followed the strife for power, even here — more the result of the teachings of the preceding perverse ages, than the untrammeled opinions of the contestors.

As long as man has ambition,
As long as he has life,
So long there will be attrition,
Contumely and strife.

"The ebb and flow of party-life would, of themselves, be an interesting story; but form a distinctive feature.

The prevailing policy, throughout, sought the principles underlying present necessities — those of security, health, and prosperity — but were not at all times as pure in their motives and measures.

"To these ends the forests were cleared, and industries placed in progress; and all the enemies of this onward march were, as much as possible, exterminated, whether of animal, vegetable or human life — the renegade and the savage, the beast of prey and nature's rank and briery growth, the usefulness of which was far outmeasured by its incumbrances.

"Out of pleasant glens and cultivated dales the curling smoke of forge, factory and mill was wafted over the hill-tops, and here and there some far-visible and marking spire pointed to a place where grateful hearts could pour out their spirit of appreciation for God's manifest mercies; and, on the Sundays, the winding paths, still through brush and often forest, leading in the directions of those spires, were dotted with the surrounding inhabitants, wending their way thereto.

"Through the dark days of savage onslaught and fearful attacks of wild beasts, of the treachery of brethren and relentlessness of foe, not without the glorious gleams of self-sacrifice and of heroism, there came an exaltation over these evils, and the gloomy difficulties were one by one surmounted — the beasts became extinct, or decimated in number, the savage saw his tribe disappear forever. and those of the white men who chose the latter's companion-ship and, worse than either, possessed the attributes of both, in turn, bit the dust, as a reward of their skulking, iniquitous careers.

"When at length the flint-rock rusted in the corner, and the woodman's blows resounded less, the hum of the various mills and the trip of the hammer in the forge

were beginning to tell another tale. How great the
changes, yet after all how sad the realization! It matters
not whether, the cruel bedizened visage and leer of the
savage, in the midst of physical plenty chills the heart's
blood or the gaunt stalk of poverty and starvation menace
the victim.

"Gradually the clearings extended, and towns and cities
sprung up. These confines gradually reached and
engulfed the outposts of the more forward and intrepid
settlers, who, in turn, proceeded further only again to be
overtaken.

"As the thrift and enterprises increased, rivalries arose
and unlovely feelings multiplied with the grasping multitude; so that at this time caste and conditions, craft and
enterprises, combinations and resources, all have their
demarkations, and become individually menacing, as they
are favorably discriminated by a government, which
should only exercise a balance of power between its prin-
cipals, not an elevation of one over any other.

"The vicious seek their prey; the indolent disregard their
obligations; the thrifty complain and with cause; the
unworthy seek, like parasites, to feed and enrich at the
expense of others. Rich men, too rich in wealth's
arduous cares, are too suspicious in regard to it to enjoy
its fruits; poor men are hateful and discouraged; the
unscrupulous, ever working on the suspicions and fears of
either, grasp and defraud in any direction; thus civilization is afflicted.

"As long as laziness or viciousness infest any members of
a community, thus so long will tranquillity be impossible,
and suffering will ensue to everyone, in the effort for
supremacy, or the danger of oppression, or, even, in the
care of bare maintenance. Thousands upon thousands,
running into millions, have multiplied in our country —

the asylum for the world. The evil-doers, banished, have
come to us; the distressed have sought solace here; the
enterprising, most of them, are here; and of the scum of
populations, which belong everywhere and nowhere, many
have been thrust upon us, as well as drifted this way.
This is a board for every game of life. But, we are best
enabled to take care of them — they come to us and we do
the rest; our examples and free institutions have produced
more good population from these outcasts than all the walled
conventicles that ever existed.

" We produce all the necessities of life, and many of the
curatives of its ills; the babe may be swathed, and fed —
and die an aged sire, enclosed in his cloth-covered casket,
all within the province of this land. Ay, many a family
that has scarcely ever gone beyond the pales of a back-
woods farm for anything!

" I will not enumerate its products, nor dwell on the
means of transportation — animal force or the mystical
power of vapor or fire — nor tell how thought may be communicated in an instant of time to great extents; all this
seems incredible to you, as it did to us when first
broached — yet, history will smile at our incredulity.

" Much of this you have not yet the means among you,
my dear colonists, of developing; although, lying inherent
in your rocks and soil, as well as within yourselves, the
elements are present, with the air, the water and the fire.
For these researches you require developments of character and of resources, for which your mutual, circumscribed contact is not enough. You may be happy, well
enough off; but, must you not use that placed in your
charge ?

" The people of the United States dress, and there is a
distinction in this respect, as well as a mark for the sexes,
substantially conventional among them. As in all affairs

of the world, unfortunately, a few lead and set the fashion, and the largely unthinking multitude follow.

"There is no individual ingenuity, no regard for personal comfort or enjoyment. Yet to the items of their clothing more time is devoted than to many things that are elevating; and much trouble is entailed, solely to excel thereby someone who may be foolish enough to feel distress on account of imagined inferiority.

"Nothing that can be fabricated on earth is too fine to give ease and adornment to the human; no food or drink too delectable. But, when the Creator of all sends one of His leveling influences — pestilence, famine, warfare, or any scourge of the kind — then the vanity of vanities disappears, and the real necessities are found few and not oppresive.

"Still, precious stones which really delight by their glittering beauty, and charming soft raiment, which is truly a pleasure to the beholder and wearer, and elegantly constructed abodes, and the downy couch, and pleasant vapors and odors, and entrancing, lulling sounds, and the delights of regalement, and of passion, are possibilities, potentialities of our mysterious organization, which indeed carry sadness in their wake. The milk and the honey of our existence is too often basely employed, gluttonously misused, and inequitably shared.

"The farmer, the merchant, the manufacturer, the miner, the carrier, the builder, with their combinations and modifications and assistants, constitute the busy class; to which may be added the musician, the artist, the author, and all those who administer to the intellect, or whose skill and knowledge contribute to the maintenance or cure of our physical bodies, or adjust the matters of our mutual relationships.

"Schools are maintained and well distributed and attended; it is sought to inculcate virtue in all minds;

the means of informing anyone of the daily occurrences
are quite adequately present. Our people affect the violent athletic sports; then there are milder games, embracing mental calculation and physical skill, one or both, in
uneven degrees; also, there are the amusements of the
passions, emotions and inter-magnetic influences of individuals in society; and the contemplation of miniature, or
idealized reproductions, the false for the real, or reflections
of existence. All these enter properly into occupation
and would not, but for their abuse, disarrange the smooth
even conduct of affairs.

"You can regulate things, but not men; spirits, like
gases, must be chastened and rarified before they escape
their bad odors. But, a bright light shineth not but in
the shade, hence, the brilliance caused by all luminaries
is what our poor nature seems to be unable to endure,
even in mental contemplation, envy and jealousy having
their seats therein. Still, we are the brightest spots in
the gloom, here.

"Seventeen institutions comprise the affairs of men and
these conglomerate and diversify: The filial relation. The
single life of man or woman. Conjugal rights. Parental
demands. Correlative regards, and justice, virtue and
humanity between fellow-beings, mercy and the attribute
of affinity with all things. Habits of industry. Discernment, courage, perseverance, and the principles of adaptation. Instruction, study and mutual acquisition. Defense,
preparation and guard. Inspiration, the guarding of men's
affairs and the relation of government, the delegation of
power and representation. Interchange of values. The
accordance of corresponding sustenance, maintenance and
degree. The spiritual aspect and the instinct, premonition
and direction of the soul. The mental development and
cordial enfranchisement. The laws of nature. Repara-

tion of or adjustment to wrongs, accident and displacement. And a corollary including honest discovery, production and construction.

"Beginning with National administration — the child upon birth finds government, the last shall be first — are found the proposing, establishing and administering powers, powers within a power, three in one. The Nation proposes its amalgamation, its delegation establishes its decree and their functionaries administer, expatiating upon the necessity of government or the advisability of coalition among our human selves —

> Justice deals when mercy fails,
> Filtering, softening, racking deeds,
> Doing acts of rigid chore.
> Call and sough then when it rails,
> Cry for vengeance when it quails;
> 'Tis not trite nor of details —
> Justice plain and pure!

"Coming down to a vision of politics, we may discern in our organization the public and domestic relations. As domesticity resolved itself to individual division, so their relations involved and evolved a polity. A system sprung up, and abuses attended its comity, or retarded its completement.

"The domestic relation is individual propriety embodying the discreet concern with the affairs of all others and things and devout contemplation of future existence. Out of the domestic the public ministrations rise, being the spiritual emanation of human association — and its necessity.

"Regarding the disease that cankers continuously in the open and hidden sores of the institutions of man, many lose heart, fail and die — flowers withered by a sirocco's breath!

"Justice is encouragement and protection to all.

"The producer, the delver, the artificer, the trafficker; the promoter, adjuster, applier and instructor—all their fruits are gathered and garnered in the store-house of governmental regulation. But when regulations disturb this equilibrium—when organization upon organization, and within the body whole, create themselves—the cancers and tumors of the physical body, that so far separate themselves from the remaining organization as to constitute localities and developments of themselves, and yet must and do retain their connections with the whole organism for their maintenance—foreign in every requisite and desire, and the worst kind of enemy, because internal, familiar and devastating in every direction—then accreting evils manifest themselves. The wheels of industry, in our country, when I left, were clogged by dishonesty, dissipation, the desire for luxury and ambition for personal splendor or power; and the consequent wanton speculations by means of trusts and monopolies—in short, those diseases which drain and contaminate the whole, being anomalous in absorbing all the foreign nutriment that is necessary and given to the body, and becoming themselves abnormal and diseased from over-indulgence besides withering the rest of the body from want of sustenance. What body can, exclusively, sustain itself? What internal disease can avoid communicating its ill to the whole body? How can you long bruise one or more parts without engendering a destructive disease there? In the absence of these, personal management would result in successful commerce with the whole world—and competition from any source but stimulates excellence.

"Thus far the government has done much to classify the people, if not equally as much as they have themselves. Yes, you say, they govern themselves. True, and it is with mismanagement or rather lack of diligence, that we

charge them — that they have allowed their affairs to
drift toward the conditions and under the control of those
powers to rid themselves of which ages have violently
battled — our ancestors have bled and died — by which
peoples have been crushed or enslaved — those of mighty
but selfish rulers, and of self-eating monopolies.

"See the folly of submission, and behold the potencies
for evil!

Unthinking, heedless, doomful throng,
With minds kept weak when exercise makes strong!
A few to cause intimidation's fear,
Intrepid reft allow your course to veer;
Shame on all valor and your hardy frame,
Fie, that your ardor be not more aflame!

"Private life, so called, consists of its various walks,
avocations and indulgences.   Yet the solid, cognizant facts
of discoveries, occurrences, achievements, wonders, ocu-
larly and auricularly demonstrated existences and perhaps
some probabilities and possibilities, with inspiration, are
the nucleus of education, which concerns itself thereby
with the transmission of narrative, perpetuation of facile
intercommunication and the developments.   The beginning is the initiation into the mysteries of and is aggra-
vated by the interminable conglomeration of the characters
of human modes and methods.   The learning is of convo-
lutions in human antagonisms and struggling to acquire
the methods of calculation in vogue to appease nature in
achieving over fellow-men, which seems to be the main end
taught, the conscience is only impressed by the omnipo-
tence of the Creator, who manifests the meager mandates
and cullings of wisdom rendered useful by men.   How
subtle are men's intrusions in the aspect of their
iniquities!

Man's glory makes good spirits merely mourn;
He flaunts vouchsafements to the dreary winds
And bids another trust to his vain boasts;
The breezes, even, sigh their spirits' woes.
Vain creature not a ruler over passion's self
Nor trustworthy when storms take their own rise
Within his mantled bosom's own turmoil:
But cries to God, the searcher of his ways,
And lies unmantled at his mercy's feet!

"You have here begun, and yours is solely, a history of the people. Continue the full, complete, connected narrative in that unbiased strain, giving your servants — which other nations call rulers — due meed, and no one can doubt the accuracy of it nor dispute the unfaltering benefit from such an institution. Precedent will then establish the right.

"Without having designated the conditions or manifested details, a tedium in one sense, yet a joy at the ample resource for employment to everyone, logically the world is not burdensome. Industrious, systematical application with intermediate and ulterior purposes of legitimate endeavors will reach to the evening of final rest and make death not what it is now but the hour of sweet repose.

"It is apparent that my old country needs a thorough investigation into its affairs — a commission to be as particularly and regularly appointed as the taking of its census. Thorough men of science and knowledge would devote themselves to the task with full powers and develop the means of much redress simply by the information they would disclose. Without remuneration therefor excepting the distinction and the value of the knowledge to themselves as eminent men and citizens their appointment would be universally hailed and the

historical knowledge obtained and thereafter maintained
by systematical continuance would be invaluable. Nothing
can exceed in benefit authentic contemporary history!
Knowledge leads to wisdom, advancement, exaltation and
the suppression of evil; an authentic report to and connecting link with is the hope of posterity.

"I thank you, ladies and gentlemen, for your kind
attention — not that one-half has been told you, but
enough for reflection, and I fear to impose myself too
much upon you."

Bowing, I withdrew to one side. The applause and
fervent, hearty expressions of pleasure and satisfaction
put at rest any apprehensions, wrapt as I had become in
the subject as I progressed, I might have felt regarding
any undue infliction upon them. I cast a look in the
direction of Kathleen — but she sat pensively gazing into
abstraction, her mind undoubtedly wandering far, far
away. in that imagined, strange country. Was I associ-
ated in those reveries?

CHAPTER XVII.

AN INDUSTRIAL RESUME.

First is power of the mechanics, second resume, third
    production's chose.
  When thought and impulse had full-coursed their
    way,
    There stole upon the horizon the dawn of day,
    In swift pursuit; and noise of click and clangor's
      sound,
    As, pending the burst storm, broke forth in tones,
    There rose the din, betokening urgent toil,
    And sharp endeavor, seeking every spoil.

Nor is content the science' searching ray, as, on its bent,
     it seeks each nook.
    There may lie hidden as the simplest thing
    And this it kens, hence often its gay fling
    As it discerns some mystery scarce unveiled,
    That its queer shape had nought to stem a hope,
    But, all of knowledge need not foil the stool,
    If its receiver will be ne'er the fool.
How soars its flight, how sinks its feeling touch down
     to the inmost depths!
    There is no vision but with lucid points,
    And no reflection, that has not its joints;
    Hence, can it pause, or hesitate to do,
    Or can it cease to jostle error's ways?
    What false excitement, superstition's fear —
    No creed is happier, than has its own seer!
The millions teemed, the millions swore their constant,
     firm behest!
    Ah, for the night, to solace in its gloom,
    To see, with no distraction, whate'er doom
    Can solve this speedy, scant, industrial range,
    To give invention to its risks and grasps,
    On, to lead forward, ever, stern and true,
    Oft, that trends froward to make, sadly, rue.
There is no doubt, the visions will reward the worthy,
     kind and pure.
    That such a scoffer was on genius bent,
    And, in his fruits, was, pitifully, shent,
    Creeds but the laws of any universe;
    One thought, one sigh cannot be lost to ane.
    Have you no wisdom as to teach the lore,
    That in pure genius can be any chlore?
This circumvision, spection is unending, great and very
     fair.
    The hand may tremble, yet devise a stay,
    The arm be feeble, that constructs the sway,
    By part to part, to shake the fundament:
    The spirit, Spirit is the power unseen,
    The all, invisible, unseen the strength of might.
    Thus, Faith is for yourself, Hope to the other,
    And Charity with all, that none can bother.

When you lead on, devise the ways as sternly, yet as
  meet, as e'er you may.
 There cannot be conjectured, nor construed,
 A single problem, other than for good!
 Contend you this endeavor then, or fear,
 That you have nought the power to endure?
 Stringe to the lists, and see that you were born
 To win as bright a pennant, e'er was torn.
A loosely garment, red, and dight all o'er a supple female
  form —
 Suggests the more, of ignorance within,
 That drives desire frenzied with chagrin.
 This heed e'er fastens to temptation's chore,
 That aught appears to waken your distrust:
 Be you, then, wary, pierce the folds, that hide,
 With your reflections, which, always, betide.
Ah, glossy raven tresses, garb of crimson hue and lightly
  dight, and face so white —
 Is that not all-inflaming, fire and coal?
 Thus eats luridity into the soul!
 And may the deadening ashes semble face,
 Which first portrayed the white flames of the fire:
 For, soon, a withering, commonplace disgust
 Will, then, have met the folly with its thrust.
How they, the picturing words, set forth each thing, each
  crevice, any thought of ane.
 You may make no remark, yet, e'er so rude,
 But, beautifully, fits a truth, not crude,
 But forms a text, as ever, just and trite,
 And suits employment, such as always right;
 For, in directness there is, always, good:
 And must, with knowledge, be so understood.
The timely application robs each and every deed of its
  seemed crime.
 But virtue, truth itself, may be abused,
 If, in their acts, not properly are used.
 Then, drivel not in cant, affected tears —
 There's nought so bad but augments with your
  fears;
 There's nothing good, that may not be mistaken:
 And everything is fair, that's not forsaken!

And language cannot err, like figure bold, speaks but one
      thing.
    Infallible, to so diverge from truthful says,
    Built course on course, in ways with reaching ways,
    It has, but properly, the forced sequence —
    One way begun, can never digress hence,
    But must add on the solvents, tricks and throws,
    Becomingly, and justly onward goes.
What makes the seeming error of one's ways, are not the
      ways themselves.
    But, choice, or disconnections we do make;
    The ways can, by themselves, you surely take,
    If you but heed the foresight to go on,
    And, by no folly, be led off your course:
    This logic, then, is truly God's device,
    That every soul may, savingly, take choice.
All conscience, instincts, natural inclinations point to
      sense.
    That is, to wise endeavors and good choice,
    And, for restraints, each owns a strong device.
    There is, so little, that can justify,
    Where wanton notions fritter, here and there,
    That judgment, soon, would cause a vile duress
    Did mercy plead not for the foul weakness.
But, brightness of this world, forever, fades — of what, or
      where, or when!
    The thought, this moment brilliant, loses cast,
    To the own thinker, when a moment past;
    And, leading, then, remembrance o'er the scene,
    Has learned a different moral by the preen.
    Oh, fadeless things we must not, here, esteem —
    If nothing else, our memories will so gleam.
This latter proposition is not true, nay, it is cant.
    The estimation, weakly, so regards;
    For, diligent knowledge this sore evil wards:
    There is in every course a natural swing,
    And is, as naturally, true to cause,
    That you have but to reck the onward course,
    To learn eventilation to each source.
The fleeting time, the days that are no more, the years
      now past!

Yet, busily, the hum of thrift goes on.
The seasons waken, each, in several turn —
The seed-time, freshly, starts its new-born life,
The earnest harvest yielding its fit fruits;
Then, rest, deep silence, save the storm, that roars,
To make more comfort garnered peace indoors.
The year has been divided, fitting to man's state, in
 miniature.
 First, weakly born (within the first few months
 In, deeply, then but slow from winter's slumps)
 At once burst forth to vigor's budding (Spring),
 Whence, then, unfolding, such the fecund seeds,
 The sterling manhood reaches harvest-time —
 Ends like beginning: Now must rhyme, rime!
What nature has supplied, man turns to thrifty, cautious
 use.
 There are embodied in calm nature's stores
 Such force and powers, that it fairly pours
 The bounties on the self-thralled style of man;
 How charily, in ignorance, man does touch!
 More offers nature, than would grant his bliss —
 He has some inkling, got from that and this.
One little atom serves a part, tends to sustain a ponderous
 mass.
 Thus, powers, spirits, turned ever loose
 From every finger-tip, from mind, abstruse,
 Dissolve and emanate, perpetuate and make
 In multiples on multiples, till all parts quake.
 Thus is the stream of increase ne'er t' be stemmed,
 For this is nature's benefit not to be hemmed.
The untold cogent factors, the unnamed potents and
 designs!
 Pure industry is ne'er without its means;
 Is never, that its thrift, but that it gleans,
 If nothing else, the some strewn remnants left,
 That may heap storehouse to its margin's fill;
 Then, comes a rest, a peaceful slumber-time,
 Now, termed a death — then, will be sweet in chime.
The middle course, the medium, the steady and the mix.
 That is the range, which serves the steady will,
 Restrains, but grants in each way to distill,

Upholds the burden, ends must bear the brunt,
Is there, in equilibrium when borne:
Thus, to all cares, the mediums solace tears;
In all affairs the mediums serve the shares.
Old gaunt Philosophy stalked, once, so solemnwise and
dreadful, shrewd.
He says, says he, "This is a sorry fix!
'Tis ages since I saw much worse a mix.
Why, bless the long-time lasting, glittering stars,
The sun and moon, and slivering earth-quaked hills,
I've pranced on planes until I'm wellnigh dead —
But, die I may not, so the ancients said.
What things would you, now, choose my fellow fine;
there, my sweet maid?
No? Hang your head — your modesty's afraid
To speak out in the meeting — where, 'tis said,
So many little children have found fault?
At this I'm not surprised, though I have said,
When you are bent on mischief, read a line,
And leave your mischief bent to fit your spine.
Well, I have wondered, when patrolling, late at night,
through many a storm.
The storm of fears, and tears and troubled hearts,
The violent commotions, renting parts
In anguish, at some pale, mistaken foe.
Now brethren, let me tell you, there's no woe.
'Look to, look to,' the ancients often said,
And this, I now repeat, was then well-bred.
I wish, my dearest, you had always better understood.
There is in eduction, construction, production
The best of concoction, that favors induction;
When once you have instanced the thought and
endeavor,
You will have discovered the powerful lever.
In action, reflection the deeds serve and prove;
In interchange, intervail all objects move."

CHAPTER XVIII.

SHIP AHOY!

For some time a question had agitated itself in our midst, with reference to the possible existence of other lands within our reach, if our craft but enabled us to make tours of discovery beyond our shores. In nautical and astronomical knowledge, that would make us successful voyagers or guide us in any positive direction or return, we were sadly deficient; and once out on the trackless main, we doubted our abilities to return; besides, almost every other consideration was obviated by our want of tools wherewith to construct a vessel of sufficient size.

Still, from desultory discussions, the idea had grown that my whilom ship might be launched; she was not badly wedged, apparently not much broken, and, although stranded by an unusual storm, fortunately had been ensconced in a comparatively safe and protected harbor during her five years of desuetude, and the appliances on board presented every possibility of her restoration to usefulness. It was thought, with our full male strength and the mechanisms our combined ingenuity might devise, we might yet proudly patrol the high seas in her. So that one evening the project was decided upon, and with a good deal of excitement it was determined to prepare at once for our intended experiment. The necessary crops being garnered or safely under way, to abide our return within such a reasonable time as we anticipated, all else could be looked after easily by the women.

Two weeks were consumed in preparations. Enough

rowing, pushing or towing craft were rudely constructed, in addition to the two or three boats on hand, to constitute a small fleet. We had simply to follow the shore-line and in a direction we knew to reach the location of the ship, and felt no concern in that quarter; and, as to provisions, knew that the net and trap would over night supply us at any time, if necessary, in addition to the stock distributed in the boats.

The fervor with which I pressed Kathleen's hand at parting might have betokened something unusual, but I had no misgivings, for I felt cheerfully convinced of the success of our expedition and a speedy safe return, already dreaming of future discoveries in the following spring, and imagining myself an explorer! There was of course, no melancholy brass band — although later, when the instruments were resurrected from the ship, their music became no unpleasant feature of our life here. There was not even speech-making; but, with emotion at the agitation of those remaining behind, many a wave of the hand beckoned the last token before dropping out of sight.

The weather being fine and our expedition uneventful, on the sixth of October we hove in sight of my old quarters, and it was with feelings of pride and joy, that I welcomed the sight of the old hulk. There she was, safe and sound, and seemed quietly to indicate that her days of usefulness were not yet over, by a great deal. The curiosity with which she was viewed by the party, and their careful inspection, were an inspiration to behold! My land abode had not suffered and my gardens were only overgrown. I felt like a lord in his own domain, and entertained with a lavish disregard and graciousness by reason of my great possessions. A poor boy of humble origin arisen to such splendor and prestige — but, that is American!

We proceeded at once to our object here, and worked like bees or beavers, incessantly but systematically.

By a kind Providence, as it were, I found a volume on ship-building, repairing, and so forth, and one relating to ship-machinery, among the late captain's effects — and I felt devoutly thankful, for these volumes were worth to us more than a continent of gold.

After ten days' labor our ship rode once more on the sea, and hoisting the bonny Stars and Stripes to its position of honor and predominance, I proposed three cheers, with the tears trickling down my weather-beaten cheeks, for the dear old flag and the sentiments it represents and protects, which were heartily, rousingly given! Those English bodies had an American spirit. Untrammeled nature conforms to the natural. How many disloyal ones at home would not have marveled at the loyalty and spirit in the country's behalf, far and almost hopelessly away!

That night we slept on the water in well-ordered cabins and bunks. Early next morning everyone was astir and the deck was cleared for action. The excitement and enthusiasm increased with every hour. I was commodore of the fleet, captain of my vessel, engineer and master machinist. The other principal duties were appropriately distributed. Old John Bertram, the sound, steady, level-headed man, was placed at the helm, and the genial, yet if need be forcible, old Silas Mason placed second in command, which put him, virtually, in direction above, as I remained with the engines. In the control of these, although a novice myself, still with some general comprehension by reason of my daily contact, at home, with machinery, I was fast initiating the quick-witted Phineas Bertram (Kathleen's elder brother) who rapidly demonstrated a decided ability and inclination that way. If there is any difference and

distinction, what is more responsible than the function
that administers and superintends the pulsations of the
heart — the motive power and its envelopes of machinery
and life! A book on engines had received my attentive
and anxious perusal, and lay near at hand, with the places
of its salient points duly marked; and never was a quantity of combustibles ignited with greater throbbing of the
heart than I endured, when I built my first fire in the box
to heat the boiler. And how anxiously I awaited progress, minutes becoming hours, and how every thump and
thud startled me, as evidences of unforeseen or hidden
danger; how my text-book was reviewed and myself
assured and reassured, and then — at last — I nearly
swallowed myself in my anxiety — the steam began to
exert its actions and the great and powerful machinery
moved — oiled and wiped and brushed, it proceeded
smoothly enough. With special messenger hastened to
the helmsman to be on his utmost guard, besides the customary or agreed upon mechanical signals, the great concern began to move. Carefully and skillfully controlled
by John Bertram, she pointed her prow and took her
direction. As night approached we anchored, placed lights
out, instituted successions of watch (the machinery, in
our opinions, or rather mine, needed watching) and, after a
merry evening of mutual congratulations and toasts, sought
repose, fatigued mentally and physically, and unstrung now
that the reaction from great strain had set in.

Fortunately, our stock of coal was still large; and I
learned that "black stuff like this" could be obtained
a distance back and carried down a stream, that emptied
not far from where the colony had their abodes, which
embouchure also afforded a harbor, beautiful, picturesque
and protected. So that cheerful prospects, all around,
emerged from the recent gloom.

The spirit of gratitude moved within me, and I humbly prayed and gave thanks.

_____

CHAPTER XIX.

TOGETHER AGAIN!

WE cruised very leisurely. Anchoring at night, and with daily incursions on land, we trapped, fished and gathered quantities of wild fruits, nuts and berries; I had inculcated the practices of drying, smoking and curing, salting, preserving and canning; with salt, sugar and condiments in ample store on board, we were preparing quite a stock of winter-supplies — more than thrice ample for our consumption and, in quality, what a choice!

The weather was delightful all the time, a sort of Indian-summer; a merrier, more genial group could not have been found. I enlivened many an evening hour, when the spirits of these benign days seemed to vie with the occasion, with my violin-playing, which delighted, as well as mystified them not a little; and those plaintive, sighing or rollicking tones, how they have strangely broken in upon the lone, weird wilderness. How often, poured from the inmost depths of my heart, they have recorded there in indelible spirit-tongue the expression of my recollections of bygone scenes, thoughts and passionate longings — at such moments my abstraction, *Begeisterung*, was incomprehensible to them. Almost awed by my appearance of oblivious absence with the fascinating *Wehmuth* of my executed tones, they said that at such a time I communicated with some invisible, visiting spirit — and, who knows, the spirit and chimes of music, perhaps.

We had timed it so that we should reach home after

nightfall, with the vessel full-rigged and decorated, yards manned, and so forth, and all brilliantly alight, and whistles sounding. The effect of such a sound and sight, suddenly imposed upon our unsuspecting dear ones, together with the novelty thereof, we could readily picture to ourselves. A projection of the shore, several miles distant, hid our approach, where lying until the shades began to settle and preparing our little piece of pleasantry, we then steamed down upon the unsuspecting, defenseless little throng, who were, no doubt, straining every auricular nerve to catch the first sound of our safe return.

Giving vent to all the power of the shrieking, screaming, whistling pipes and the deep, horrible soundings of the fog-horn — imagine the consternation of these women and children, at these demoniacal renditions and at the appearance of the glaring, looming yet beautiful apparition!

Knowing the water to be very deep close to the rock-bank of the shore, we ran alongside, anchored and ran out the gang-plank. Acting Captain Mason, swinging a lantern, passed over to land — all of the others remaining and standing in a blaze of light on deck — and, inviting all on shore to follow him, preceded and lighted them on board; eagerly and confidently following him, mutually joyful interchanges of greetings followed. I was the only one not present there at that moment, being still engaged below with the management of the engine. I was afterward told by a humorously inclined, quick-witted old chap, that Kathleen peered about for me!

But the "captain" of the vessel received his due share of homage and consideration, when he did appear. Headed by my assistant engineer and fireman, the whole group, excepting myself and two or three of the elderly men, paraded the vessel, from lookout to steerage, and the excitement, amazement and curiosity were edifying. My lively, witty assistant was quite equal to the showers of inquiries shot out.

At the last, the doors were thrown open, and they were ushered into their first taste of artificial elegance—the beautifully lighted, and magnificent dining-room, where a banquet had been spread in anticipation of the happy event and midnight festivities, with all the marvels of glass and china and silver service, fine cloths, brilliant illumination in gorgeous holders, including incandescent electrical lights, all these things so "heavenly" to them.

I presided, upon solicitation from all, with Kathleen at my side—as happy as a king, and, to all virtuous intents, the same as one.

And on the serenity of that still night with no sound, save the note of a nightingale, and the murmur of the incessant tireless breakers, anon broke peals of laughter from within; and, if the memories of departed, who had occupied seats herein in life, occurred to me or suggested themselves to anyone, yet the waves of reflections or sadness must soon have vanished.

I looked at Kathleen and thought what an auspicious time this would be for a betrothal. But, Kathleen did not yet seem, to my tutored mind, to understand what it means to love, hence I looked at her with a mixed feeling of chagrin and despair—but a silvery rim forever appears on the heavy clouds of the future, and a bound within my bosom bespoke happy things to occur—yet, a tinge of melancholy marked the terrestrial aspect.

CHAPTER XX.

THE SCHOOL-MASTER MAKES AN IMPROMPTU SPEECH.

SHORTLY after midnight, Mr. Talbot, the teacher of the school, arose, setting down his bumper, cleared his throat, and said that upon so important an occasion, one that marked a new era in their lives, he felt he had something to say — and, with impressive mien, proceeded:

"Brethren and fellow-merrymakers, it is with a deep appreciation and consciousness of the proprieties, as well as the unusualness of this occasion, that I perceive its import as well as direction.

"Lingering, all our days, on the verge, on the borders of civilization, it is but recently, that we have received an inkling of the possibilities of man, which lie dormant even within us. We have now the first great direct evidences of his accomplishments — still regarded only as experiments by their authors.

"Our immediate progenitors emanated from that dawning civilization but were snatched from it and separated here by the elements, when their lives were to blossom into its fullest realization. But they have reared us to its standard by account, example and we have maintained the same as nearly as tradition has enabled us. We have heard their words and regrets, cherish their dearest memories and at peace their resting place is as quiet and rest as tranquil as anywhere on earth.

"What is our condition or what was it, when Almighty God sent this our friend into our midst, not until he too had been made to feel the weight of the burden of ostracism, in its heaviest form — that of total solitude; that he might give the more incentive to us, by the depths of one extreme taught the exaltation of the other, the highest and best in the world.

"It is true, we have zealously preserved all we ever knew and heard, and have added a collection of useful local knowledge; we have chronicled our doings, which in a busier world would be regarded as trifles unworthy of remembrance — but which are the sum and total of our history. In the fifty years of my life, what has been our progress? Are we to-day fitted for and equal with the society which our fathers and mothers left? No, we have deteriorated. Within these few hours, we have received a practical demonstration, a loving glimpse into the procedure of our brethren, somewhere, beyond these surrounding seas — they have progressed.

"True, were it not for this self-same ship-building (man's arts bring him his smarts), within a specimen of which we are now enjoying ourselves, none of us would be here. Thus, so far, we have been injured, yet, again, benefited by it. And conceive, as, thanks to this practical example, we are now better able to understand the accounts our friend has vouchsafed to us, what delights and pleasures, what luxuries, what entrancing sights, sounds and sensations, the arts and sciences in their high state of cultivation afford to the communities of our fellow-men! The store of this practical knowledge, whence comes it? Is it the evolution of one province, one nation? Nay, every corner of the inhabited earth has had part in this garnering — frustrated and scattered, or nursed, fostered and fanned into life again; and the results, periodically, speak as the special opportunities favor distinct developments.

"We might remain here in our seclusion eternally, passing hence by the laws of nature and succeeded by our progeny, only to work through the mazes of doubt, experience and experiment to where these civilized nations already are — from which point we might start, were we with them, or they united with us, and had we a choice and union with their knowledge.

"I favor intercommunication of the freest kind throughout the world — I feel, that the people of the different localities possess diverse characteristics, have various local opportunities and facilities: that this world is a whole, in natural parts and functions, not separable without ill to the rest, and should be operated concurrently. That the greatest blessings flow from a healthy whole, smoothly, co-ordinately working body — no matter how well any part, in particular, may have developed, it cannot bear the entire brunt; it will either be an isolated spot of health, preyed upon and surrounded by disease, which is ever reaching out toward it and sure in time to encroach upon and consume it, or it is, itself, a well-defined diseased development.

"Now, when our noble ship courses o'er the main, and our studies and observations are stimulated by the possibilities it opens out before us, then we shall cast hither and thither for an enlargement of our vision, and increase of glorious powers of peace by intercourse with all our fellow-men, for our and their advantage and betterment, that God's aggregate may be enjoyed by all, as he intended it should be.

> Tell me not of little, curtailed range!
> The spirit shall traverse the universe.
> We are God's favorites and his house 's our own,
> He wishes us each cosy nook for joy
> And has devised each place as such a nook.
> Would you displease him by your ignorant cant

Or by refusing to employ his store?
Does he construct in parts not of a whole,
Himself the whole of all the glorious parts?
With lack of knowledge we abuse our gifts
And though the groveling wretch excites your ire
And your contempt arrays your goodly points,
Behold in that example the distress:
That poor unfortunate lacks a balanced creed,
Bereft of power his might is more his need;
Employing but few of all exceeds with some —
Since nature's scope must have fulfilled its glume."

At the close of this speech, we attested our deep appreciation. Mr. Talbot was the distinguished personage of the hour, having dispersed the last settlement of gloom with the first ray of light, but he bore his honors in the staid manner of the reflective, imperturbable philosopher, as was his unostentatious, truthful, fearless, lovable character.

We retired a happy-hearted set — all my guests, in the staterooms, on the vessel; our prospects had brightened, and our motives were pure.

CHAPTER XXI.

THE FIRST KISS.

THE ensuing winter, which was very severe, and long, was, nevertheless, a very busy and interesting one for us, engaged as we were in the closest study and daily drill for our contemplated cruise of discovery as soon as the weather should again become pleasant. We had explored the coal-field, already referred to, and a part of our population was engaged in coal-mining; the product, of first-class quality,

was laden on sleds, shoved down on the thick, solid ice of
the little stream, which transported it to our vessel near
this stream's mouth. A few others were storing the quantity of ice for the steamer's ice-hold; whilst others yet
were fishing, and trapping game for supplies and raiment,
the skins being variously dressed and adapted, in addition
to which the ladies were giving enthusiastic assistance in
their own ways. The command being entrusted to me, I
endeavored to proceed systematically, with as little as possible left to chance, and as we progressed we all felt that
our preparations were substantial. So eagerly and persistently did we engage ourselves, that we were through
before we could depart; but each day seemed to suggest
something more and much was acquired of general benefit
in our other affairs. Thus, we added much to the comforts
of our abodes and their enjoyments; we discovered min-
eral deposits in our mining prospectings; we learned of
valuable water-powers; we discovered oil and even natural
gas; salt deposits were found, and our hunters, now excited
to especial zeal and attention, often stumbled upon veritable mints of valuables, of no further benefit to us than to
lay the foundations of a rare and, finally, complete mu-
seum, itself an industrial history. I was the practical,
untutored experienced man, while Mr. Talbot was rapidly
becoming versed in the scientific and literary lore thereof
and rendered us invaluable assistance.

Beyond a doubt, agriculturally and minerally we had a
rich country, amply adapted to give sustenance and happiness to millions of population.

My previous knowledge and experience, naturally,
enabled me to perceive many advantages, that had but
to be turned to account, and there followed, of course,
many improvements.

I had these otherwise dry affairs interspersed with festivities on board the vessel. There was so much of abiding interest there: the fabrics and jewelry, utensils, china, pictures, style of dress and head-gear and a thousand articles for the women; the fire-arms, tools, machinery, appliances and other things for the men — piano, guitar, violin and all the musical instruments' lessons — and the ladies, on one occasion, attired "in fashion," equal to a masquerade. That life at this time was by no means dull goes without saying.

Passing over this Spring's flora, her gentle breezes, hummings and carols, and her poetry maligned by those who could not tell Rhine-wine from a bottle of salted sea-water, we shall proceed to the eve of our first voyage of discovery. How we all had become concerned in star-lore, had repeatedly scrutinized the ship's charts and endeavored to grasp the portents of the instruments; how we watched that beautiful, glowing sunset, and knew, or thought we did, that that was west, and figured out, somehow, our relative direction from the rest of the world.

Only myself and ten of the hardiest of the men were to go, and, as an exception, the old helmsman; Phineas, my valiant assistant, was now to become regular engineer, with Samuel Talbot as assistant; old John Bertram to attend the wheel, with two substitutes, Ira Mason and George Bertram; I commanded, with Ebenezer Mason, the eldest of the younger men, as lieutenant, and James Talbot did the cooking. Our force was small and, therefore, it would have been useless to draw strict lines on our several duties, had courtesy, even, permitted it, for our division of labor was only in the nature of expediency, nor was there any distinction in the pride each towards the other felt therefor.

The generally merry group was quite subdued on this eve, excepting myself, of whom all possible encouragement was expected, as a matter of course, and excited no comment; the intrepid band were heroes, yet, the objects of much yearning attention from those who were soon to be separated — perhaps, forever. This kind of anticipation was entirely concerned with those about to depart — with no thought that death might as well invade the little circle remaining behind and strike as cruel a blow. I felt a presage of good from our voyage, and did much to lighten the oppression by my arguments, sanguine statements and demeanor.

Sweet Kathleen — well, I caught her gazing at me, I thought, rather longingly, and, as though casually, I drew near to her, and in a moment when there seemed to be a general distraction withdrew her, by a suggestion, from the others. In the bright moonlight, as zephyrs played with her soft, fluffy hair, and the mighty ocean seemed, contentedly, to roll: "Eternal, eternal," we slowly passed on, her hand in mine, then — her frame quivered — my arm gently stole around her waist, and, drawing her blushing face to mine, I —

A pure kiss — ah, how, still, lingers its sweet ectasy,
And thrills me through all life with memory's bliss;
I breathed my soul upon those chaste, warm lips,
And, yet, inhaled the nectar of her heart
Oh, moments heavenly, when I yielded mine,
Thoughts so divine, when her soul came to me,
As bosom throbbed to bosom one brief spell —
And, yet, I leave thee for awhile, heed well,
The seal has closed our compact, I am bound
To cherish never other thought, than this,
Sweet maid, pure love, in thee my ways entwine.

Silently we stood, gazing out to sea, her bosom heaving as though with some inward commotion, which seemed partly suppressed; she was closely clasped in my fervent embrace, her silky, beautiful head resting against my shoulder — at this moment, her younger brother approached to announce the desired presence of all of us at the "All Hail and God-speeding" banquet. After that, at parting, I had only the opportunity to press her hand· ·the pressure was quiveringly returned.

CHAPTER XXII.

VOYAGERS.

A MORE auspicious morn could not have fallen to us. Boldly we stood out to sea. We had planned a directly western course, without any reason therefor other than a mere choice of lot. More heroism and determination, than physical strength sustained us through our trials and trepidations. Seasickness began to manifest itself as soon as land disappeared from sight, and the cook's occupation would have been gone for the next two days — even had he not been first, and worse afflicted than any of us. The smell from the kitchen is, ordinarily, enough for me on any kind of steamer out in motion, so I succumbed with the rest of them. After this healthy but unpleasant purgation, we enjoyed the benefit of learning that there may be times when death, even, can lose its terrors. Poor cook was the last to regain himself, and such cooking as was done until then, was desultory indeed.

All were becoming practically familiar with their parts, and, as is always befitting in any vocation of life for its honor and success, were developing their several duties into objects of pride, when, on the evening of the seventh day out, wind arose and the waves began to dash high, when every nerve and muscle was strained to bear

the tests for our new accomplishments, and nobly the good
old steamer bore herself through. Veteran tars could not
have been more nonchalant — than we were after that!
Afterwards the little storms, that traversed us, caused us
no fear.

Well, we ate and drank and were cheerful and merry,
recalling, always, that to Providence we owed our entire
guidance, and could feel as peaceful as the sleeping nurse-
lings, in an abiding Faith.

Forward plunged our intrepid monster, and we could
count numerous knots the hour and many miles the day,
but we were making no efforts to run very fast; our ship's
log kept a respectable, if, for the time and occurrences,
somewhat voluminous chronicle.

On the evening of the fifteenth day we had inventoried
our stock and, for the first time, discussed the advisability
of returning; when our trusty lookout startled us by the
announcement of a light or fire on the western horizon.
The sun, was hinted; but, that being improbable, at 11.30
p. m., some of us mounted, and through the glasses
thought we, too, could distinguish something luminous
there. The excitement, then, became intense — and suddenly the idea of danger flashed into our minds almost
simultaneously. We held a council of prudence, therefore,
and decided to push forward. Sleepiness did not trouble
us that night, as the interesting object did not disappear.

With the disappearance of the gloom of night an imper-
vious fog enveloped us. We deemed it well to stop, keeping out our signal-lights, and sounding our fog-horn, at
the same time anxiously trying to pierce the surrounding
density. About noon, the fog lifted, and away off ahead
of us still, a dark rim seemed to be visible; we hardly
dared to believe our eyes; and yet was it not the fulfillment of what we had devoutly trusted?

Experience the meagerness, the fickleness of our faith, by no less an object lesson, than our emotions and incredulous fears at the attainment of our ardent desires!

Misgivings began to present themselves as to our possible reception; but we felt there was no alternative, certainly no turning back now — and, with a prayer for our safety and for those left behind, we stifled every other emotion, suppressed every consideration, excepting the one immediately before us, and proceeded as rapidly as we could, all hands on deck and to the fore, except the engineer and his assistant and the sturdy rudderer. Arming ourselves with fire-arms and other weapons, of which, with ammunition, there was no dearth — we stood arrayed for discovery or death! Approaching, apparently, a lifeless expanse, until we feared to go nearer, a boat was lowered and, manned by myself and five others, rowed to the shore, where, I the first to leap on, this little detachment of us trod land once more.

There was no time for exultation over that, as a little distance off we saw the ashes of a large fire, still warm, and — detected footprints leading to the water's edge, and also indications that some larger object had scraped there, on the sand and conducting into the water, probably a boat.

Whither they had gone, nothing indicated — the water leaves no track behind, of those who have been borne or engulfed by it. We returned to the steamer and reported to our earnestly awaiting companions, and then concluded to coast this Newland, entering upon our project at once.

That evening, as the sun was reddening the few fleecy clouds with a brilliant hue, we drew near to and perceived a set of habitations, orderly arranged and bearing evidence of a system thereabouts, and a distant sound to us, of activity, reached our ears. At last, what a thrill of anticipation or doom!

Anchoring out, not far from this shore, I again with five ventured in a boat, alert to every indication, leaving the remaining as a guard to the vessel and a reserve in case of emergency.

CHAPTER XXIII.

NEW FACES — YET, EVER, OLD THEY SEEM!

Is man not man, maid maid, woman, lad or babe,
Whate'er geography locates their states ?
The visible form is flesh, bone, blood and shape
And reasons wrestles in a human crate.
Then he's your brother, she your sister, while
No dissonance can shirk your duty's sense !
Columbus, you recall upon our shore
Did they not teach you then that human love
And human thought could flourish in the wilds;
And if some passions coursed within their bloods
How muchly more they learned from your cohorts ?
And you lamented how much natural grace
Dissolved before the advent's paler face !
Your chains are *jangling* to teach the creed!
Philosopher, from you we have the truth
Indomitable courage is our God's Love;
Requital in your fellow-man's reproof
The curse you felt, but always blessed your God
And sighing, Mercy, mercily forgave.
Thus honored moulderings have filled your grave !
Oh, idle man you trend with caustic stuff,
You lead a life that is not clear enough
In freedom's measure not from right to swerve.
In ev'ry Nation note the men of fame,
Speak, in each clime is wisdom not the same ?

Then if co-ordinate men of fame are like
Conduce such matches, that each friction's strike
May cast a light upon this worldly gloom,
That is, raise standards then all men thereto;
To wrap within the higher recompense
Makes equal man to man from clime to clime,
As goodly men, where'er, will, always, chime.

THERE is a bond of sympathy, a real relationship between men of thoughtful, deliberative minds, that makes them coeval and equal, wheresoever chance in its indiscriminate choice has placed them; and the contemporaneous discourses in the several countries each honor their respective masters.

This moral or conclusion seems to arise herefrom, that distinctions are merely intellectual. Thus, to make your neighbors useful and pleasant to you, elevate them, if you are above and it is possible to do so, or elevate yourself and them together. Integrity, which is based on true enlightenment, promotes harmony; and general integrity is not promulgated by factional strife.

We were well received at what we discovered was a busy town. Our advent aroused in these people curiosity and superstition. To our delight, their language was a fragment of the old English tongue, and was sufficient, with gesticulations and pointings, to conduct a fairly intelligible conversation. I shall briefly sketch their history hereafter.

The town was of goodly size and constituted their principal fishing port; it was moreover their capital and principal market-town. Their population was over fifty thousand.

These people bore evidence of having been isolated a long time. Certain features had become marked by the long continuance in a new climate, and new habits; but withal

they must be described as a simple kindly dispositioned
folk, with a natural but artless shrewdness and perspicuity,
by no means to be despised. They were medium sized,
quick, active, keen, and possessed of indomitable courage
and persistence, that bordered on abandon in their determination to accomplish their purposes. I afterwards
learned, they represented a thorough intermixture of the
English, German and French nationalities, with predominance of the first, all of the humblest of their respective
countries' classes, embarked as poor emigrants. Fortune
deposited them here, to evolve a government from themselves, who had been under the cruel lash of the dominant
classes at home so long that little more, at first, than the
mere instincts of dumb brutes could have been expected of
them — but displaying excellent parts, as the long kept
dormant and abused faculties dared to peer above the
inculcated slavery.

But that broad breadth of insight that belongs to the
more enlightened had not yet reached that expansion, for
want of opportunity and knowledge; but, nevertheless,
they were a credit to themselves, an example of untrammeled nature in its orderliness.

After a short time spent in their company, at the landing place, we bethought ourselves of the anxious suspense
and curiosity of our companions remaining on board the
vessel.

The news of our arrival had spread over the town like
wildfire, although precipitated upon them with an unto-
ward suddenness, and a great throng pressed about us, as
under my leadership we boldly stepped on shore, and several who appeared to be leading men and were treated
with great deference by the crowd, extended to us their
hospitality, but in a manner that evinced their feeling of
awe. We explained our situation briefly, as best we

could, and received their marked deference and some show
of confidence, as far as they were capable of understanding us. While surprised, apparently, and mystified, they
put their best foot forward, so to say.

The lights of the vessel were now visible and served us
as a goal in the growing darkness; we rapidly proceeded to our friends with the good tidings. As our boat
pushed off, the mass gave a cheer, as though of delight or
admiration.

Those on board were breathless with excitement, as may
be imagined; which gave place to great exultation, when
we told them of our impressions and surmises. We
retired at once, with the precaution of a double watch and
subsequent reliefs, and were up before dawn had fairly
broken. After a hasty breakfast we set about putting our
vessel in the neatest trim. With sunrise, first one, then
another, and finally quite a little school of boats — row and
sail — began cautiously to approach us, for the evident purpose of inspection. We hailed them, as any approached
near enough, and beckoned them up; but none seemed
willing to venture — superstition, thus, being so readily
allied to ignorance, for, otherwise, they seemed to have no
fear of us or our craft.

After awhile, however, and as the crowd on shore began
to thicken and grow each minute, as we could discern
through our glasses, we perceived a larger, more like a
gala or festival row-boat put out, seemingly manned by a
number of oarsmen. Swiftly this pretty craft tended
directly toward and ere long had reached us. Someone
standing toward the front called to us something we did
not understand; but, suspecting a formal visit from one
in authority, we motioned to them to approach as closely
as possible, at the same time dropping a ladder of rope
down the vessel's side, which two of our party descended

and, springing into their boat, aided its crew in securing
to the hooks lowered from the vessel to it. Then five
important personages ascended, decked in their garbs of
state and office, and were heartily welcomed by us.

The head man addressed us, gracefully. He said, substantially, that after our departure last evening, at a
meeting it was decided to treat with us and extend every
courtesy, and they had been delegated to impart to us
their kindly intentions.

I responded on our behalf, that we esteemed their good-
will very highly and should contribute all in our powers
to the desired result. Thereupon we suggested, that
their men might also come up; but to this they quietly
shook their heads—evidently, degrees of society were
here in existence, and it grieved me forcibly to be recalled,
thus, to society's blemishes. To my friends this was of
course the first practical demonstration of the establishment I had told them of, and was received with not a
little astonishment, accustomed, as they were, to pure fra-
ternal regard, in practice and beneficial policy.

Then followed a round of seeing and sight-showing on
the vessel.

Business in that town was suspended that day; I doubt
even whether the people ate; and the news ere evening had
spread many miles into the country, whence people at once
began to come in. As time went on they seemed to lose
their first assurance, and on reflection after witnessing
our manifestations, innocent and unavoidable enough, were,
evidently, questioning the propriety of their beginning.

They were a good folk, and their simple hearts dreaded
a possible foreboding from the heavens.

Learning the water near the shore or landing was very
deep and there was afforded a sheltered cove we aroused
to greater energy the unextinguished fires and soon had

steam blowing off in volumes and great clouds of smoke gracefully curling upwards and the vessel in motion towards the shore. The alarm on board and on land was magical—horrible. The rowers in the gala-craft help-lessly in tow were in abject consternation and impreca-tion and prayer mingled. Is it to be wondered that they esteemed the monster a living thing and ourselves imps of its construction, despite our friendly and arduous assur-ances of man's contrivance?

At this time, it was more interesting for me to behold than to describe the motley assemblage, edging and push-ing forward to peer at us, as we stepped on shore. Seeing that the monster, our vessel, had become comparatively quiet, and was no longer approaching, they had mostly ventured to return.

As everywhere, nearly, in this world, caste existed here with no qualifications of pity, and showed itself plainly in outward appearances and mannerisms. But, in this hour of one common concern, rags and fine raiment, the ballooned paunch and gaunt spareness hustled each other or stood, pressed closely together, side by side. They had not escaped the inculcations of their ancestral experiences.

Can you appreciate my feelings at once more seeing a. multitude, as my memories darted back to former occa-sions of popular excitement or announcements, which I had witnessed? No brass band enlivened this occasion; on the contrary, an oppressive, awful silence reigned instead of any sound or noise. Individuals in uniform led the way for our advance, and we were conducted to a large wagon or car, capable of comfortably seating us all, yet primi-tively constructed, and drawn by about twenty donkeys hitched in twos, led by three attendants, equidistantly distributed. Donkeys, I will add, were their only beasts of burden; and goats furnished their milk products, besides fabrics from their hair and skins—and their flesh, too, at times was eaten. They were thus far better off than my friends.

We proceeded through the principal thoroughfares, the passages on both sides densely lined with spectators, to an edifice of greater pretensions and significance than the rest, and suggestive of a majestic sombreness and over-shadowing—it might well have been the monument to the specter, that has arisen from the sorrows of past ages. This was the Governmental Residence—that is, here resided the presiding officer, together with an oligarchy of ten additional members, and their families. A common table was served in a court, which in summer was open overhead, in winter closed.

The architecture was grotesque, yet served convenience. Off to the southeast, connecting directly from one corner by a covered passage, was another square building, larger than the former, and consisting of but one room or hall; this building was so located, that the passage entered the nearest wall, the northwesterly, by a large aperture in its center, and stood transversely to the southeastern corner of the other building—and was so presented, because, their projectors and architects said, man's oppression of the unfortunate and the weak extends to the four cardinal points: this shall ever be a reminder, that in this court and legislative hall the utmost corners shall be sought for justice, and the greatest reach of a square, the extent between the diagonal corners, is thus squarely fronted upon; their surmounting motto was, "The Earth seeks round in mean ends square." The effect was of course curious, and shows their ideas.

All public business was conducted here in open session. Here the laws were passed, courts held and every order issued in a loud tone of voice, resounding and distinctly

understood in every part of the hall. Nothing in the way
of secret societies existed here. The enactment of laws
was simple and brief in number and anyone might, during
the presentment, publicly urge any repeal or new enactment. It was, therefore, in one sense a much simplified
popular government, in another quite arbitrary; their needs
were simple and simple remedies were required. The
terms of office were for life and embraced no other business for the incumbents, nor allowed any. Upon the death
of a member, a new one was elected by the majority vote
of all the electors, being only males and restricted to real
estate owners — that is, having arrived at a requisite age
they must own unencumbered lands. Encumbrances consisted of a kind of registration of indebtedness — from
judgments in their court or freely attached liens. This
caused electoral disqualification until these records were
lightened. I presume this was to encourage independent
thrift and extension as well as to promptly regard or avoid
such obligation. Originality brings with it necessarily
some peculiarities. (There was ample scope for the owner-
ship of realty by everyone, and this provision was, evidently, to encourage husbandry.)

As their territory was large, to facilitate justice, as well
as to accommodate people by saving them long trips to the
capital, the country was divided in districts, and these
eleven appointed two persons in each to act therein as
judges and sub-governors; and twice each year the eleven
made the round to three distributed regular points, where
they heard the appeals, or inspected the judgments rendered by their subordinates, and completed the whole
national records therefrom, and listened to addresses by
and from any of the people; subsequently, all these
matters, so accumulated, were publicly announced in the
hall at the capital. There were no lawyers, each person

becoming, in fact, cognizant of the laws by direct concern
for him or herself; an accusation or prayer for redress
and defense were publicly stated by the parties themselves, or in their absence by a friend, and anyone present
might state his or her knowledge or views on the subject;
no oath was required, but, where it was shown by a number of creditable persons' statements that anyone had
willfully lied, punishment was meted out according to a set
of criminal statutes. These were their salient points —
primitive yet withal effective, because they were honest,
zealous and open to the world. Their affairs thus were
not inequitably conducted, and as, at the stage we found
them, their ruling men were unselfish philosophers, who
esteemed as the highest honors the knowledge and establishment of truth, it would have been sad to disturb this
tranquillity by suggesting improvements, which would
have been to precipitate a new, unknown order of things
—and a good reform is bad before the subjects are prepared for it.

Reaching the entrance to the hall, and having alighted,
preceded by the president, we, following next and in turn
followed by the ten others, were led to the raised platform,
and first assigned to seats at the table, the president occu-
pying his, and the others remaining standing. The vast
room soon filled and overflowed with an admirably behaved
audience, standing because of no seats. As the president
arose, a hush fell upon the assemblage. He spoke in a
deep, powerful tone of voice, with musical intonations;
substantially, he announced to them, that we had suddenly
come among them on what he conceived to be a search-
journey; that we were evidently enlightened beings and
seemed to carry the universal assurance of intending them
no harm; that we were, probably, from some land or
country, of the existence of which, it would be remembered,

they had traditionary cognizance and had, often, vaguely
conjectured; that it was, at least, due, that we should be
courteously and considerately treated, and that therefore
they would consider it an honor to entertain us, and hoped
that all would contribute to make our sojourn as pleasant
as possible.

A ripple of assent followed his conclusion.

Thereupon he led us through the covered passage into
the other building.

CHAPTER XXIV.

FEASTED.

A TRULY delectable repast awaited us, spread with
inviting nicety, with a garlandure that evinced a refined
taste.

We were presented to the women, and all seated themselves at the festive board, each judge with his wife to
his left; we succeeding, in a row, at the chieftain's
right, who sat at the head of the table.

Servants attired in white brought in the viands, in
courses, on platters made of burnt clay and some shaped
out of hard, medicinal-propertied woods. Our plates were
of a peculiarly hard, whitish wood, shaped round and
scraped smooth with the sharp edges of shells and rubbed
and polished, until they were really beautiful.

A broth, flesh of fish, wild fowls and game, preparations
of some succulent roots, which imparted a pleasant flavor
and agreeable easiness to the digestion, and other indigenous vegetation, besides goat's-milk and preparations therefrom, were served in succeeding order with the precision
of epicures. A kind of barley-meal furnished their bread.

They possessed salt and sugar, and, also, a delightful liquor, agreeable to the taste and exhilarating, without being intoxicating.

We enjoyed the repast exceedingly. It was interspersed with gay good-humor and excellent sallies, marred only for us by the difficulty of intercommunication. I understood them better than I could make them understand me.

After we had all regaled ourselves, I arose and, speaking very slowly, said that it was a source of very great pleasure to us that we had found human beings, and especially of such advancement. When we might have encountered savages — we were agreeably surprised by enlightened, humane people, from an intercourse with whom we expected much benefit in the future, and hoped to contribute our share to the common fund of the general weal; that we desired to extend our hands of fellowship and true brotherhood in any enterprises, and offer every facility in our powers for their beneficial use; that words could not express the feelings of our hearts, and we should, certainly, insist upon entertaining as many of them, in return for their kind treatment of us, as could be conveyed to our welcoming shores.

They understood me, and the next to the chief, an elderly, white-haired man, gracefully and briefly thanked us for our manifestation of satisfaction.

After we had arisen from the table, the children were brought in, large and small, a healthy, rollicking, romping lot, who, whilst a little abashed at our unusual presence, sparkled with curiosity — such are children the world over — as they shyly glanced at us.

By their table etiquette, the children with their guard, a dignified matron, always waited until their parents had partaken, for their meals.

We were next shown the apartments at our disposal, a
series of ten rooms, set apart for guest-chambers for any
distinguished governmental visitors — which heretofore
had been confined to those of the country districts.

It was then suggested that we should take a survey of
the city; but I first begged that our three companions left
on shipboard, who had thus far missed these ceremonies
and pleasures, should be allowed to come ashore and enter
the party, and said that I would take the place as watch,
they being unused to such sights; whereas I was by my
previous experience differently situated. Although demur-
ring to my severance from them, upon my reasonable
insistence they yielded, and we were driven to the landing, whence we speedily rowed to our vessel and soon
had effected the intended transfers. I wanted to gratify
these three companions. I desired also to learn the effect
of the simple intercourse between these excellent specimens
of detoned people in their receded conditions from the
progressive civilization their ancestors had eminently or
as purely as possible emanated.

That I regarded a protection requisite on board, was not
the opinion of these people's predatory inclination, as they
manifested but good-will coupled with curiosity; but it
must be remembered I had dwelt long enough and inculcated in me after birth in my native, most highly and
exemplary civilized surroundings and experience the
acquired prudence of established insincerities. I may say
the habit of suspicion, then and there, hung tenaciously to
me. Whether or not this propriety continues I, now, far
removed with no expectation or hope to return, to you
ascribe for solution, who are in the distant land of civilization and my former habitation. I may be instrumental
that an intercommunication between these people and
yourselves will ensue, when I pray you to treat them as

brethren, and not, ever, treat my fellow-man with distrust.
Simplicity of manner and plain confidences do not attend
outraged trusts; but the last-named foster a contrary
sentiment, that, thereafter, manifests itself in every
transaction of life, much to any harm, carried, even, to
the echoless wastes.

Then, I wanted to think, to ponder—and sweet Kathleen arose in my mind and demanded a devotion.

I watched them out of sight, saw the commotion among
the dense crowd of people; then descended to the engine-
room, making a careful inspection of the condition of
things, and found them in excellent order. Phineas took
such a pride in his vocation, that he loved his machinery
as though a mate to him, and proved his regard by the
dress, the dazzle that shone from every part, the result of
his diligent rubbing and polishing, and the whole moving
without a jar, from his careful oiling and adjustment.
Returning on deck, I threw myself in a large easy-chair, in
the shade and facing to the shore—and reflected.

Here were a primitively acting people, civilized in a
measure, yet, upon the whole, not advanced or rather not
progressive but in fact deteriorated. In some respects
I preferred their state—their simplicity of manners, for
instance; still, may not that be only relative to all their
surroundings?

Would I willingly forego the pleasures and delights of
a higher civilization? No. It was not homesickness, for
I had no particular home to return to or any marked
attachment to attract me thither, but I could intelligently
attribute the feeling, first, to desire of the glory of the
whole; that failing, of personal achievement; and to the
healthy, active energy in man, which craves this fulfillment of the highest destiny on earth.

God gave to the human family the earth and the seas

and the skies, and their attendant functions and offerings, intermediaries and blendings. From them man receives his first common resources — swayed, thereafter, when mere necessity is supplied.

Necessity again levels mankind — witness the ship-wrecked when raiment and food assume their proper sphere, that only of comfort and sustenance, and shelter that of protection.

A natural, pure sentiment dictates a division of toil according to adaptation and best calculated for the general good — yet who is to apportion the several duties? A spirit advances, first, cautiously, then another, and are countermet to be restrained, somewhat; but at least a war ensues between the different representative ideas, desires and exultations. Indolence on the part of some, insatiability with others, add to the derangements. Oh, this interminable entanglement, that the human heart, mind and soul cannot exist without employment and solely, somehow or other, diverted from its proper chan-nel to rush blendedly, hither and thither, increasing, thereby, their respective confusions. Few quietly, pain-fully for a time heed and ponder and strike in the direc-tion to regain the proper course, all bring care and trouble, when everything might be smooth and pleasant!

Somewhere, within the confines of this earth and powers are vouchsafed to us the same results beneficially sought, easily, safely and pleasantly accomplished with but a pure, mere manifestation of desire and but its happy accompaniment of joyful exercise.

I watched the fisherman toiling at his net, nearly cap-sizing his boat in his strenuous efforts and thus in peril of his life; another toiler labored in the sweat of his brow, as he belabored his lazy old donkey, who gave indications that she was very tired, also, of life, and very listlessly proceeded to pull along the heavily laden cart; but here a merry young maiden skipped lightly to the water's edge and, darting down, dipped a vessel into the ocean's brine, bearing away her trophy with the measures of her foot-steps marked out and accompanied by the sounds of her voice in a gleeful song.

But the June sky and breezes, cool and pleasant, carry-ing murmurs upon their wings, subdued my senses as I slipped into a drowsy, oblivious doze.

I was startled by a sound and call, and looking whence it came, saw the fisherman alongside in his little smack beckoning to me. I gathered that he would like to come up so lowered the rope-ladder, which he fastened to his boat and then ascended. He was a man about sixty years of age — hale, hearty and muscular; he would have meas-ured five feet six inches in height, a large size for these people; his hair was long and gray and he wore a full bushy gray beard. He was clothed in a singular suit made of one piece of goods, cut with arm-holes, through which extended the bare arms, the piece slit up at the bottom in the middle to the length of his legs, and the ends to com-plete and hold the encircling of the body and legs fas-tened together by leather threads or thongs run or seamed through. His large feet were bare, his bronzed calloused hands large, and on his head, fronted by a broad and high forehead, was a wide, flat head-gear, made of the same material as his other garment and stiffened a little, by some means, in the brim. He addressed me in a conglom-eration of speech, but was respectful and diffident. I judged him of German descent and thought to detect Ger-man words in his utterances. I could estimate, that while hesitating in his manner, mayhap out of deference or dis-cretion, he was a courageous personage and not easily moved by superstition.

He indicated to me that he did not regard us or our craft as emissaries from the devil, pointing down, or as scourging visitations from above. I gathered thus the drift of comment among the people, as well as a remnant or indication of orthodoxy in religion among them.

Seeing that he was curious, I conducted him all around, but his dazed, puzzled, yet often admiring looks were comical to behold. He ventured not a remark, not an exclamation. When we again reached deck, he hurried to the ladder and quickly disappeared over the side of the vessel, much to my astonishment; but directly I saw his head reappear and a moment later he stood on deck with a receptacle, of some kind of rude wicker work, full of small but choice table-fish, which he deposited on the floor, and, uttering something, accompanied by a kind of curtsy, turned, descended the ladder, loosened his boat and had soon paddled around the steamer and out of sight. I placed his present, which was an evidence of his appreciation as well as requiting generosity, in the cook's receptacle.

I took a pace around the vessel in true watchman's style. But all was quiet and serene. I ate a little supper, as the glowing radiance of the skies betokened the sun's good-night—that same sun I had seen in Ohio, in whose shield it formed one of its emblems, light, in whose rays I had basked and blistered my back in the brook's ripple, there it was, and within the last twenty-four hours it had lighted the visages of former acquaintances and friends, where, I could mentally locate, but not find them, they physically have found but could not locate me, and Kathleen's brow and sunny hair, too, had been kissed by some of those rays. I wondered if I might intercept these with my lips, or had they remained on that sunny head charmed thereby by their own resemblance—I was in love and I knew it. I drew a loving, quivering bow over my sensitive fiddle, as I fondly laid my cheek on its smooth surface, and sent forth a wailing melody.

The breeze was toward the shore and bore the fantastic tones thither, and as the twilight was dimming the view, I, with my last glimpses thereby, saw people gathering there — and what their startled, wrought-up feelings were in these days of our strange presence at the weird sound-wavelets, I can only announce from what I afterward learned, that they believed they heard some angelic bird from the celestial shore.

I don't know how long I played; but I continued to pour out my soul in " Home, sweet Home," " Kathleen," " 'Tis years since last we met; or, Her bright smile," and numerous others, besides improvisations, in which I could best interpret my incomprehensible nature, completely lost in reverie, when a lusty cheer awakened me to the fact of my companions' return. I had even forgotten to hang out the lights (subject to their surprised censure, had they not been too happy but to overlook anything) and hastily lighting a lantern (we were very careful of matches in those days, using a wafer, which was lighted at the fire, in the cook-stove, at least, kept glowing always) held it that they might see their way to come up.

All were delighted with the afternoon and evening's entertainment; everything was so novel to them, and to see so many persons alone a revelation. The difference between ourselves and our children is, that we have become accustomed to our ordinary sights. Frequently a body of legislators are no more decorous, than a lot of boys in an unsuperintended school-room ; the latter have an absence to excuse them, the former nothing. They had no room or time to feel any vanities of distinction bestowed upon them, nor had they, as yet, appreciated conditions of caste

or degrees in society, trained to different reflections by
their own guileless institutions. This primitive enlightenment is what we must seek again to attain—for to
them each one they saw was of their brethren. This
bespoke the real truth and best as it assured in their
unbounded delight at worldly contact a widened sphere,
society and comprehension; they saw the objects attained
without reference to their varied ingrediences to emanate
solely from the human mind. They recounted to me with
great, almost childish, enthusiasm all the happenings during their parade; children, maiden and youths strewed
flowers on their way—the minutest details seemed not to
have escaped their notice—and commented favorably on
the industrial advances; whereas I, just previously, had
in my own private contemplation noted the retardation of
progress here.

CHAPTER XXV.

DISCUSSION.

The transpired is an indelible occurrence; history is infallible. Forgotten; but, it cannot be extinguished—except in oblivion and, thus,
seems largely the Past.

EARLY next morning, they seemed constantly to advance
upon us in the initiative, we received a messenger who
informed us that the goverment wished an interview with
us, and asked whether or not it pleased us to accede to
their request. I answered that it was our ardent desire,
and invited the whole body with their wives to our vessel.
   The cook, with two assistants for the occasion, set about
providing a special spread worthy of our guests. In an

hour from that time they were seated in their barge of
state and being rowed toward us; on this occasion we
motioned them to remain seated, whereupon I and two
others descended, and, fastening their boat to the lowered
hoisting apparatus, to their new alarm lifted them, boat
and all, bodily from the water and deposited them safely
on deck. We then politely requested them to step out
and down to the deck, which they did with alacrity. Let
me describe their costumes of state for the occasion, which
were, if unique, not unpicturesque, and certainly serviceable and decorous.

One of the first things that struck me was the apparent
modesty and morality of these people. Still that need not
be surprising since, it is often repeated, many primitive
people were introduced to vice by their civilized discoverers; just as to-day, it is said, much of the populace of
the Chinese — who probably antedate us in so-called civilization, to treat some genius and device as such, having
reached their individual culmination, and therefore incipient decay, long since — now on the wane — can give us
revelations in that direction astounding, even, to our
enlightenment. Therefore, vices grow with our progress,
more, than keep pace and encircle the front to cause the
early culminations successively transpired traceable to
this, underlying, principle. The recession of true or the
substitution of false religion.

The United States is the best, of highest promise and
the most enlightened, religious country on earth; free
from bigotry and intolerance to discountenance religious
hierarchy and pure against a mere oligarchy; to stem by
faith the preposterous claim of temporal organization.

The will of God is, that man should not control man,
because He Himself gives freedom, except by the free
intercourse of his presence and agencies. The claims of

special guardianships are unruly. A great many may claim successorship to merely designated conditions. Through faith all things are possible to everyone without distinction or human intercession save the humanitarian principle to and of Christ: the Redemption. This is religion, philosophy, science, conscience — the free agency God has implanted and allowed.

These people were, thus, in the first stages of or rather emanated from a state of civilization,

> He knows the most, who speaks from sorrow's ken,
> Whose words are jewels hewn from out the dross,
> Where, therein, hiding, he might know his loss;
>
> But, he has suffered most for, hiding, thus,
> With all his brilliance pent-up with its rays —
> E'er, gleam again or pass through hardship's frays,

that transplanted in a few specimens far removed from the locality of birth was to rear especially a promise to their children. They had to solve the question of existence — as we that of restraint. No human automatons to do their work and their mere enjoyments of the usufructs and, yet, pernicity of social distinction was apparent — hence, slavery is not beneficial to the wielder and is a curse to the community.

> The good man speaks the truth;
> The wayward tries from heart and birth —
> Conglomerate they both say true.
> The one sees brightly in the gleam of light,
> The other in the dread storm's flashing flight.

Recurring to the items of dress, I learned that the materials of their fabrics were grasses, wood or plant-fibre and goat-hair or wool. These they ingeniously handled and skillfully and artistically arranged—the first thing humanity has seemed to learn is how to cover its nakedness, to hide its most artistic outline—the simplest of procedures and best apparel made by the simplest of people, and the greatest of vanities, covering the real cause for the only pride we ever had cause to possess—our beautiful bodily resemblance to the highest ingrediences and powers in the universe.

As to-day it chances elsewhere that otherwise ignorant natives of some favoring climes can produce fabrics of a texture and artistic coloring that make them of prime value and delight in the world, not to be duplicated elsewhere. So, I found here, that in the working of these materials into clothing-stuffs they occupied a pre-eminence, truly distinguishable, and in clay manipulation and hard wood-wares they had obtained high proficiency.

The ladies' garb, on this occasion of eminence, seemed to consist of one piece, general or connective, but made up of three materials and dexterously worked in or woven together where they joined, forming a perfect, graduated blending of color and texture and fulfilling the evidently desired effects. The stuff was thin, not raising the heat of the body, but otherwise dense. The style or fit curved gracefully high up about the neck and throat, then hung in loose, interblending folds down to the waist, and was confined there by belting; the sleeves were full and airy, leaving bare the shapely wrists; then followed what might be termed the divided skirt, gathered and held closely at the ankle, over high kid-leather encasings of the feet, in natural color, following the natural shape of the feet, with soft leather soles, thence upwards in ample fullness to the waist, making an easy, graceful and delightful garment to the wearer. Their hair, which was thick and inclined to waviness, was very fine, glossy, and included respectively the several shades, and somewhat fluffily hung loose, reaching to their shoulders, and was plainly brushed back. Everything about their personal appearance, face, ears, hands, finger-nails, beautiful, white, healthy teeth and their whole attire supplemented their exquisite taste and betokened habits of and strict attention to cleanliness and neatness. The men wore bushy beards, and hair very similar to their wives, though not so long, and coarser. Among the more advanced in years gray commingled with the jet or gold, as the case might be. The attire of the men consisted also of one piece, fastened together down a divide or opening in front, being made to fit very snugly, but not uncomfortably, to the body, from the good fashion about the neck to the fastening at the knee, with a sash-belt about the waist-line to give a dressed appearance; their legs were enclosed in kid leggings and goat-leather shoes clad their feet.

The men's suits were black on this occasion, while the ladies affected various shades of color suitable to their individual complexions, in which they showed such good taste as to excite rapturous admiration, the blending of shades and harmony of coloring not being an unnatural intuition in the human family, if individually allowed what might be called the proper instincts and relations therein. The goat-hair materials in these instances were more for the strengthening the places for connecting the different materials where the strain would be greatest, as, in the equable climate, the use of much of it would have made the garment too warm. The dignitaries of the world indulge their pleasures in the semi-guise of public affairs or in the more intimate relations gain the knowledge to inveigle themselves into confidences, though at this stage the craftiness of man comes to the fore. Routine is inevitable and the next thing was our exhibition.

After the formal greetings, being an occasion of state, the visitors at once entered into unrestrained appreciation of the situation, and seemed entirely free from embarrassment, having no doubt been assiduously schooled thereto, in view of the circumstances. Each part of the ship and the exposed parts of the machinery shone and appeared at their best. Everything had been put in readiness, and, raising the anchors, each man at his post, the machinery was started and the vessel moved. A sort of quiver at first seemed to seize our visitors, but they were anon lost in astonishment at the wonderful operation, at length enabled by analogy to conjecture a power of the mechanics, and the surprises of their new experience; they marveled at everything we had and did, undisguisedly. We had decided to treat them to an excursion as part of the entertainment, the day being delightful and the sea calm, and, as none of them had ever been out of sight of land, to extend the trip that far. Their glee grew as the minutes passed, and reassurance manifested itself more and more with familiarity. With their easy, quiet tread they seemed fairly to glide, in their graceful movements, over the vessel, as in their animation they darted hither and thither, with a view to every vantage point; and as a gentle lurch of the vessel, on this quiet day and sea, would sometimes almost upset them, the incident but added to the zest of the novelty.

We regaled the party with most lavish outlay, away out in the outlying sea out of sight of any other habitation or foot-rest. Our choicest viands were prepared and served in our best style, in selecting which I tried to exhibit as much as possible the tastes and arts in vogue in the United States. A number of toasts were drunk in bumpers of our excellent wine. On the whole, they enjoyed the feast very much, although the dishes were as novel to them as our selection from our store could make them; and, with the effects of the libations, by way of novelty, too, which however we judiciously curtailed, the jollity and good humor of the hour might be said to have been "unconfined." Excitement, probably, spared them any feelings of sea-sickness, aided too by the exceeding calmness of the sea.

We returned to our anchoring-place as the dusk began to come on, and it was a happy group that stood listening to our parting words, preparatory to going ashore.

SCIOMACHY.

The shadows, falling as they dance upon the leas of wealth,
Contrive a cruel fascination's mystic bond
And, hence, they spread, throughout, their fantasies with
      stealth,
Which lead to visions, whither, nought trends fond;
As in prone man his spirits rove in chambers three,
Those borne to impulse, soul, to heart and mind,
Therein to scourge their fetters, emanate, thence, free,
Thus, they will rankle, ever, in their spirits' kind.
All progress stayed on elevation's highest plane,
There, one straight course is this for life inane?
Peace, didst thou rest upon a mortal's crest
Or cease the tumult of his anguished breast —
Was e'er his soul with blissful joy so blest,
That not another hour frightfully did wrest?

        So, was a man:
A little shadow dashed forninst his brow,
A mist-enveloped gleam came to his mind,
So, tired and fatigued it scarce could shine
In its scarce, living, shiv'ring, trembling, light;
Yet, he felt luminated by its frangent ray
And posed a head-light with its flick'ring torch!
        The daring culprit,

Rasping, every hour from birth to doom —
Does he conspire to end this teeming earth,
Or does he wish to plunge a poniard, life,
To still its impulse and its pulse for trade
Or does he rant?

No period, soothing as the last-drawn sigh,
No sigh, so longing as the last-sought hope,
No hope, so fearless as its wished for end.

SCIOMANCY.

By shadows we may measure heights;
But, heights contain themselves.

All visions tend but to forecast some news,
The fascination of the mental views
Wrought on a sensitive endeavor of the mind
Are not unworthy; but, portend of kind.
The simple child has fancies not its own,
It borrows from its lights and inwards sown
Deprive it not of that sweet, sated rest,
That loves to nestle where it lingers best;
All musing hours are shadows cast before,
They trace each subtle passage as of yore.
When, then, the muser scoffs at his own guile
Or pensively develops many a while,
Thereby, prepares the strokes for master-hands,
He has not challenged what his life demands —
How many would have worshiped, such, his hours,
How may we disregard their unguent powers!
How weary, weird the thought of utter bliss,
Like to some maiden, yearning for a kiss
From her fresh lips just burst to woman-state —
It may prove pleasant; yet, it may abate
The would-have ardors judged not for their pair:
In life meet system is its prime affair.
Thus, in the bud or winter of all life
The thought is uppermost, oh, seek, ah, rife
Is all that of the future care, to rest
Is but the assuage to seek it best.

When portents hover o'er their inklings wide,
They do in fashion all their charms bestride
And point directions, whither, mightst thou steer?
Or being courseful thither shouldst thou veer!
One reck'ning gives conclusion to amounts;
But, these give drift and body to accounts.

On the next morning the government officers appeared
early, for the contemplated discussion. They came as a
body and organized for public business, to which no other
considerations were admitted, thus manifesting their earn-
estness. They were unaccompanied by anyone else, and
showed as much eagerness and impatience to proceed with
the objective business as politeness would possibly permit,
and to this end as considerately as possible waived every
other attention, that we thought to bestow. My companions were not a little astonished at these business-like
methods, or what appeared to them the severities of practical life without any mollifying social features, in the
direct attention to matters in hand; they felt confused
and inclined to keep aloof, because of the newness of the
evidences before them. But this latter was very foreign
to my purposes with them, for divers reasons. Amongst
others I wished to note their natural temperaments
untrammeled as they were yet by any artificial abuses
refined by society into fine art with severe technicalities
and their natural penalties instead of pure, unswayed
tendencies of promise primarily endowed by the Creator;
then, I wanted them to experience, in their own vigorous
state, the responsibility of the contact with calculating
minds, disciplined to a routine and serrated by elements
that have brought into warfare ignorant requisitions
of unnatural alliances. Besides, there were their own
interests and requirements, of which they knew their
necessities by experience, and, as their wits would become

sharpened, heated by actual friction, possibilities would unfold themselves, better understood and appreciated by them, because of their assistance in developing and discovering them; concerns bring ample store; also their knowledge would be enlarged and memory awakened.

Repairing to the dining-room, which was the coolest as well as most appropriately arranged place for our purpose, I proposed that I should act as general secretary, and the second in order of the judges to preside, since the president himself was to conduct the remarks on their side. Our helmsman was to do the "steering" for us here, too.

It was to be expected, that, besides my notations, I should keenly watch all the proceedings, and be heard from in order, representing as I did a third interest, and to be called a friend to everybody in my knowledge and independence.

We were seated at the long table in the center, the presiding officer at the head with the president judge at his right, myself to his left, Mr. Bertram next to me, then, respectively, on our sides the remaining persons of each party in successive seats. The white-haired but yet vigorous president of the governing delegation arose, and with a graceful yet dignified bow to the chair and to the assembly, with the elements of courtesy and proprieties, sequacious to culture, even the natural exhibition of human character, he began with the happiest allusions to the auspiciousness of the occasion and its agreeable revelations to them; and, in language equal to that of any accomplished diplomat, in the customary happy commonplaces and preludes, indulged delicately in complimentary references to us, our achievements, enterprises, prospects, and the promise of benefit they, humbly but unmistakably, recognized in any future intercourse we might graciously accord to them, instruct them, share our products for anything we might esteem of use or enjoyment of theirs. To these sentiments we politely bowed in modesty our thanks.

Proceeding, the speaker said that there were several things, that became inevitably apparent and impressed themselves on every reflective, earnest individual in the daily as well as periodical occurrences of affairs. It was required of all of us, that we be diligent in order to know what is going on and for that reason likely to take place and to suggest expediences; that unforeseen accident may, ostensibly, thwart seemingly well-laid plans; but, that this latter proposition is doubtful, anyway not as well established as known, that our faults have their natural sequences and almost every disaster can be traced to preceding human fault, not referred to in a spiritual sense, readily waived . because of the infrequent effort made to understand it; but the material, although not as potent. He hoped for and believed in evolution — a rational, comprehensible evolvement into higher and better affairs, but his subscription to the doctrine was largely consequent upon previous downfall or retrogation by reason of disaster or misconduct to or on the part of our ancestors. Manifestly victims of a retrogression of race, they could perceive in the supposed progress of the world periodical recoveries from abjection and the degeneration of the old to be supplied by new energies. That it were easy to estimate ourselves better than our predecessors, that is, advanced upon their knowledge and practices, to argue that we have improved or bettered the natures they have transmitted to us — did we not witness in ourselves the unmistakable evidences of deterioration or temporal suspension of progression, from allowing our principles to relax. From indolence or vice arises want of knowledge and strength, wisdom, industry and — success; as a studious government officer, with the welfare of the populace at heart, he found those elements of social disease, those cankers in humanity, traceable to our own transmission and imparting, though hampered by the wilful errors of our ancestors and some extraneous natural causes.

Situated as they were by the wise provisions of their forefathers, they esteemed the establishment prudent by their training and knowledge of no better, they had ample leisure as well as the power, trust and opportunity to put any principle to test, which their diligence and forethought could suggest and prosecute. The transition of narratives ascribed to their predecessors strict integrity, industrious propriety and investigation for true knowledge, which adduces morality and makes its maintenance a free and urgent choice; that with indolence in the individual, thereafter in the concourse they discovered the first indications and invention of vice, whereas those engaged with the true affairs of life were filled with odium at these harmful dispositions, the result purely of cultivated taste. The legitimate functions are crowded out of the space necessary for their administration. In this extent, perhaps degree, improvement is possible, evolution a fact, a regeneration, renewal, reacquisition of the pristine glory of man, when he was pure. Mercy, not the will; to regain the early vigors after a determinate destructive influence on them, all the joys of manhood as one blessed — a progress possible, a rehabilitation. To avoid these cataclysms is feasible.

That they felt these conclusions to be natural and evidential: secluded here for generations, evolving from themselves whatever woe man inflicted upon himself, they had no source of evil from beyond nor any view to succor from such a source; and, if a deterioration became noticeable, or, even, a source or degree of evil existed, their range was not so great, but that the result was attributable within a circumscribed limitation. That the shades of human existence became unavoidable for reflection by their magnitude in the small frame; the world brought things around to us and was lighted provided to and by ourselves. In the confusion of ideas ignorance spins mysteries for want of reflection and manipulated by unscrupulous persons created false doctrines into great climaxes. These were begotten in iniquity and born in venom, reared by our cultivation and use a dosed remedy or agony and destruction. No explanation for an incongruity otherwise existed. Where, then, were their further knowledge and susceptible transactions?

"You, excepting the Secretary, have had a still more limited range and less elasticity of human connections, and that is shown by your still greater simplicity and mutual love and consideration in regard to affairs which have happier fruits than ours; and our friend, the Secretary, I can conjecture from analogy, can and will tell us of still greater complication in transactions in those larger fields, where the greater number tend more to the downward course, than we, even, imagine — because they bear down on each other and there is the greater number to do it. I contend, in my primitive way, that human intercourse and desires are the result of instruction — thus, that by instruction the best conditions of our respective relations and affairs should and could be inculcated, looking to, then as now, the one result, practice; the human heart responds generously when its comprehension is pleased — I hope the Secretary will bear me out from his larger range of knowledge, as we have come to the conclusion and in favor of the free schooling system, out of that arises respect, from that religion — not intimidation. How may our people be restrained from lowering tendencies, or their massing alone from contributing to that weight and result, and their present state recur to their proper elements of buoyancy?

"The question is, whether, in addition to and after these pleasant social exchanges, further communication between us is advisable — whether that intercourse shall be only nominal or merely friendly; shall extend to assistance in calamity and danger, and no further; shall be a strained relation of suspicions, and the profits, arbitrarily, that can be derived from the other; or whether it is to embrace every feature that can contribute to the general welfare from the means and articles the Creator has variously yet conjointly distributed over this earth, for our enjoyment and the balancing of our and their powers.

"The first burst of sentiment and heart-felt loyalty says the latter, of course — reason is never far behind it, the former being God's unlaborious presentment, the latter your exercise — and reflection says so too.

"My dear friends, there is no doubt that you can help us — in morals that is sufficient reasoning for the executor under the will of God and the good of men though the beneficiary may not, in mere propriety, urge it — by your knowledge, your connections, your resources, your possibilities. You can turn us and ours to account, for ourselves — and we think we can be of service to you, beyond this beneficial exercise, and beyond mere amusement. This is the law of the universe.

"In our greater number — because of thereby greater circumscribed opportunities, I should say more multifarious necessities draining on our resources and curtailing individual portion — we appear to you more solicitous and perhaps are. Still, we have our numbers in construction, assistance and employment to offer you. Perhaps we have less occasion to be selfish, as our vision has been enlarged to abhor its baneful effects. But we assure you of our earnest good-will, and willingness to contribute, numerically and specifically, in full measure and as an experiment of us if desired, to establish with you, and the world, our good faith. The expediency, the means and degrees of interchange remain, solely, to be adjusted.

"Of our resources you have some adequate idea; probably, have discovered the dearth of improvement, that we might well be expected to have made or be making, and have marveled at our ignorance. We have nothing approaching such contrivance as you here possess, although no doubt we possess all the means therefor. Oh, knowledge! The facilities thrust themselves at us; but, we have no comprehension. We forcibly feel the wonderful existence of our ignorance, sigh for emancipation, which, next to the Heavenly Power, can only come from contact and intercourse with the aggregation of the people — *all* of them are necessary to the healthy, created whole — outside of our immediate pale. Can there be any question of benefit for the whole in every race, if their several peculiar functions are freely and rightly employed? Improvement is thus in all experience engendered and born, and what troubles then arise are due to the lack of attention and nurture.

"We, in our own people here, are composed of several nationalities — humble and obscure subjects, yet thus greatness exudes — whose peculiarities are known to us by some still perceptible traits that crop out here and there, despite the freest intermingling of blood. Records in the history of general blood lie not. Practically we know no other history.

"What we know, at all, from an outside world is tradition of those first locating here by mishap, perpetuated by the successive generations, how correctly we do not know.

"But, you have opened possibilities to us — we are like a newly discovered people, snatched from an incipient heathendom. Think, how your posterity, your dearest earthly objects, might sink to such a decline Where? Remove the locus by wisdom and design! Why did not progress materially favor us?

"But, kind friends, open the ways for us — we are your prisoners, but not your criminals — to satisfy the cravings that disturb any rest within our seeking souls! Show us the possibilities of the earth — and we will prove to you the glory of Heaven — mercy and gratitude — as you have witnessed it, and we will aid you in embellishing it as you have never even dreamed; or together, aided by the mutual light, that we may shed or invoke, beaming with the gladness thereof on earth and in Heaven, the divers constellations, we will endeavor to enlarge our visions, our very stripes will become luminously light ('the stars and stripes'), and we shall *comprehend* and embrace the beauties and joys this earth is certainly intended to contain for us, could we perceive. But we must enbound it. Become acquainted with our people and we with yours, and, together, we will search the utmost approachable recesses of the earth; we offer you ourselves, for the search, and only ask that you share the surplus with us, which will give us comfort and joy. Kindly let us hear from you, and we will add our views on anything that we have inadvertently omitted, or you may wish to know from us upon. *No single nation can ever prosper* — unless it embraces the world!"

He sat down, and we were so astonished by his unexpected quality of discourse, that we remained silent wrapped in awe by the grand spectacle of this eloquent, earnest old man, growing grand and luminous, until his visage was one, either of fascinating attraction or terrible

glow, according to the beholder, but with the evident light
of truth. He pled the human cause as the result of his
almost unaided reflections. Contemporaneous observation
and the meager, unintelligible accounts sifted down to
him accreted with much foreign stuff left him, still, unself-
ishly to plead for the unbiased elevation of the human
race. He regarded the means with an entirely different
motive — by which, otherwise, selfishly, so much doom has
been wrought. His remedy for the ardors, cravings,
yearnings, of the soul was knowledge — not of good *and*
evil, but the former to eschew the latter; this was not as
remarkable as the suggestion, that inferentially the human
races had a common, mutually comprehensive role, from
the many, seemingly incongruous parts to conclude practically to a happy whole. Was this abstract, unbridled
philosophy?

I slightly turned to Mr. Bertram, as though to call upon
him to express the considerations of our little colony;
which movement he understood, and gravely arose, deep
in thought, as though a field of new ideas had unfolded
itself to him. His fine physique contrasted with the
somewhat small body of the old judge, and his large, well-
shaped head and lofty brow gave him a majestic appearance, from which fairly beamed and glowed the benignity
of a virtuous life.

> Ah! vicious visionaries of maid or man
> Within your countenances, which to scan
> Gleam fearful names.

"Friends," he said, "we have hearkened to a grand
exposition of what the books and the outside world evidently call unselfishness, as touched upon by the honorable and venerable speaker. In our midst we know or
knew nothing of those things that seem to disrupt all the

so highly desirable relations of the human family, except
as some vague, hardly understood rumors were handed
down to us, or we read; but hearing does not approach
feeling, and since here, for the first time, we have seen a
multitude of people, whom we could not but esteem as
something different and unknown to us, in our image but
to be regarded as strangers and without familiar friendli-
ness or relation — here, for the first time, dawned upon us
the friction of such contact — practice and history speaking together seem to us at present but poor instructors for
emulation. We have had our natural foibles, but not
acquired vicissitudes.

"At this period, when we have heard so much, already,
of the anxieties to which one is to be exposed by becoming
a part of the world, their divisions, subdivisions, and individuals — and, on the other hand, can ponder upon, from
experience, the stress of solitude or circumscribed association, and the lack of those productions, evolutions of the
necessities of numerous co-inhabitants — what a perplexity
is ours!

"Cowardice would turn back — only to pine for the
opportunities missed. Something urges on to the mystic
fray — perhaps to save some souls with the new vigor in
the battle. Conscience and thought are not reprehensible
and fear no doom; doubts enfeeble the constitution and
quake, that the inmost impulses lose the purity they might
purvey. In expressing an astoundment, pardon me, my
dear friends, we would rather not have spoken, but
yielded to your urgent requests as a requital for your generosity. We wish calmly to review the situation, you
bestow caution upon it, although you sigh; we have
unequivocal confidence in you. Would you betray that,
we should acquire a new insight into the workings of the
heart though not our own versions of its functions, for the

natural developments in us have not led us that way or
to such considerations. I do not desire to dwell on the
sadness of life, nor do I yield to morose tendencies, but
clearly onward there is a light, success, with a little rub-
bish in the way, which I push aside with my foot, and
proceed to the goal. Our natural necessities seem to be
supplied, excepting such as appertain to the spirit; these
desire variation to fulfill their destiny, because the means
therefor have been placed here unmistakably for their use,
and they have a right to yearn for their own. And yet not
all of the *physical* wants are supplied, either, since the
different localities must produce several articles, distinctly
and really required even by our physical conditions.

"We, you" (bowing to the judges) "and ourselves, differ
from the Secretary in that we deplore the lack of opportunity, in being deprived of the numbers and the expansion
incidental thereto and the receiving of new ideas; whilst
the Secretary laments a narrowness of sentiment in multiplied restriction, the over-crowding of populace, and
deplores the struggle, that ensues for existence in the
inadequate circumferences insisted by their practices to be
maintained as sole ends and means; on the one hand is
the solitude, from which it is sought to escape; on the
other, the oppression of being too closely crowded;
between the two is the salutary mean at which both
should meet, and, working thence, reap the undoubtedly
happy results of all equilibrium. We have not yet learned
to regard everyone with suspicion, nor does it seem intelligible to me that selfishness is a wise course, as, creating
suspicion, it exposes every individual to constant warfare
and doubt even in things of good; neither do I behold in
it the elements of prudence, or of even temporary profit,
since I cannot conceive that one in such acquired condition
could lead a practical, feasible life. Self-protection and

grasping are opposite elements, and the former would be unheard of but for the latter, for what care nature involves is but in its ordinary, self-regulated concern, a pleasure to accede to; but it is wilful human agency that consciously and maliciously disrupts, without any self-explainable reason, the regularity of affairs.

"Our colony, each individual thereof, is individually ourselves; would one starve or perish or suffer, that the other could, in the susceptibility of his complete nature, forego the sharing of the mishap? It is incomprehensible to me, that I could shield myself and see one of them lost, but, my impulse, my judgment, my esteem and consideration would place me at their side to combat jointly the threatened danger. What could induce otherwise? Wrong inflicted by me. Whence this wrong? From a mistaken judgment, and bad judgment arises from mysterious conjectures and false experiments not natural impulses. Though, from the heart spring evil designs, in the even temperament, elevation and tireless tendency of the soul in its struggle for its destiny is always the prime impetus for good. This is the highest and only implanted law, marred solely, and eternally injured by gradual, total suppression.

"While with you, my honorable judge, thought has concerned affairs temporal, we have principally wandered in spiritual realms, since temporal affairs did not disturb our tranquillity; our brows are unclouded, since by the spiritual food we acquired the most necessary parts of our nature from God's unquestionable store; not till we hear of these things of which you inform us, did we know how happy we were, by comparison — not an aristocracy of happiness, but a pitying soul, to which pain and suffering are more manifest than to the reality. That the fisherman should drag his net, the laborer dig, we esteem pleasures and recreations, not hardships; but when the spirit is made to

suffer thereby from scoffing of other persons — as long as
ignorance or superstition or brute force can maintain these
shackles, the distinctions of the social scale, then the real
evil becomes apparent. How it does grieve one to hear of
these conditions — how it must yoke those who feel them
— but onward, we will share your doom, shall endeavor to
distribute to you of the stock God has given us; must
learn your sorrows, perhaps, but our principles forbid us
to eschew you, our natures bid you welcome.

"We will throw open to you our ports and our enterprises; we will exchange opinions and products, and form
a coalition with you against the only enemy of mankind's
welfare : a besotted, sordid, benighted mind, with its indolence and intentional perversity. The multitude must not
tolerate the viperous individual — or with the scorn that
withers he will grow and multiply. The commonalty
must be very defective in the existence of misery, and I
venture the so-called honorable are the most depraved,
with or without religious guise, or the things would not be.
For, whither the head turns the eyes may look — possessing, individuals necessarily wield for good or evil. Inculcate thorough intolerance of vice, which seed will *again*
rear the physical and mental *man*. Contemplation can
discern happiness far off — reach out to it, reach out to
it — and, we welcome you to us."

Mr. Bertram sat down, and his shining example of
human disposition unmarred by the sickening flaws of
civilization was enthusiastically received, especially by
the judges, who hung on every word as it was slowly,
distinctly uttered, appreciating every sentiment; for the
first time learning that pure thoughts the world over are
without distinction, as they could so well themselves
understand the workings of the human heart. The speaker's cordial invitation to them to participate with them in

their joint affairs filled them with great emotion, the more as the speaker seemed to comprehend that their hitherto happy tranquillity might be disturbed or agitated by the elements of deterioration the preceding speaker had outlined as existing in their more multifarious midst. That true manhood and humanity uttered itself, and most nearly fulfilled the destiny of its origin, there could be no doubt; the selfishness he descried and discriminated could not be laid in any part to his charge, since the most deliberate humane reasoning explained his conclusions.

All now turned to me, and the task imposed upon me, in view of the preludes and the expected solutions of many practical problems that now presented themselves, filled me with a little quaking of fear so that I too might have fled in the first trepidation of the august moment; greatness is not as much appreciated when thrust upon us. I had been so wrapt in their discussions, that I had not thought for myself, being entirely unprepared for the surprise of their handling of these topics. Still I managed to catch enough of the fervency and realize the import-ance of the occasion and the prospects before us, to be keenly alive to what might be expected, and to formulate, as well as the time admitted, the circumstances with which I had formerly been familiar or at all acquainted. The mind may be very active, when an urgent concatenation draws it into severe conclusions, as you all know. Under such scrutinizing expectation as was now directed to me, such pleading confidence, attention and solicitation, I almost trembled like a schoolboy.

"Kindest of people and noblest of friends," I began, "there is system in everything; somewhere, somehow, in some degree, within this world, there exists that alterna-tive for everyone of good and evil, and the worst, most debased of criminals, natural or from any acquired cause,

in his or her appropriate situation, would be so docile, so
honorable, as to grace the very best of mankind. The lack
is misapplication to the proper turns of affairs. The
woman is not complete in her happy nature, until the man
has been accorded to her companionship and the two
together form the mutual partnership, physical and mental, as well as, more remotely, spiritual, for their common
elevation and the welfare of mankind. What errors mar
this principle of perfect unity, or the benefit from intercommunication of true parts under naturally proper conditions, are those of ignorance, wilful disregard, and violent,
useless, silly experiments. Spirituality requires no great
or any show. Its grandeur is manifested by itself and
annihilates merely temporal affairs. It is best judged by
its simplicity — not the mere assumption thereof but its
act. The greatest nonentity with possible potence is society's taste, to act without detection its test and creed.
Envy dogs its every footstep, hence it welcomes hypocrisy.

  "A symbol or an endeavor is vacant, that does not with
a sensitive elevation raise therefrom the elements of
discord that surround the unfortunate mass. Many
thoughts pass in a moment; but ideas flourish, when the
incidents have connected into a complete chain of transmission in which the vastness of the envelopment and concourse have been regarded. By this the system becomes
freed from the dross of neglect and the uniform propulsion
is satisfied.

  "Adverting to recent incidents, kind friends, do not fail
to read aright the appearances of regret or of wilful ani-
mosity. The sensibilities of a vague effort are not aroused
by idly cringing to local conduct or experience, frequently,
heretofore, expressed in pitiful moanings of the spirit.
Many days ago, when on the verge of despair, the turmoil
of affairs and the recollection of it, aroused a spirit of ani-

mation to resist the anarchy that was fast displaying its
tentative fascinations for the evanescent faculties. But,
with the recurring light, the possibilities of hope and
the cheerfulness of a reunited, feasible effort revived the
the desires. How silently the factors move the insight
into these seeming mysteries and carefully progress it
over the uneven ground. This is no greater than the
power of expression, which, if it fails, is a blame to the
incipiency of signs; but the spirit, the heart, the mind,
will ever contend within their limits. Enlisted for years
in the patient, suffering tranquillities of nature, the arrival
is at the portal of discernment or despair. Heeding the
quivering, seething, undulating mass there is no stop, no
enclosing the elements of corruption; but they must be
purged, ejected through their natural channels.

"I shall pass to a consideration of our temporal affairs
with the premise that no individual lacks the power to
succeed him or herself in the little discriminations which
fill the additionals of our lives. There is no unbiased
estimation of a deliberation or a dilemma to estivate a
happy existence. The interlockings of life are unloosened
or strengthened according to the existing exigencies.
Wearily you drag or rush on the path of necessary recti-
tude or lovingly linger in the rouged light of momentary
bliss, the effluvescent tendencies and exhibitions indicate
the decay of the firm matter and strong fibers of your
character and accord their sustenance. The undoubtedly
erroneous flourish for a time in your regard and neglectful
privilege; sometimes your forbearance, patience, construed
by them into right; your necessity, sometimes their deliverance: but the laws can manifestly only favor right and
leave their untrammeled enjoyments for a time in wrong
only in consideration of the burdens of right to be crushed
by curtailment of, or their intrepid contrivings.

"You have never felt a desire for mal-administration; you do not yearn for direful adventure; when aspects are murky, you do not rush to individually established gods of meager taste and false ideas: but, the fountains, the flood-gates of your sorrows pour forth anathemas, and you cry aloud, fiercely piercing the wild storm of your emotions, that the Power that superintends and wields a mighty destroying influence over all constructures, has again sped a menacing distress into the realms of bliss. Obliged to tranquillity in commotion, enthralled every moment in painful anxiety, the endeavor strives to grasp the illimitable in its frenzied efforts to perceive beyond its narrowed prevision. Fearfully it racks every constituent of power, delves in the bowels of woe for a bated seclusion, thrives on the disgusts of conventionalities until the ingrediencies of conception are exhausted, when the throttled, gasping victim expires a burden of an impoverished load. This is the wail of wrong. The meager details revolve about the firmly implanted stake, that thwarts every effort to remove it, holding relentlessly to the bounden fetters, which, too, refuse to yield their duress or to transplant into other sordid fields. The pasture is that of selected grace and none other. Thus, the development of an inner grossness supplies a care-worn field in the sterility of production, which, again, dwindles to a dead exhibition of withered hopes and dreaded expectations. A cant comes to the rescue and describes the votaries at the stake as victims of an unbegotten cause and furnishes even unseemly bier-holders in their excoriating anguish.

One single thought with which they wildly guile their
    feverish hours
Is sometimes more there fraught with sad, regretted
    plight.
Than burdens millions upon millions of true toils;

In no event but all is such mere gloss
Spread ten times o'er by envy's thoughtless task.

"How severely doubts enter into your lives is shown by
the repeated vain declarations of undue distinction; the
struggling tender to each other of a trifling share of the
fruits of one's own spoiled energy, for a return that cannot
be measured but by the discontent of the ungratified
desires. There is no escaping the conclusion, that the evil
of intent is not beggared by the developments of the sin-
ner; he fosters every thought and transcends every deed,
that not an impulse of detriment is allowed to escape in
his perverted construction of obligation. Could he envel-
ope this world with an inflexible band of flinchless steel,
he would feel inclined to encircle it with his desires. The
evil of these contentions, the destruction of the simpler
allotments to each individual part, have turned affairs into
a chaos, until not even the heedful know each and every
discrimination to be made in time.

"What is duty? Not the sole thrift for individual use;
but heeding in the upward, onward steps to the goal an
extended reach to take along all, who will not successfully
struggle to escape. By this precaution is supplied with
the strength of surrounding good parts, brave deeds and
noble friendships, and exposure of the bad and protection
of the weak, despite that now and then a traitor recedes,
which will be solely to his own detriment.

"The differences of the several concerns of life contrive
themselves into so many worshiping follies, that the mind
is overwhelmed by the abstract delineations; perhaps,
when the glories of achievement have fallen at your restless feet, in a moment, plunged into the intricacies of a
further discernment, the gloom appears greater than before
because of the little dazzling light that has suddenly

shed its beams where the refractory powers were least
developed. That brilliance should emanate from the outreaching and over-reaching between two destructive, pernicious agencies, is one of those strange facts that throw
the whole into that impenetrable gloom from which it cannot evolve itself. It is visibly affecting, that affairs for
better are blocked by the unwillingness of practice to be
purged of its hardships as though life depends on con-
troversy and not on real needs.

"Lastly, not a sigh is breathed that is not borne into its
realm of discreet consideration. Could anyone doubt that
a grief-stricken, woe-begotten heart could escape its griev-
ous impulses, such a one would fear to attempt to pene-
trate the causes that led thereto; such a one would not
tread with benign confidence the mazes of dread and
despair, or dare to asseverate that the ends of all justice
meted to the wandering creatures any measure of redress.
The unequivocal effort indulges in no such fallacy, the
tireless ardor of the soul knows no security of favor nor
yields a moment to such misanthropy until overwhelmed
by agencies which subdue it to their course. The hour
reckons this one the hero, the mighty premier, who has
once more agitated the main for a new bearing billow of a
scene upon its angry crest — shortly dashed asunder and
gone except a little moisture and spray to soak in or
evaporate. A few more faint regards and the power of
endurance will break. Soon the esteemed ambition of
hopes will have dwarfed into the significance of aroused
resentment to vile encroachment. In an hour the development of a life may grow naught; a gentle whisper
turn the tides of any intended flood of thoughts; but, the
reverence due to God is fruitful.

"Experiments are right or falsely represented to delude
into unwariness or attempts to gratify a mistaken direc-

tion by blending affectation of the belief of the useful
with dread of exposure of the faultful. Genius may come
or be the result of wild dreams; but, when its benign
influence is felt the little scoffers seek to array themselves
along the potent factors. Hence, that the progress of
affairs is not more systematical. False hopes of a vainly
glorious age!

"You will now extend your commerce and perchance
your domain; you will seek to rival your neighbors, then
to exceed them — your young vigor will attract and go out,
and will be your excuse for ignorance and arrogance alike.
You will not hesitate to thrust upon your new neighbors,
or cast against them the improbabilities of the existence of
another reckoning power, than your own judgments; thus,
the fallacies of life will repeat themselves, as they have
recurred for ages before. An extension is made to you of
gratitude and gradual endeavor; you are not supposed to
comprehend the former or abuse the latter; you are led
into a sphere, where the elements alike and facts and figures favor every vagary, that may infest the idle fancy.
If you are prepared to face with intrepid courage and skill
the inevitable results of a social contest for a fitful elevation, you have chosen the realm of man for your warfare.
A few considerations will thwart or discourage your intentions. What is the polity of sovereign benediction? Do
you contemplate, in the unfolding fields of enterprise
which stretch before you, the objects of usefulness that
cry to you to raise them to their proper levels?

"Despair not; mankind is not hopelessly lost. Trended
in part that way, it has been unscrupulously swayed. But
an element is growing, developing, that will no longer
grovel before a few depraved assumptions of mankind to
abject all the conscience and every instinct of generosity
to less than a beastly level. With that more powerful

factor the unmitigatingly unfortunate cannot stem the
tide; but, a pitying provision will have for them an
asylum with the predominating pure impulses and the
feeble conditions of our nature will yield to faithful,
patient attribution and attrition to an elevating power and
to the prayer of a saving grace.

"Extend yourselves, spread over the contiguous terri-
tories, and know no stay to your virtuous endeavors save
the sleep to waft you into silence and bliss, whither
thoughts may hie with burdens; but whence they return
not laden.

"Your estimation will be the appreciation of results, and
a few firm resolutions to abide the evidences of principle
will invest themselves properly and necessarily in your
prospects.

"The measure of your interchange of values:

"Can you, restricted to yourselves, produce everything
necessary for happiness and welfare? If so, your limits
need not be broken, unless humanity on the outside cries
to you for help — then you cannot be happy within, without being brutal.

"A few leagues hence lies the domain of this handful of
people, compared with you in numbers, as a drop in a
bucketful of water; yet, possessing an area of territory
utterly useless, excepting in a trifling part to the whole,
for any and all of their purposes. You have more than
ample territory, yet, for all of your concerns, but you lack
the knowledge to properly develop your resources, and
therefore are in want where there is wasted superabundance. Still you esteem yourselves in want of more
improved territory, labor and possession, when your own
is more than ample, while my friends here, still more
primitive, desire your company. But you have no advancement in this alone, as their small additional labor would not

contribute materially to any development of your resources, while their attraction of your populace would diminish your force and but raise them to your level. Then you do not stop there; the first step is proper, provided you intend and do carry the matter farther, otherwise you will be more happy to remain as you were discovered, with a request not to be discovered again; as to foist new ideas upon either of you will be but to entail the labor of learning them with no valuable consequences, unless the sequences naturally are observed. One will suffer more than the other by unequal advantages, which will rebound against the latter; and, finally, causes for strife, on each side, will develop, all traceable to folly in its origin. Thus, you may have ignorance in the lack of certain knowledge, which latter you must unearth. There the advantage of your present union becomes manifest — increase of territory, kinds of resources you combinedly have understood and exhausted and now deplore as a dearth. In your blind visions you have not observed your teeming opportunities; but, a combination of you will enlarge your comparisons. New mental faculties bring renewed considerations and you have further starting-points nearer to desired discoveries. Not at all foreign to the general principle I may shed such light in my power, when the doctrine enunciates, that different frictions are caused by new contacts and additional advantages adduced as every discovery is of something good by the great Creator.

"Now then, having embarked upon the search for knowledge as the requisite to be sought for your necessities and enjoyments, we will take it, that we have together discovered another, a savage country where dangers threaten us, but with our advanced appliances, we hold their onslaught at bay until we can parley with them, or awe them suf-

ficiently with our greater prowess to win their fear and
respect. What benefit is this to us and to them? I
will express my opinion.

"You see, at a glance, these savages need the benefit of
your contact for their improvement; if not, then you had
better adopt their modes, for undoubtedly there is a choice
in favor of one or the other; but better, there is certainly a
measure of benefit to be derived by each. Topographi-
cally, they also have some resources that you have not,
others that you have exhausted, and you are like a man
renewed in his energies by a sure, ample restocking of his
stores; never fear, in true virtue, you have ample to
exchange with for what has no value to them,
because of the superabundance of that particular kind,
whereas they have exhausted or have not certain things,
that will add much to their real, enlightened delights in
life and spiritual elevation, as well. Then, you are nearer
to other discoveries, because, on the expedition we are on,
knowledge, idleness is not encouragable; also, we may
have approached nearer civilization.

"You proceed and you now arrive at my old country.
Imagine the curiosity, in the present condition of affairs,
you would excite! I, myself, could not escape therefrom,
being become in such lapse of time rusty and out of style.
You come to a nation whence every source of knowledge,
that is ascertainable in this world, can be reached. It was,
originally, the most enlightened aggregation and government of people ever assembled together; selfishness was
nought, and what measures of circumclusion were adopted
were merely temporary efforts of desperate resistance,
adopted as a desperate extreme, not to be maintained.
Tending to liberality, which reaches out to enlightenment
and prosperity, lighting the way ahead for itself by its
own luminosity, it proves the glorious power of example,

and the happiness it brings with it. What it has barred herein is only by its own restrictions to foster a few selfish interests within its bowels, whence its excruciating pains, to be met by necessary purgative or result in death.

"In search of indolence foster protection and vice! Never before were the wisdom of past ages and their knowledge handed down as to us — to employ their virtues and shun their vices. In the crucible of aroused indignation the oppression of humanity by man was crushed and consumed by the burning shame it had engendered. The votaries of oppression have always exercised the excluding dignity of high protection by government. A sovereign does not want another admitted free — but the idea of a sovereign people is a myth where exclusion one against the other is practiced.

"If you wish to quell tyrants, encourage competition, their mutual devouring will be your salvation the world over. Our country had mapped out the most enlightened way to emancipation. Do they again want high protection, that fosters sovereigns and ignobles? There is a world-wide bond of sympathy between the people, between whom every contact is jealously guarded by those who exempt themselves from their common struggles. Palaces are reared on the ashes of cottages to make room — groans are not unmusical to some ears.

"The imaginary lines of boundaries are but to rear so many ambitions and put on violent commotion and destruction in heated cauldrons so many confined quantities. A range for distribution provides the only means of escape. People's minds as their products must travel — the constrained family habitude or intellect does not manifest the glories of man's nature.

"Those who most zealously guard protected industries, because of their direct benefits are personally the rampant free-traders — those very products, their means, are lavished any and everywhere upon any enterprise and for every pleasure. The life-blood, that is confined in the victim, when at length drawn at pleasure for use or vice versa is freely spread over the world — to distribute its stench perhaps. A foundation laid in God in not the pretended but avowed principles scrapes the contents of the earth to its bowels. Everything thrusts itself in the way for use, benefit, and the spiritual emancipation recognizes and hails enough wisdom to allow the dormant powers to become known.

"Willingness and not ability, instruction in the place of ignorance, are the wholesome lessons to share with true hospitality the unavoidable rewards, the humble, diffident, but true proffering of the best of each. Thus, in the double, laudable object to open ports, the noble, elevating attributes of human nature are gained, assistance and knowledge fulfilled, and society and zest for life created. In short, free to the world, permitted and then accorded, Christian here and everywhere, is there a wrong to be recorded, a hate to be engendered? Christianity not practicable — then abolishable!

"The liberality, which is none at all at best but a plain duty to self and mankind, spoken of, creates friends and coadjutors, unavoidably. By this means alone distress is abridged. The great luminary searches into the smallest penetrable corners of the universe. Retardation is the restriction of conscience and good science: poisonous remedies are better antidotes, than nourishment.

"No government should foster a single condition; if industry or general folly bring elevation or grief, the merits or punishment are therein. Government should not interfere with the natural rights or contracts thereof. Being no crime therein, prohibition is useless. An asylum of mercy should be practiced and not mistakable force, if necessary.

"Whenever we shall recede from this luminous way opened before us, the interest of the few will not compensate; but, we shall be forced to witness the most awful gloom. The grace that has beamed upon us is not for selfishness; when wandering over the earth as homeless traders for denial of this grace, as history may record in an instance, we may sigh, that we denied its boundlessness, in a boundless endurance. We sigh for exclusion and our king — God forbid!

"Shall a few shallow spirits for aggrandizement create a besotted power and be maintained by slavish restriction or slavish, worse, persecuted exclusion? Wisdom has no delight in the revelry and debauches of the aggrievers. Let the hitherto unthinking multitude attack this vulnerable point. The people immured into slavery, their masters have a loftier spirit over them, which extends and enters into alliance with the like the world over; the visions of these controllers are unrestrained, their means are *boundless.* Credence is exceeded hereby; but, repeated investigation would unearth the awful truth.

"Such ideas are barbarous in civilization. The secrets of the dungeon, the cruel exile, stealthy inquisition, close conclave, intrigues combination in the view of the world are premanifested by suspicion and meet its condemnation. It is but the wile of the individual at the expense of the whole.

"The instigator, who long since has borne the utter odium in addition to the common woes, is hurled from his ill-gotten pleasures by his own disappointments and fallacies.

"But, having arrived at this port, you have entered a great country — made so by God's blessings and nature's

courses; marred only by man's contrivances. You should
be challenged there but for the most laudable purposes —
we did not, *and shall not*, hurt you by our free entry here;
a certain consideration is properly demandable from you,
that the country may be in a position to accord liberty,
satisfaction for yourself, your business and property and
your legitimate pleasures.

"But on the other hand that tribute in substance should
be hospitably scrutinized by your host, should be so
reasonably gauged that nothing unreasonable or impossible should be expected from you in your conduct, either,
while on your visit.

"Exclusion means internal festering! The best appearing are the soonest ripe!

"America is for the Americans; but all may become the
latter, as these are of all, when, upon their due supplication, we annex their territory: they gain more than we
lose. You have not erred, when you have come to us for
the greatest amount of intelligence to be gained at any
one place, although it is not to be gainsaid that outside of
this point there are many, very many, places full of things
of true advantage, also. A reference may articulate a
truth both ways as well as one relative proposition.

"What will you offer in exchange? Remember, nothing
will be furnished you without recourse or value, and that
alone will furnish you constant employment and profit; a
free-trading nation cannot be bankrupted! You have
territory, now, that you have already united, a great
extent of it, more in fact than you yourselves have any
definite idea of, and you can, very acceptably, offer two
things.

"You have, already, heard, indefinitely, that an excess
of population, so to speak (formerly this was usually gotten rid of by wholesale murder, called war, for the delec-

tation of potentates; then, too, they rid their power of
so much menace) exists within the narrow range, in
which they seem to insist everything must be conducted
according to some set fashion, or not at all, and the result
is that with many there is a constant struggle to meet or
successfully thwart the clashing interests and unavoidable
contacts-within the narrow range. God has provided for
population — man has curtailed the range! That they
possess an unlimited range of territory, which they might
improve before bringing yours into requisition, leads us to a
discussion which may later be taken up in the abstract,
and brings you now to the idea of development.

"You require something more — you need a certain
amount of communication with other conditions and all
their incidents; and both you and they are benefited by
the intermingling of their several products and, thus,
engender a new life — the old succumbing at a certain
stage for the benefit of the new, not able itself to prevent
a determination of affairs. Parturition is a painful joy,
but, borne by the most glorious of mankind, gives the
impetus to evidently intended results. A happy combination favors a lovable issue. *All places need the rest of
this worldly space to distribute their surplus and foster
their employments.* God never sends a cloud over this
earth without its blessings — the negro and darkest
Africa bring refreshments to this garden, as it is new life
that carries on existence of affairs.

"Reform is the healthy emanation of happy admixture
and the fruit thereof — new brain, new knowledge, until
the diseased and weak are provided for. This is the nude
in art, and as essential as the quivering, shivering
mass, that poses therefor.

"Upon the details of things, the most expedient and
initiatory are adopted; subsequently, everything is treated.

You assume everything to good use, and add to the usefulness by the emergencies, that suggest improvements.
Beware of spurious issue.

"Now, then, you may offer the following considerations
to the United States why they should cheerfully receive
you, to wit: Upon the first aspect, you take up for your
use and consume many of their articles of almost every
description, which they have constructed for the very purpose; you have opened to them an encouraging avenue,
consequently, they are pleased and undoubtedly benefited
by the result, which, it should be assumed, they appreciate as a satisfactory fact. *That some should employ,
outside, beyond, everywhere and the room kept up for continued in rigorous, successful, beneficent employment, therein
lies the sole principle of happiness in life, individual,
mutual, universal.*

"And acting upon this truth, the United States offer you
the facilities of the application of all their industries, to
instruct you in the beneficial use of their products until
your experience and understanding make these two things
profitable to you; and you will have offered a locality
where the skilled men of their nation can find employment (and think, yours, too), the field being more than
supplied at their home if the consumption is restricted to
the home market, and seeking aid with high emoluments
if it is not. Otherwise, that field of endeavor, where the
heart as well as the mind may be desirably exercised,
would be cut off but to a favored few, or you would sink
into apathy, gladly hailing the end of your enforced days.

"Every corner-storebox has its philippers and fillupers —
every individual under some circumstance is a linguistic
host. Upon your premises you are an orator, although
the top of a stump may be too uneven. Here the free-
booters mount with acrobatic skill, though the hardy

woodsman, who in preparing the settlements also prepared the 'stump,' is not nimble on its surface. With no premises of their own they here call for the strategetic events and become *free* fellows at your home with the request to rule and live off you. They desire to cut off supplies from elsewhere, that no time be given you to rule yourself in the attentions they require or the 'rest' they wish periodically to enforce upon you without a chance for succor. In this way they may leisurely balance their accounts with and charge the difference to you with interest. These have never been your friends — neither to the newcomer seeking admission to the higher realms of man nor to the subjects of their prey. The only free, comparatively useless property they find here is the 'stump,' and appropriate it and call you forth for a barter or trade. Where do they get their provisions but with their coadjutors whilst drawing you from the defense of your homes and stores? Let not such wiles draw you into the denuded wilderness for the unknown terrors of a combat, with a foe in companionship with the unprovidential and grasping, whose fort is the power of menace. Your castle is your joy, fortify your virtues, admit your friends and fellows in general interest the world over, and the host you will muster will debar all 'domesticating' wolves.

"Where you are hopelessly general, and not specifically pure, you start with infatuation for a few, end with adoration for all, and reach the issue, happily, if before death or destruction in the meantime. But where you faithfully admire all, you enjoy their company and they reward your faith. In this conscientious intercourse with a nation you will have developed your means, produced your resources, mutually afforded knowledge and facilities, and the mutual assistance has distributed your stores to unbounded satisfaction and employment. Your foreign relation is indeed happy and auspicious. If trade with restriction can be beneficial, without it must be multiplied.

"Why is it, my humble friend, that kingly houses and the powerful seek to unite their family interests? Is it not for local power regardless of the foreign substance of the force? Does anyone question the motive of such mutual alliance of power?

"A happy stimulus for surplus productions, and therefore the best employment of forces, is the application to dispose of them.

"Now, then, you may come to a point where you both have so completely supplied each other with your mutual supplies (no formal agreement, no reciprocity, but necessity is the compact of enlightened procedure) that your range has, again, become limited. What is possible of thought is feasible. You will never become limited except by utter impossibility, and at that time the provision of the great Creator comes in with the end of your trials, with acquittal, if you are innocent.

The dolor (or dollar) of your needs in your house must determine the sense (or cents) out of it; but, you must go out. Your house cannot supply itself for or from its own construction, still supplies others through you that you may inhabit it by them.

"But you shall, we will say, proceed to France, to Germany, to England, to Russia, and the several other countries and nations. (You will wonder why there are so many names; I will tell you, To quarrel about.)

"One might go on and adduce, interestingly, the several kinds of productions the various countries are respectively capable of offering to the world for exchange or such they are incapable of producing; how the different climates, topographies and zones possess divers faculties for the developments of knowledge and resources; that the people in their race peculiarities offer inducements and mutual advantages—all of which would be fascinating in the narrative. Then add thereto the advantages of inter-mingling of products from all these various sources and you again have before you the pleasing problem, that leads but to the one happy result, the creation of new life to delight you, unlimited, varied, restrained solely because our possible uses cannot embrace all. Yet, swiftly, unin-terruptedly see—let the world first come to you and erect the power-house whence to conduct this electrical portation, grant the space for such a beneficent result and the profits enormously will be yours. The world now awaits a general enterprise to give its bounty. The intellects that can henceforth devote themselves to this investigation and welfare of the world have a happy and unrestricted life's work before them. The lack of employ-ment is the lack of enterprise.

"Thus, you will linger long and patiently, with enthusi-asm, confidence and delight, inquire into, perceive and learn the divers facilities, and will receive their possibili-ties and developing powers, and, in return, offer them your field for their experiments. Thus, ever working for each other, a strengthening in the chain, yet a flexibility, each part a complete *little* self, a link, yet a uniform, encircling, beautiful whole, as durable as all life. Then we shall not be compelled to quibble over foolish unestablishments, strained circumstances produced by narrow views, but only perceive the measure that is accorded to existence. Here we can abduce the true evolution, that is to figure for this life.

"But you suggest the sordid motives, the inequality of different people and conditions—the disparagement in the case of one over the other. The difference alluded to is largely of estimation and entirely of forced inadaptation.

Because one soil produces what another fails is not a difference in production but results. Not even this for the second will produce equally as profitable. Everyone is fit somewhere.

"The whole resolves itself not to the fiction of difference in true parts for humane purposes but the establishment of propriety, and this is an unmistakable thing. Perverted by fault and ignorance appears in your daily experiences; yet, no thing is so trifling as not to be embraced by this underlying principle. Everything is a part and legitimate in its purposes. An absence would leave an imperfection, as the vacancy from the principle would leave nothing to be considered.

"You trade; you cannot live off yourself—cannot cling to your own parts for protection. To be connected even means to be torn and crushed with the disaster of the support; but, alone, affright is sufficient to quell the senses.

"To flourish means to benefit and be benefited by. Can you deny man's benefit to you? Have you not made him what he is and will make what he remains? What would you resort to in his absence—or pine eternally?

"In a proud moment a little individual success elates, envelopes the fancies, that hardly a sickly gleam of intellect is left. Every likelihood is then burlesqued and we presume on distinctions, where it is shown none truly can exist. The same law, that is raising, giving to the other, maintains the identical prestige—more than that even in its time and space. But, where one result necessarily leads to another, your neighbor becomes illimitable, unless you eliminate yourself. Be not duped by a momentary use; to-morrow's sun may not only shine on a different scene but your circumstances will lift you to the common sphere despite every protest and contrariness. Appreciate your surroundings, comprehend them by EDUCATION.

"You speak of weaknesses. Alas! God pity us, and there is where we need His pity. You say truly, 'our weaknesses,' for they are our property, our production. If we wish to point with pride to anything, we can proudly asseverate, 'Behold our handiwork; our genius!' —and no patent-right will be denied us, because of any like invention, or one that will supersede us in that respect.

"The best is not always for you; sometimes a very mediocre fits your best and is all that is required, the best being preserved for those who need it most. Because of our pride we are weak; when we are passionate, angry, indolent, perverse, and refuse to persevere where the goal, undoubtedly, promises the most delightful ends, we expose ourselves to, not insinuations only, but charges of our transgressions and consequent imbecility. One or the other, or more than one of them usually infest our practices, and are the stumbling-blocks which plunge us into ignorance. First we excuse, then seek to save whatever good emanates. Virtually our affairs are in chaos, from which the extradition of what is good is the so-called invention of ourselves. We vaunt our discoveries and seek to protect them for ourselves—dependent on others. We mingle the fruits of our successes with chance, fortune, experience, accident; but, the accepted consequence of pure knowledge is not a fact.

"One ponders and wonders; yet cannot charge perversity to man covertly with insinuations as is frequently done, but must judiciously take a bold stand. The search for principle is not discouragable as it saves from malignity the many candidates for the honor of true manhood and womanhood.

"The sneaking, creeping viper is the most certain foe! The open scourge is a blessing, compared with the terrors

of a hidden death. But, to return to the *consideration* of
our weaknesses, we owe, not to ourselves but to our neighbor, compassion and commiseration — ourselves should
aim to purge ourselves of our iniquities, not so much in
grieving over past offences, but in rehabilitation and a
renewal, as much as possible, of the pristine strength.
Your silence, in your countenance, speaks your desire.
Your example elevates. Your wish guides.

"Wealth is your desire? — wealth, and power, and the
attributes and the incidents you choose to ascribe to it?

"That seared withered old man, who has spent a life of
licentiousness, of debauchery, of dishonesty, cruelty, cold-
blooded dissimulation, and yet withal, and even by these
means themselves, collected what it pleases you to call
wealth, has enjoyed himself in that way, and has also
accomplished more than you, in the common race for the
same object, that is, wealth.

"Has the anatomy of such a one ever been dissected?
I mean now with a view to the question in hand.

"Assuming, that you are diametrically opposed to his
course: look at him, he bespeaks his life. That you
term their's enjoyment, therein lies the dilemma. They
have annoyed their neighbors; but, from the estimation
alone of their neighbors have they derived their prestige.
In other words, fail to perceive any reason for a man's
eminence by his selfish acquisitions and you crush the
incentive. Your envies and bickerings afford the very
results you deplore. Eschew caste. How many know the
eminent minds and able men, that exist. Those who have
an abiding faith in principle suffer little or none herein;
but, are pityingly, solicitously, prayerfully grieved.

"That old decrepit, disgusting, unrefined, ignorantly
mannered man, assumes a position from his mass of dross,
and ascribes to himself, really, candidly, a virtue, a dis-

tinction, and exhibits an evident contempt for your relative position in 'society,' because you cower and cringe to his assumptions—hence his position, his so-called *powers.*

"Now, my anarchistically inclined friend, this is no solace for you, as he borrows no glory from and, hence, has none to return to you; neither could you give or consent to be given that which you never had or, in any measure, controlled. If your ideas of division are based on absolute right—you are wrong; but, seriously now, that old croak is miserable; depreciated, or falsely appreciated, worn out, disgusted, 'no more worlds to conquer,' because he has exhausted *his* ability, and has no desire to vacate these premises where he has some gleams of fitful joy.

"Bad practices destroy good manners.

"The quantity of delicacies at a rich man's table is his surfeit.

"I, it will be remembered, but a short time ago had a plentiful supply, yet lacked everything—in spirit.

"As a rule the delights of the table have become sordid, soured or commonplace. The meager appetite of one is no cause for complaint of another in his ravishing desire because he has and the other not—the former is surfeited and lacks the enjoyment, the latter is in dearth and suffers; the occupation of the former is without a desire for gratification in consumption, while the latter's seemingly calls for greater supplies. Herein is the enigma of the relative existence, fostered mutually by restriction and idleness.

"Thus the elementary principle of life becomes disgusting. With downy couches, elegant equipages, service, there is no delight alone; the absence of these is no deprivation although their pleasures are beyond question, because their possibilities are for use. But in the conduct alone lies success and mutual enjoyment.

"Now, as conducted, the exultation of the one over, and the envy of the other at possession, create the only appreciable zest, are too the only causes of friction, and lay the foundation of the pernicious social principle underlying this fictitious fabric. That only the unfortunate complain is no comment on the silence of the others. Sooner or later the burden falls between them and then the general anguish becomes manifest. Distribution would be favored if possession were not exalted in the minds.

"Property would be a burden were it not the adored manifestation of selfishness. Its limitation lies in the industry of the others to acquire other and not to tender a high regard, in hesitation.

"Where were you begotten and born? The world is the field for the righteous, heaven its storehouse. Because you can see no further you conceive yourself in gloom. But read aloud the promptings of your heart and you perceive everything. They say to you, Vain man, your foibles trouble you not enough. You chase shadows when a little forethought would conduct you upon another course to await the things the shadows have forecast. Or you would go to them. An inspiration enlightens the heart and mind and glows through the soul. It is from heaven; pure are then the motives, leading but to right. You have no right to complain; not a destructive, violent sorrow is considerate to the several principles, but it is enunciated these must control for properly onward propulsion.

"No man is wealthy, but collectively that accord, privilege, appellation has been made him. Withold wisely this consideration, make him again your equal by your undistinguishing regard, first in your individual opinion, then collectively, and you remove his exercise of his relative situation.

"Or remove yourself from his immediate contact and what price remains not his social sacrifice? Leave him his matter but deny your companionship and you thwart all his desires. The higher intelligence must come from you. Let his price be refused.

"His wealth is only a relative position to yours in the opportunities you grant him, which for his delectation lies principally in your jealousies, where, in your fair-mindedness, ought to be pity. Your estimation is that makes a rich man proud, haughty, cruel. His exorbitance is your knavish connivance.

"Let intelligence supply every calling, education find its avenue in each, and the otherwise humblest virtues will exalt humanity to equality and abolition of caste.

"But as long as pre-eminence is generally sought in caste, it must be allowed, and the burden of ungracious life continues.

"Earth is for the good; but where all are wicked, folly metes the share to the wise — and wisdom may be as sordid as a hog. How would you, then, quell the riot of a rich man? We have discussed what makes him rich: your esteem. Now, let us see where his esteem arrives, if he ever has any. Transplant this rare flower from his gardens, you will find him a rarely indigenous plant, a fungus, an overgrowth, of doubtful beauty there, but perhaps some drug or a manure, still draining the earth of more of its fruitfulness, than he can ever alone contribute to it again. Take him where the blooms are of another order, and in a clime of a haughtier, hardier, more majestic growth, and whither languishes his desire? If he is at all enabled to exist alongside of the substance-draining, over-bearing, shadowing plants, when they fall he is crushed beneath, perchance, unless he is so withered and shrunken, by that time, that they cannot touch him even by disaster; or the new soil and food are death and destruction, themselves, being inadequate in substance to his enterprise. He passes hence into insignificance. Among his equals he is no peer; with his superiors he fades from light; with his light, alone, he illumines no other's path. Away from his power he sheds no beam, whatever; and when cold death embraces his chill heart, it is no welcoming touch, for, it is not the cooling, delightful zephyr, that wafts ease and blissful enjoyment in rest to an earnest existence spent in fruitful garnering of an even harvest of delight and plenty.

"The spirit of man may be ever proud, but his victors are his insatiable desires; he may desire all the possibilities of this earth, he cannot hold them all at once, and yet his insatiety will disturb his every thinking moment.

"He yields not, this mortal, to the necessities of the day, but, racks in the night, and he goes down into the darkness of his gloom and despair a wrecked mortality, unfitted for the strife of the morrow. Let him live in social enjoyment of right.

"It is not necessary to speak of this or that iniquitous influence; it boots nothing to refer to these feeble indications of the unfavorable tendencies of man, unless a mighty effort, a stern endeavor and desire uphold and uplift the knowledge, that presents itself to view in these visions. It is useless for me to augur you an enlightened, beneficial time, if you do not, in the first instance, realize your important, active engagement therewith; nor can one premise a condition of things to be, unless there are directions to point out the tendencies, that may bring about such affairs. God made us for a whole, and mutual esteem and social quality.

"*No single nation has ever prospered* — and none embraced the world."

I sat down and was at once touched and moved by the appearance of anxiety and dread that had settled itself upon the assemblage, for to them appeared, for the first time, a possibility of a worse state of affairs, than those they were now trying to escape. Their gaze was abstracted, especially that of the judges, and several had drooped their heads. My friends were evidently bolder, in their hardier manhood, and uncontaminated, in any measure, by previous social relation. I suggested, at this stage, that dinner was probably about ready — and, establishing my surmise, the meal-gong sounded its not unwelcome summons. I offered, during the noon-hour, to prepare a series of resolutions, which should, in brief, outline the skeleton of a preparatory or provisional compact, that no misunderstanding should mar our much-to-be-wished pleasant relations, as in all human relations the clearest understandings are the foundation and basis of progress.

They acceded to my proposal, and under the hospitable leadership of Mr. Bertram presently filed out of the room — a somewhat subdued set, willing to concede that life certainly presented some perplexing anomalies — ah, when emancipation is about to ensue, ever the worst of the first fears of despair; then, glorious happiness forever, rest!

Left alone, I was plunged unrestrainedly into the depths of my pent-up feelings and experienced the sorrow of regret — there came to me, again, one of those times, when we are burdened and borne down in the heaviness of our spirits with deep, afflicting ponderance on human affairs.

But I had not much time to yield to doubt-creating theories in the short space before me to determine expedi-

encies in the highly practical, important occasion before
us all.   It was *all* of the world we were treating; it was
but a small concern, compared with many great ones, that
are before the larger world — but, importance is not measured by its extent, but its bearing.

I formulated as follows :

"1st.   The affairs of man are in chaos.

"2d.   A mutual consideration imposes an interchangeable esteem.

"3d.   Esteem and consideration are, mutually, indispensable.

"4th.   Under the direction of a benign influence a solemn realization may be accomplished.

"5th.   Individual desires and tastes merit their careful
attention.

" 6th.   It is an undoubted principle of good, that intercommunication be fostered, not restricted; that good-will
and well-intention be manifested without reserve; that no
burden be cast upon another, which is not willingly borne
in return; and that the highest beneficial result is to be
anticipated and realized in the pure development of
comprehension.

"7th.   That the ports are to be thrown open; that each
accord the other an investigation into the other's resources,
to satisfy the doubtful ones, although, there is no question of
faith and, therefore, knowledge in the many and majority;
that the facilities of development be mutually accorded."

When they returned, it was with brighter, beaming
countenances.   They were profuse in their offerings of
condolence at my enforced absence from the good things
they found prepared for them, but I waived their good-
natured sympathy, and began at once to read to them
these several items, at the conclusion of which Mr. Bertram added :

"8th. Plain expressions raise no uncertain distinctions."

And the whole was adopted with enthusiasm and heart-felt joy and thankfulness, the gloomy forebodings giving way to the certain, enlightened future, that dawned upon the world, thenceforth, as a new basis upon which to join their old affairs.

CHAPTER XXVI.

THE RETURN HOME.

Political economy with early domestic propriety is the field for the future man.

Those who complain loudest are usually the worst — reform must begin with them and their complaints. Never profit without principle or you will generally be mulcted despite of it thereafter.

The sound that lingers were it many dreary miles away,
No joy, no scene, no grief can rob its name;
Nor thought but has a fondness for the erstwhile day
And "home" remains the beacon-light to gleam.

WE spent two more days with these people, who were daily manifesting greater confidence in and regard for us as the facts became generally known and understood, and their liking for us increased, when they had learned, also, our further amicable intentions. Already their imaginations were becoming fired by the promising outlook; while the authorities lavished such attentions upon us, as proved their high opinion of us since our formal, consultory meeting, and the evidences they had then derived as to our sturdy, resolute views.

We had again quietly discussed the matter among ourselves, and entertained the unanimous wish to extend every facility to advancement in our powers, and our every conduct and expression towards our friends and whilom entertainers exhibited that resolution; all of which had the beneficent effect of putting everyone in the best of humor, and we mutually enjoyed the freest intercourse with one another.

We met and became acquainted with their leading people in the several branches of their industry and callings, and found them, in the main, as we had found their rulers, to be possessed of brave, simple, kindliest characteristics as outlined. A people may safely be judged by their rulers.

That they were a people who promised much in their integrity, industry and intelligence, we became more and more convinced, as their reserve wore off.

One day was devoted to an excursion, or, better, incursion into the country for a distance, to embrace a view of their husbandry. We found here a neat arrangement of all that they undertook in the way of farming and gardening. Their products were not so very numerous; they comprehended and used, advantageously, the sciences of manuring, and draining of surplus water, therewith, too, internal ventilation where necessary.

The farmers were a neat, industrious, intelligent set of people, who furnished the *basis of all supplies* much more unmurmuringly, than I had ever beheld. It would be needless to go into any further detail about these people at this time, especially as our subsequent intimate relations with them will draw forth all their native qualities, in the narratives that will necessarily follow concerning them, interweaving themselves hereafter so closely into our whole history, public and social, that the favorable consideration of one will be to compliment the other.

One more incident remains to be told of this memorable trip and successful discovery.

On the eve of our departure, having all in readiness to

go early next morning, we were informed that the people
wished to entertain us, "as they humbly were able," by
an exhibition of their national kind on festive occasions,
which, for this occasion, they had endeavored to make
extensively elaborate. About five o'clock in the evening we all repaired to a shaded spot, for the sun was still
high and shone hot rays, where the "picnic" was to take
place, and were very politely ushered to the elevated seats
of honor. The judges and their families, being likewise
accorded distinctive recognition, were picturesquely
grouped near us—but upon us all eyes were turned, and
to us was especial effort directed.

The first thing was the distribution of a libation among
the honored guests, who, besides the judges and ourselves,
embraced the leading citizens, the fore-men and skilled
and directing operators in their affairs and traffic. This
was, truly, a delicious decoction, and was as refreshing as
it was palatable, and by no means stinted in supply—as
the gods would be presumed to prepare for a feast. And
a feast followed; young maidens, of about fifteen annuals,
fair-skinned, beautifully featured and gracefully moving,
with their beautiful, loose-flowing silky locks fluffing in
the gentle breeze, and clad in a gala-costume, red-tinted,
and, in this case, sandaled bare feet, did the service in a
winsome, graceful manner.

It was of that kind of spirit, which is exhilarating, but
not stimulating, unless it be beneficently so.

What a wonderful amount of narrative could hinge on
the contemplation of these people, who seemed simple
enough at first, almost primitive and uninteresting, if a
devotion were to be tendered their every entertaining
detail.

But now followed an exhibition that excited my greatest admiration and was marvelous to me as a new

development or exposition of living art. Purely the embodiment of their own ideas of graceful demonstration, and in nowise even suggesting an impropriety, the spectator was not only entertained and delighted by the spectacle, but experienced a sense of relief in escaping from mere conventionalities of life. Yet a refined tone of morality pervaded the atmosphere and evident intention of every movement, so that one was unrestrainedly drawn into a noble, exalting and invigorating realization; the first, or primitive, spectacular entertainments seem more to pattern after nature in its purity, but are afterwards sullied by indiscreet ventures. That the taste may become morbid, is evidenced by the deterioration too often witnessed; but none so depraved, who cannot appreciate a noble exhibition forcibly rendered.

Arranging themselves in two lines, fifty on the side, were maidens from the ages of sixteen to twenty, none exceeding these limitations, which was, as we were informed, a particular, though, perhaps, singular part of the order; at the completion of the twentieth year, the whilom member stepped out; on the sixteenth birthday anniversary each maiden became a member of the order of "The Rays of Light," and, while the exercises to be performed were to be learned, as a consequence, the order was so delightful, that every girl looked forward to the time at which she was to enter it with great eagerness, and retired from it with regret. *Their* debut in society — but such a beneficent society!

Other sports and pastimes there were, besides this one displayed to us, as they informed us, going into detail thereof; but our stay then did not allow further entertainment of the kind; and the youths' exhibition remained for some later date.

After their attitudes of initiative position were struck

(in physical development there is moral taste) each one
moved in graceful poise with military precision, regarding
their relative unison, a further evidence of their native
taste and cultured eye for harmony in coloring and shad-
ing and form. My friends, who were in the extremest
state of excited expectation, as this was their first experience of this kind, greeted with a surprised exclamation
of wonder and awe-stricken delight, the beautiful appearance of these charming ranks.

Their raiment had the gloss of silk, though the material
was not quite as flexible; but, in coloring, nothing was
left to be desired in the harmonious blending of the
brilliant dyes in the severally constituted groups. This
artistic effect was more potent, because the different roles
from their history and ensigns were thus to be portrayed
and, nationally, to be impressed on their memories.
Whilst amusing the faculties you can inject more pleasure — by seeming calamity bitterly tasting but more
pleasure after. Here truth and joy were happily in their
natural union.

After the first bow with arms folded reverently, as
though appreciating the sacredness of their missions in
this world, the nimble feet quickly bore their lithe, easy
burdens over the fresh green sward, which had been
closely trimmed for the occasion, and their first figure
was assumed: their national flag, or ensign of colors —
and so beautifully and correctly was it given by these
delightfully appearing maidens, that I was ready to shout,
"glory," myself. But restrained myself for the time-
being, for demonstrations of so-called applause did not
seem to belong to these people, at this time; they seemed
to regard this exhibition with a serious mien, as though
attaching considerable importance to it, although their
delight was apparent. That the best was here expected,

soon was manifest, and we ascertained that their best performers had been selected for this entertainment; all were handsome.

Their ensign was an angel (a happy relief to me from the usual figures of animals, selected, too, for their most terrible propensities, queer inculcations for the human mind, *intellectuality*, and heart) or, some might construe it, a "goddess of wisdom," and was beautifully and realistically constructed from this tender plant, this beautiful mass of humanity, so skillfully interwoven and supported one by the other, that the perfect image became apparent and the several identities of the human persons forming the ensemble were lost. With the aid of their mantles of pure white or gold or green or purple, they completed the whole picture so quickly, so dexterously, so ingeniously, that one was fairly bewildered and could not perceive just how it was done. Like so many active, healthy particles, they industriously fittingly blended into the one grand whole — typical of the well-regulated life, and the figure the emblem of the grand and beautiful protection of a union. Their banner represented the guardian spirit of progress and success.

Everyone of the hundred was utilized; some to enter into the figure directly, others for the footstool of fleecy clouds, while banks of soft clouds surrounded and formed a background for the figure, set off in one corner by a rainbow, also their emblem of peace. Could anyone make a distinction between them in the beautiful whole, the united beauty of which was not individual vanity? Why should there be difference by caste in life?

How they accomplished all this is a matter of skillful detail, and could only be done after the most systematic training in the delightful art, each to know her proper place and to maintain it. Some bearing or supported by

several, or in a measure by all of the others, none could
be said to reign, all were lost together and none perceptible alone, yet everyone requisite. The statue was of
heroic size; the head of the figure was formed of the
heads of five at least of these, not otherwise distinguishable charming ones, but so dexterously did they insert
here and there little articles of artistic employment, of
illumination, by artificial light, that instantly, so well understood they their parts, a shining visage beamed brightness and glory, not cold stone, but living in living parts, and
quivering or pained with the souls therein, while the hair
of the pure, golden blondes, who formed this uppermost
part of the figure, made the natural halo — incipient
angels one angel. Then, as I have said, there were the
"cloudy" base or footstool and background, all arising
simultaneously with the figure, in fact giving it its buoyancy, and at the last the brightly-hued rainbow completed the serenity and beauty of the scene, all composed
of these living, distributed bodies. One of the features in the clouds was a long plume, which, when
properly adjusted about the body, formed an exquisite
ornament to the costume. This allegory and significant
introduction completed, with ample time to take in its
beauty, the illusion vanished like a phantom; but in so
doing assumed another figure, and was even in the transition state a representation. We became aware that the
whole was a connected series, and demanded our continuous attention. When next there was a halt in the
movements — the whole was an ocular demonstration, not
a sound was uttered — we beheld the entrancing spectacle of
"sleeping beauty," or, I take it, their charming idea of the
creation of man, that is, the establishment of earth with all
its wonders and delights and fruits. The world over this
charming spectacle is engrafted on the heart, the same

original genius. A beautiful brunette maiden, the largest
and most queenly, full of figure, was reclining, garbed and
draped in the neutral tints, which shed off and subdued
from her raven tresses, that luxuriantly and wavingly
clustered about her head and neck and down to her
shoulders, framing her white face and large, luminous,
black eyes. The whole effect was one of virtue and inspiring innocence and consequent bliss. The luxurious couch,
as well as the brilliant frame, with the rising "sun" on
the margin, was the same human arrangement; beautiful
shrubbery stood and bloomed forth, with startling, bewilder-
ing suddenness, all about this roseate couch, in all its dewy
freshness, as these maidens adeptly posed and seemed to
lose all their identity, in the fairylike, incomprehensible,
yet visible transition into beautiful blooms. Now a sudden
gyration, a moment before a general gentle stir, as though
the impulse from a fairy-wand, or the soft breeze that
stirred all vegetation, with a true vernal burst of glory,
this fanciful garden, waving in purity and wafting its
incense hither, burst into existence, in the midst of which
this beauteous angel, also, blossomed out into the rarest of
productions, the human being. She was, in reality, the
last to appear upon the scene, but so immediately and
sequently as not to lose the earliest preparation of the
beauty about, so completely a dearth without her perfection, that the order was scarcely perceived in the wonderment at what had so delightfully taken place.

A moment later, and while rapt in cherishing ecstasy on
the view, the whole was turned into confusion, and this
beauty disappeared so as by magic, into a veritable chaos,
that a cry of horror was scarcely suppressible. One
or two of the party, our younger representatives, for-
got themselves so far as to utter a low, spontaneous cry of
chagrin at this transition, and when, a minute later, all

was again in repose, it was no longer the bright spectacle of restful bliss, but the seeming reign of brooding terror. A gray, murky tinge (a first indication of the agonizing brain as it were) of shade invested every coloring of the desert landscape; a dreary object, at length, raised out of the scene, and a fixed, awkward female figure, with disheveled hair, seemed transfixed with immutable agony as her wild, glazed, fixed look seemed to gaze into vacancy, there was little else.

Gradually, almost imperceptibly, a bright spot here, and a barren, desolate, despairing place there disclosed themselves, only to vanish into the reverse, a realm of sordid glee, and the quivering humanity, visibly flitting, sadly burdened.

Not a sound had thus far escaped the performers; nor was there any resort to artificial light, or shade in any way in depicting this gloom, which was realistically produced, as well as the preceding brilliance, by their adroit use of coloring in their garments and arrangement. Thus far truly an exhibition of simplicity had been given with means not outwitted by their ends in the fac-similes of great events.

In an instant, without any forewarning whatever, or any apparent effort at transition, the whole aspect burst into a scene of angels, immaculately clad, and seeming to float on white, fleecy, golden-tinged clouds, when there broke forth a marvel of harmony and sweet tones, that made everyone, not excepting myself this time, heave an involuntary sigh of relief at the promising, succoring light. How happy to dwell on the unfolded glory — a happiness willing to forego a taste again of the pristine. Sordidness, morbidity, must but appall the taste in a bilious appetite. Joy is in the pure domain.

This singing, which was a song of praise and glory, I

have never heard excelled, each word being articulately uttered by that great chorus, who sang in unison, but, such tone and inflection! and each expression, full of meaning, was accompanied by tinkling sounds made from sea-shells, and metallic substances fashioned almost from their raw state, and some from wood, arranged in chords and registered and toned to certain scales, and, in their use, each at a proper time, these gifted musicians were wonderfully adept.

Then followed a fantastic dance, in which the nimble feet moved through the intricacies of the figures with unerring precision and unsurpassed grace; this representation had but just been created, showing their exquisite readiness, the adaptability of all good training for an emergency.

They first vividly portrayed, in this pantomime, their consternation and surprise at our sudden unheralded appearance; next their delight at the revelations we brought, which latter exhibition increased in ardor and happiness as our future prospects had unfolded themselves; last an evident opposition or regret at our departure from them so soon, with indications of the uncertainty of life, but faith in the revived hope, fittingly and touchingly closed this view.

Then followed, as if the aggregate of them had been shot together, and all life stilled in them as in one impulse, another representative scene and closed this highly entertaining, marvelous affair, which ever after lingered in our memories, as we often dwelt on the numerous features, and, I must confess, many an hour have I philosophically lingered upon this lovely tournament of female grace, winsomeness and adaptability. Who would not wed a "Ray of Light" under such circumstances? Physical culture and mental endowment — a toast to the "Ray" and the Turner forever!

In the last scene there loomed up evidently their other
divinity or reverse ensign, a somber, handsome figure in
black; the brown, thick hair enveloped in curls the large,
shapely head, while a kindly expression shone from the
face, a ready, burning flame of indignation, or a tranquil,
wary, scrutinizing reflection; this was intelligence, and
embraced in the one, justice, charity and progress.

> Intention speaks from every lineament
> To honor him who thinks and acts aright.

The setting about the central figure was appropriate —
the surrounding scene subdued, but not hopeless; and a
faith, like the little snow-flower, fresh and vigorous in its
chill, pale surroundings, cropt out here and there, conspicuous, despite the seeming identity with the evenness of
the colorless and lifeless embodiment—down below it
knows and draws its sustenance, preserved and refreshed
by the dampness and chilliness --the tears of cold despair,
from the cold draughts of the world.

I am free to say that I never witnessed an exhibition
more fraught with demonstrative instruction, and, at the
same time, delightful entertainment. Even religion should
be allowed to waft its spirit into all the conjectural flights
of the most intense imaginations.

Imagination is not an idle fancy, but, a busy flight, in
every instance; in no instance is it a drawback, if the
results are calmly harmonized with actual experience of
fact. Our anticipations must not only be excited but our
judgments invoked thereby.

More refreshments followed, now, in addition to the
liquid, a light repast, consisting of some kind of small fish,
dried, some of their kind of bread and a sweetened cake.

Thereupon ensued the most amusing part of the entertainment. A queer, drastically appearing little man, who

resembled intimately the accounts of so-called wizards, and with a long, flowing, black mantle, and a high peaked hat of like somber hue, and carrying a long, black, hooked staff in his hand, entered into the center of the space, but a moment before so charmingly occupied, and was at once greeted by the multitude with welcoming shouts of pleasure mingled with familiar, good-natured expressions, as they seemed to hail his reappearance, as from an absence. He was evidently a highly appreciated celebrity. I felt not a little curiosity at this strange appearance, unhinted at before, and no less an interest in the still stranger man, whose very look and gesture marked him different from the others.

> God utters often by a chosen piece
> Within his own reflection's pause.

Striking a dramatic attitude, which was at once greeted with shouts of approval for it seemed evident thereby that he contemplated a humorous rendition (the nature of his efforts could never be predetermined, so I was afterwards informed, in this strange man of pure genius and his first indications were carefully noted to ascertain the nature of that to follow, when the whole proceeded, sequently enough—a kind of inspiration for the several times being—and the audience was thus prepared to set their countenances to the serious, comical, or semi of either, as first appearances predicted, for, in either event, the subject would be handled and the tone maintained, which would portray the feature in life under contemplation, with a success that never failed to produce the legitimate effect of a well and appropriately rendered object), he began, in a squeaking, high-pitched voice to recite:

"THE ADVENTURES OF A MEDDLESOME WOMAN IN A
LIFE-TIME OF WOE."

" Dame Nature fiddled never such a tree,
    As they would have you know,
As rose from out a rose,
    Without a thorn,
As spirits hovered o'er the lea
    To set in prosy this game tree.
Nor does it, e'er, behoove your simple self
    To speak a word, but, that has its own creed;
For, if you do, you will have ne'er a need
    O' sarcophagus.
This vixenish, venerable old dame was mild,
    Mild for her age
(And, also, miled, for passing many a stone,
    And milled where they had jogged)
But, still, she had the fire of the flame,
    The flame of youth,
Which broke the veins asunder with her burst
    Of tenderness.
A cruel narrative conveys this tale, once,
    (She's now several score)
'What then,' so says this mail,
    'Are you in dread?'
'Of what,' she snaps, and fire darts her eye,
    Her slumbering eye;
'Heed, wistful wight', her hagly finger quakes,
'Heed this, I say, heed this' —
    'What would you have me, dame?'
'To perish, to go beyond this realm;
    To lead in abject misery a life,
To grovel with the snakes and lizards, toads' —
    'Nay, toads you mean not, toadies, aye?'
'Ay, that so be it; you may toady to a stick,
    I'll none o' ye, I'll none o' ye!'
So be it, damey, then, so be it;
    You'll none of me.
But, let me tell you of a little incident,
    An incident of woe —

'I'll none o' ye, I'll none o' ye!'
    No, that I know;
But, yet, I shall narrate you one grave woe,
    The woe of dread.
And slinking, shivering to a mortal coil,
    She reels upon her doubts
And throws a wisp of straw
    To catch the breeze,
And make all doubtings doubly sure
    And fears and fees.
List! trembling woman, often didst thou scream and rant,
    Of what, thou know'st not,
Of which, thou car'st not;
    But, this thee bootest:
Thou'lt ne'er know peace, until thy eyes see clear,
    Thou'lt know no rest till then;
Thou'lt not mistake within thy heart fond love
    For wicked glee;
Nor feel the impulse of a joy,
    Which lifts,
Until thy sorrows shall have purged these hence,
    These drifts of woe.
'Ay, I have wandered o'er the lists not e'er in vain,
    I have not sought, but found;
My wisdom is not driv'ling to mere caste,
    I am not proud— *nor downed!*
Nay, you may fear me, or may fear me not,
    I am not downed— *nor drowned!*
But, when I shake these shagly locks,
    Out drop'— 'drop downs.'
Yes, feebly you have trudged by many a side,
    And, scarcely, have you touched the beam,
As many a weary heart has faltered, fled
    The saddened life between.
No sorrow was so great, as when bereft,
    You felt this strangely clinging power cleft,
Cleft from your means,
    And you then sighed the sorrows of your life,
In lifeless dream.
    But, to a tale of more and joyous woe,
That is, no words of slander,

But, of sport;
For, sport makes all this life one merry round,
    And finds therein much truth on subtle ground.
Then, to some sport, some light and humorous fun,
    The thought now hatched, the frolic is begun.
A woman's life is much like salt and ice,
    She's flavor's seasoning,
But, is to man his worst congealing force,
    When she's perverse.
Like to a summer's rose, she blooms and fades,
    Like to its thorns, she stings, when touched;
But, while the odor and the ardor lasts,
    She's queen of joy, like, beauty, is the rose.
Yet, withering the touch does blight the gleams,
    Which turn the happy hours to moments, scarce,
And can torment the revelations and the scenes
    Of whither, that her love and beauty went,
Calm sight, queer realm where nought is seen,
    Save that lost joy, that stole a furtive sheen!
Such capers steal the hearts of men away,
    And steel their hearts.
A winsome smile drives sorrow on its course,
    A short beguile makes sorrow all the worse.
When nought appears, save fancy, in a dose,
    Then, fancy, soon, had better be morose.
This is the maiden sweet, the matron and the dame,
    No thought is uppermost. save that, the same,
Which favors or ill-favors any suit;
    Which raises where the drooping spirits fall;
Where dwells the heart's fond fountain,
    Where leads, where lists his all,
There, there she lingers, or she leaves him, dropt
    Like to the leaf, that she has blown and cropt.
Once, I was young, so, hollowly, speaks this man,
    Once, there was joy and love, whence now this
        ban?
Once — yes, I can recall,
    Recall some things, of note —
I can conceive the most infallible hour,
    When silence is concerned with musing feats,
And not a sigh brings film to eye, nor tear

Arouses one small impulse of a fear.
Oh, woman, woman, cropt from Paradise,
    Oh, creature, creature, left to fond surmise!
I would not have you change one whit from this,
    If you were not so much concerned with bliss.
In fact, I rather glory in your fraud,
    For, having lost your coronet, you sighed, and
      hawed,
Until himself was captured, this same scamp,
    Who, for your sake, has turned into a tramp.
But, thus she scampered, leading life a trial!
    Nothing so bad, but turns for good,
If you yourself are right; but, nothing so good,
    That may be bad,
That may not turn the penchants of the heart
    Into the stream of woe.
I'll say, kind sister, temper not my steel
    To pierce my heart myself.
I like to see it, I love to see it, this fine carriage, this gay
      rig,
    I dote upon her haughty behavior!
I am as fond to see a pretty child
    Of nature —
I am not fond to see her pensive fall;
    But, I would raise her to the realms of Heaven,
In all, that her behooves and her does call.
    I am as, silently, fearful as a stone.
And I am tearful as the dewdrops,
    Nor weep a whitless more.
Whenever there is salt the ice must melt;
    Hence, woman cannot long restrain her tears,
Her little anguish and her borrowed fears.
Unless congealed in waters where the brine is weak,
    Compared with overweening cold.
But even there the genial warmth will glow and burn —
    Some time, a time, come from above,
Below, about, and turn these icelets into fountain rivulets.
    The deepest glow in woman is her thought
Of freest impulse, and her love
    For fondness' sweet desire;
And these will burst through every gloom and rime,

No thought too rigid, but is her warm theme.
But, what a chase, thou lead'st me, maiden, what wild
   lore
  Dost thou indite to musings and to sprites?
I might yet follow, yet, I know no more
  Where thou mightst turn this failing trudge of
   mine,
No more, than thou were'st dead, or ding.
Yet, I would suffer worlds to know your heart—
  To know it, mine!
In concentration there is force,
  In comprehension virtue, if you waste no sub-
   stance,
In drawing to the center thereabouts,
  But, grows with stretch;
Thence give to one your ardor's sweet attentive sense,
  And, giving every incense of devotion's call
From one grand round of knowledge and reflection's self,
  Place to your grace what graceful is itself.
One woman is as fond
  As many fair;
One smile more to be prized,
  Than laughter from a hundred hoarse-grown
   throats
From hollow sounds.
Would you taste of the sweetest of all inspired love,
  Drown multitude of sins to make a sough.
  Life is a dream,
A dream of women—
  Her grace, her winsomeness, her smile;
Her happy hours, that lead us to beguile
  Us into woe.
Sad, sorrily do we beshrew her cause,
  Worse, worryingly do we forever pause,
Pause at her brink, or, bridged it, over goes,
  Or to the chasm plunged in utter throes.
What fearful picture I do paint of bliss.
  No woman is so lovely, but she fears my paint.
I would not paint her, were she nature's elf;
  But, when she shrinks and shrivels, she does
   that herself.

My nature is as fond, and visage wise,
    As he, who has a dozen several wives,
And I had none;
    For, none to have, is one yet I may get;
But, to have some,
    And, ever, yet, regret,
That such and such a one has, e'er, been got,
    Is better to have none, and none to fret.
But, having one, 'tis best to have no more,
    For, more, than one, lead life a divers pace
And much diversity lacks solemn grace.
    But, best it is to have one, sure and true,
Such inward bliss no man will ever rue.
But, should she prove a burden, cast
    It off, the burden;
For, she will sing as sweetly as the meadow-lark,
    And soar as high,
When clear and tranquil is her sky;
    But, do not touch her vanity with your fork,
That prongs with several tendencies your tact,
    But, be as noble, when you guide her heart,
As he, who treasures but the unguent fact,
    That hearts were made to cherish, not to break.
And I would ne'er be crabbed were my core not sour.
    How many times I've pondered o'er a throb!
It is the everturning knob,
    That gives admission by the opened door!
And I would utter greetings from within to those without,
    Who would come in;
But, how I dreaded hesitation at the door,
    I knew not, happily, or, whether, sore.
In pending evils oft the thoughts run wild,
    As they course over this and that, when chilled
They are as plightful as their doubts,
    And, when they hesitate, they thrive no more.
Fond maiden, had you, ever, recked a beating heart?
    If not, you've wrecked a many a waiting life;
You've been a fire-brand where straw was rife!
    Rife, for, it was straw; and straw, because,
This life is withered and bleached, cropt of its head,
    When through the threshings grains were sought
      instead

I'd be a farmer, and my flowers should be wild —
  This gentle sprout, this handsome sprig,
That overwhelming, gorgeous rose
   Should flourish with the dewdrops and the
    honey-bee,
And, sinking low, with perishing there
   Enrich themselves for future consonance.
One short and brief, consoling thought — once more;
   Soon I'll be hence, and those, who follow o'er,
Will not have lost this consonance, to tread the path,
   O'er which sad fright is one and all the same.
If this white hand should reach from out the gloom
   (Or, being dark, should loom best by the moon)
Its tender touch yields its own guiding sway,
   I'd be as happy as the live-long day,
Which finds no fault, recurring as it may.
   I'd be a lovely child, coursed towards Heaven!
But, when she falters, oh, my May-day queen,
   I'd rather, that an earthy worm
Had wormed my hide
   At finished pilgrimage.
If you can gather to spend all with one,
   You've gained the bliss, completely, to your own.
A point's a point, and several points prick sore
   Where not the sore sought with the easing prick,
When more applied, than one there for in vogue.
Then, let me sing this little warbling lay:
   Calmly, calmly, sweetly is the day,
When sights and thoughts in harmony, when plaisance,
   not delay,
   Will bring the mind to fulminate — its play,
Its joyous play.
   When little objects tremble in the balance —
When they constringe to every other sign;
   When higher objects, than the creeds, are lower-
    ing
To lend their welcome shade —
   A child's so simple thoughts are true;
A man accomplishes to rue.
   Kind friends, we bid you now farewell, farewell;
Though you may course o'er main, and steal at night

The same continuous course as by the day,
Unsleeping hope and faith shall guide you —
  Shall guide you hence and hither;
For, when returning thoughts bring listing sighs,
  'Tis well to have the avenues remain the same.
But, as all memories dread evil things of Past,
  Ill were it to deny to us your joyful stay.
But, may your memories dwell with ease and joy —
  Whiled where you joyed, there happy was delay;
And what sole grief was felt
  Was, when you went away.
All happy thoughts range with a grief so pure,
  That hearts, in feebleness, can this endure."

And this strange man glided away, all grace and ease of silent movement, so that an air of mystery seemed to attend his vanishing powers.

The exercises completed hereby, we had arisen for the final ceremonies of farewell. I was presently informed that the man who had just entertained us, desired an interview with me, and I was equally very anxious to meet him.

This individual was their poet — their master-mind, their philosopher; it was he, who had instructed the "Rays of Light" in their beautiful maneuvers and was the guiding spirit of the organization — who could develop the poetry of motion, physical combination, as well as lingual expression.

That he was queer and eccentric, is but the resulting estimation placed upon all natural genius; but as the undoubted leader among these people, he ranked beyond any misconstruction.

He approached me with a quizzical look in his wizened features; his brown eyes shone with intelligent and luminous brilliance, as their dark tints contrasted with his pallid features, and his long, brown, fine hair and whiskers gracefully draped his evenly shaped head surmounting a thin, sinewy body, that appeared flexible and wiry in his costume, which so appropriately set it off that I was at once lost in admiration of this "typical impersonation" of genius.

Close proximity dissolved the illusion of grotesqueness in his appearance, which he was successful in manipulating to the sight at a distance. In person, then, he was handsome, refined and noble; and, as his reflective gaze seemed to comprehend my very existence, it was with such a kindly light, that I felt drawn to and with full of confidence in him. Such a man, who would befriend woman, virtue, and whose undaunted might is a terror to evil-designers!

Advancing within respectful reach, he proffered his hand, which I seized in my fervent grasp. He cordially said he was overjoyed to meet me. Expressing my unfeigned delight at what we had beheld of him, I stated that my regret was not to have known him previously; he smiled gently and replied that the auspiciousness of an occasion had much to do with agreeable impressions, and that he had hoped not to render himself obnoxious.

Leading me then apart, and slowly walking on, he began a conversation which has remained memorable to me. "Young man," he quietly resumed, "we look towards you for a great development of our people, and a lifting of the veil that has so long surrounded us; in the opportunities, which will follow our mutual intercourse, do you guarantee us your personal endeavor, the exposition of the refined mental faculties, the exposition of faith, the expressions, practically and in instruction, of candor and routine, such as a mind can disclose in its revelations from a search into the orthodoxy of faith? Our spirits will meet on joint ground."

Thereupon he pressed my hand, and had vanished almost instantly, turning abruptly and disappearing in the direction my back was turned to.

> Life is too short to waste in idle proof,
> Too brief to ponder in a misty quest!

Did his spirit reflect this to me?

Too astonished at the suddenness of the affair, I hardly realized his act, yet am forced to admire the force of his tact — intent as I was on his speech, and impressed by it as I am forever. My surprise and confusion increased when in my hand I found he had left a small book and a rudely fashioned ring of crude gold. I placed these two objects in my pocket and sought my friends.

They had witnessed the scene with astonishment and marveled considerably at what could have taken place between us. My pensive look, upon my return, was by no means reassuring to them; the judges themselves seemed concerned for me. I was so deeply impressed by the mysterious mesmeric influences that this man seemed to carry in his wake, I felt for good, elevating, and I loved him, that I was anxious to return to the ship and to enter my bunk to ponder and reflect, in solitude and darkness, upon those kindly eyes, which beamed pity and compassion in their every look; whilst an embracing wisdom glowed in the aspect of his countenance.

Ten of these people had been selected and eagerly agreed to go with us to our home — an elderly merchant, wife and two daughters, aged, the last, respectively, about eighteen and sixteen years, three skilled artisans, in their clothing, building and utensil works, and an intelligent young farmer and his bride, and the bride's younger sister, a maiden eighteen years of age.

By the way, they had an orderly, rigid institution of

marriage; in fact, were a people prone to strict morality, and encouraged early marriages in their young people, universally and in general, for that sake. Their physical culture wrought wonders in their moral and healthy developments.

Having gathered all of the intended party together, we proceeded to the beach, accompanied by the entire concourse, where the final adieus were affectionately interchanged, and a God-speeding shout given us by the multitude, as we drew off the shore; soon on board we at once made every preparation for the night and each promptly took to his or her assigned post or quarters of rest, with an early start in contemplation the next morning.

With the first break of day all were astir on shipboard, but a fog hid the land from view; without waiting for the fog to lift, we concluded to raise our anchors, and with a farewell blast of our steam-whistles, were directly steaming out to sea, and homeward.

Our hearts were gay — we anticipated reunion with our loved ones; when we could recount to them, knowing their appreciation, the wonders of our journey and exhibit and present to them the tokens from our new friends and field of enterprise. The natives of this part, who would, furthermore, emphasize and make more realistic our discoveries, were enthusiastic with the prospects, the novelties, and the measure of distinction they were enjoying — and they were not disappointed, the world exceeding all expectations in the wonders it has and may have wrought. We had made no savage discovery nor a ferocious development. We learned to what man's misfortune may sink him in the propensity of the masses, led from, or his course swayed; in the desert, savage wilds the natures conforming to the surroundings. Individuality is the exercise of self.   The reflective powers of the only creatures capable are so lowly at ebb.

The space of the world is required and an exposition of its contents no less and therefor.   They are potent to this effect and increase our knowledge in our time.   Well it is to magnify a thing to see its details, not to engross it beyond reality.

Fie upon any prohibition!   Replace it by liberal education and *manfully* prosecute the latter.   Tend to the purity of all provisions!

We may flatter our vanities; but, the World's Fair admonishes our mutual esteem.

Chicago, art thyself exhibited a fair;
Fair to behold where enterprise built stays
And worldly artifice match living grace,
As it demonstrates daily moving view
With any art or science brought to sight;
Worth such a fair alone the seeming price.
Ah! while you teem in priceless tone such arts,
The enterprise and science known to man —
Alone can rear such works so near the skies
And tower with your teeming mankind's sprites,
The western star, to which such wisdom scans,
Is luminous truth and full of earthly lore,
Is rife with Heavenly pinnacles for worth.
From off those lofty roofs range with the sight
To where the groveling mankind lists and waits,
And casting thither shed thy rays of light;
Descend then from uncertain, dizzy heights,
Reared for the aspect o'er the rounding gloom,
To spread such possibil'ties o'er the Earth
As leveling to bring on general Light. —
So courteous entertainment graced thy board,
That lords were all — and lordly they accord.

CHAPTER XXVII.

HOME!

WE steamed directly in the direction which our records prescribed to us, and the return voyage was uneventful.

We were anxious to finish our first tour and make it a complete and successful one; besides, inward yearnings were driving us with haste thitherward, where we esteemed kind hearts beating for us and daily anxious eyes were scrutinizing the horizon for our safe return.

Thus we continued, rapidly and favorably, until on the twelfth day towards evening we saw a dark outline in the distance, which we correctly judged to be our welcoming haven. We steamed on until the shore was very apparent; but the shades of evening were fast settling, whereupon we called council and although hardly able to contain ourselves, for eagerness to rush right in, our cooler reflections and counsels prevailed, that the undisturbed night's repose would better prepare our loved ones for the happy surprises so near in store; and we, also, would be refreshed by rest, so we argued, though, I believe, a fallacy, as the prospects of the morrow hardly favored sleep in our excited minds.

Dawn brought out our eager preparations for the *denouement* to ensue on this memorable day, fraught with happiness for many hearts. Our garments were made as pleasant looking as possible. Our ship-deck was cleaned and polished up, and everyone was in scarcely suppressed excitement, including our guests, who could not have escaped the mere contagion. After swallowing a hasty, scarcely regarded breakfast, we slowly entered our cherished bourn.

Kind reader, have you ever felt a misgiving; a loaded, heavy feeling, that seemed to smother your heart, that seemed to press down on you until you would have cried out?

As a disappointment, an ill, even a so-called sorrow must have its spirit, so these must travel and disclose themselves somewhere in their existence, as omens; perchance, their whispering admonitions are to strengthen and encourage the soul to meet these inevitable happenings; perhaps, to feel the pulse for its enduring stay, or to fathom and prepare the mysteries of all life.

Should the head bow in sorrow, may the heart shrink from the task before it? But the soul, the translucent spirit should ever pierce the seeming darkness, that would enshroud with feeble mysteries the light of brave conscientious endeavor!

Our approach had been seen and was communicated to all on shore; we could, through our glasses, see every demonstration of signaling they were capable of making, as at length we signaled them with our whistle, and, having approached near enough, could hear their merry shouts. With a full pressure of steam we made quick headway, but made our way around to the mouth of the little stream, where, it will be remembered, we had a natural harbor, and safely stowed our vessel.

There, too, the approach to land was so near, that we had previously constructed a permanent gangway out to where we could bring the vessel, and thus make a ready and easy landing. Perceiving our course, the multitude, a small multitude now compared with the "crowds" we had just witnessed, made its way hastily to the harbor, where they all arrived some time before us. But all anx-

iety must at length cease — or new take its place — and so
we drew in and greeted and interchanged shouts upon
shouts with them; scarcely within touch of the end of the
landing-gang, when the rush onto the deck began with no
attention to the strangers on board, who stood with
wonderment and excitement depicted on their countenances. Strong arms enfolded quivering, happy forms,
whose arms encircled swarthy necks in passionately, tenderly loving embrace; or hands were grasped, and childish and baby lips uttered their glee.

Where did I look?

Kind reader, in vain!

My greeting was very cordial; but I needed to ask no
question, and did not, to interpret the pitying looks that
in my anxiety I readily perceived — and when the mother
of Kathleen burst into tears with her head on the bosom
of Kathleen's father, I standing very near, I needed to
make no attempt to hear, "our Kathleen is no more."
The strong frame of the man and father shook, as he
half-turned, then bowed his head and face on the
uncovered head of his wife as he clasped her closer
to him, seeming to understand, as though full explanation had been given by those few, sad, heart-rending
words.

I said nothing — but turned away towards the hitherto
neglected guests of ours, and speaking a few words by way
of attracting the attention from them, made them aware
of the moment when they should be duly presented; but,
before that became my performance, I was considerately
relieved, in a few well-chosen, heart-spoken words from
Captain Mason, and I retired — for, in all that throng, I
was the only one in sorrow: my *all*, my only special object
had vanished.

I was calm and no agitation had come to the surface, if,

in fact, it had gained time to exist, except that a slight pallor may have betrayed something unusual.

After a while, the sixteen-year-old younger sister, who seems to have thoroughly understood, as well as from the confidences of her sister as her own observation of both of us, the tenderness of regard between us, told me briefly — it required not many words to narrate how a swift fever had despoiled the flower of my deeply awakened, purest affection, the natural, spiritual, supernatural impulse between man and woman; that regard which underlies the fundament of all existence of virtue and happiness. Her words had often lingered about me; her eyes roved in the direction I had gone, and in her delirium was the rapt joy of an united bliss between us!

Yet I was unmoved save that the pallor in my countenance may have increased somewhat.

At the festive board I occupied a silent but not undignified seat; the subdued nature of the otherwise festive occasion did not even disturb my tranquillity, and the speeches brief though they were, by the school-master, Captain Mason, and by one of our guests, were happy and facile enough in the allusions to the many commendable living issues and the happy accomplishment of our undertaking.

Kathleen's mother, tearfully enough, towards evening found opportunity to inform me of the particulars of the sad demise which had occurred shortly after we had left— left her in health and buoyant, expectant spirits, expectation all excepting our own possible loss — and now her grave was already beginning to grow green, under the covering and hiding garb of consoling nature.

I presume that evening was interestingly spent by hosts and guests; but I had busied myself with writing and the completion of records, which consumed, at least,

so many feverish hours, and I hailed the moonlit night,
having not dared to gaze upon the gorgeously beautiful
sunset of that benign evening, when nature vied with the
most tranquil happy thoughts, but I stole out to the grave
of my sleeping darling.

The early autumn was beginning to dry up the grasses,
and flowers and herbage wore a matured look; oh, how all
suggested the ripeness of harvest-time — ay, harvest past,
and the few remaining stalks blighted.

MY DARLING'S GRAVE.

Death steals one furtive glance, then, slinks away;
But, bears upon its wings the shining ray,
Which it has borrowed to light up its glance.
Ah, how it bore to angels what an angel were
In all the purer part of hearts; it leads the darkened path,
Which lighted is by such a soul as this,
Unveils the gloom to utter, blithesome bliss.
That this meek silence should, here, reign, to mock
The would-be anguish of my soul, just robbed
Of its own kindred spirit, led to its altar
By this spirit of its binding kind —
Good God! the sigh is not assuring to the mind!
The throb, which in the heart brings pain
And, momentarily, is fraught with threats,
That, ever, not a soul shall course again,
But, cursing, shall forever, thus, refrain
To yield its spirit to its spirit's chime,
Is plunged in depths of misery from time to time.
Time shall not cease, where misery therein pent.
Eternity, forever, flees its bourn,
Nor stays in limits where the hearts-yearn burn,
For, nigh to Heaven, not to hades, is rest.
That solemn search, eternity in quest,
Errs least, when feeble with its timely touch.
Nor is one solemn evidence so full of fear,
That those, who will, cannot alway forbear.
When led unto the portals of this sleep,

That to the ethereal realms takes spirits hence,
What consolation is there left, to seek
What remnant, visibly, is left behind,
When, to its earth, it soon must be confused,
Of earth, its prime delight, hence, there so used?
But, spiritually flee, too, with its spirit's flight,
And there commune, too, as it must there dwell
In bliss, in joy, in glory unconfined!
A brief duress, then, following, thus, its bent,
Your spirit usefully will seek the hour,
When rest is welcome to this freedom's bower —
Such rest, which flees no healthy exercise.
Ah, gnashed and torn, no heart will long endure,
But, healing not, will soon be felt no more.
The intervening space the mind must spell
With thoughts and deeds, accomplishments, as well —
No happy hearts have ever wrought grand deeds,
For, happiness to indolence misleads
And brings more sorrow than it e'er has cleft,
For, during it, it oft forgets to help;
Or causes grief by, usually, its neglect;
As, being painless, it thus never recks
The other's cause, nor apprehends his becks.
But, where the heart is porous from its pains,
That darted have in all its quivering walls —
There is each passage for the message-woes,
Soft, inner couching for their sick-nursed throes.
On furtive joy some sorrow may steal, swiftly, in its
        stead;
But, winnowing grief can leave no chaff of joy;
Yet, from the mist the radiant peace and promise may
        glow,
When gloom, again, has burst to show the light,
Whose slanting beams shed on its rays aright.
Successive griefs build up a strengthened man;
Succeeding ones but break a woman's heart;
Thus, taking them together and apart,
The thing that welds the master, wields the seam,
The two together make the strong esteem.
Death is no monster, black, as, though, it seems,
Or lurid, in the wildest fancy of some frames;

But, is the innocent child's soft, soothing rest,
To which it yields, fatigued from ardent play,
And sinks, profoundly, to its blessed allay.
Death is a calm repose within its state,
By which the soul goes in untrammeled flight
To yonder pale. Nought comforts a troubled heart,
At this dear one's departure to the realm,
Save preparation, that leads to the same.
The earthly night's repose steals no dear friend,
Because, yourself engaged to the same end.
But, when the severance is disunion's cause,
In mind, intention, effect, in divers laws,
The sadness of the moment recks further days.
Yet, silence is not gained by wild career;
Just as repose is troubled by wrought cares,
Or trembles, sorely, balanced by grave fears.
So must the soul be tarnished, or be wrecked,
Which, in this life, has its calm radiance flecked;
And, solely, purging itself by sought grace,
Can, only, thus, its afflicture efface.
Nor is the night, which brings the sweet repose;
The day, before, makes that, which, then, you chose.
And, with its evil, so, the night grows long,
As with the evil unrest there is strong,
So will the tempest, thus, endure its night;
But, if, e'er, day, depends on other sight.
If first from gloom there into light was launched,
And, rounding out, gloom is again ensconced,
The figure full, gloom will, then, never end —
Eternity will, thus, fore'er, depend:
Mean bright will stay, ends meet in gloom endure,
And dark and light will be forevermore,
The one attend the other — space the universe.
And every sign and thing rounds its full course,
And, for that one, complete is for its corse.
New hopes, fresh joys, rise from each fallen hope,
This we esteem; but, lost are opportunities lost.
For, light, forever, fades away,
To leave in darkness what may decay.
And wrongs, conceived, give birth to direful deeds;
And these must flourish, such as each thing speeds:

Thus, if, forever, each thing must advance,
Your creed cannot dispense the wrong, perchance —
In Mercy lies the only seat of Bliss;
With Faith thereof the spirit's stubborn part
Made soft and pliable to fit the joy,
That tender is, hence, cannot bear a crush ;
Which rounded is, thus, must have flexioned touch
To fit unto its surface without crease. —
Oh, Mercy, render my poor Faith so pure,
That, despite sorrow, I may, hence, endure !

Kathleen had towards the last been almost engaged with kind words of my memory; her ardor had unfolded to full devotion for me; and in her delirious, last moments she was wandering with me over pleasant places. Her affectionate, devotedly tender sister was charged with the several messages; and her mother bore the information of Kathleen's love.

Life wore a more sedate aspect than ever before; I had nothing before me but an earnest endeavor, and to any vow in that regard the spirit of my departed yet ever cherished darling was the only witness, as with my head bowed over her grave, I attributed every virtue to her memory, and my body lingered, in that still midnight, over where her loved one lay shrouded in the cool earth underneath.

CHAPTER XXVIII.

A CALM LIFE.

Folly spends more than the rich garner and indolence fastens on vice as consuming barnacles. "Mechanics" do their "stiffly" taught task. Transmission is the effectual action of self-constituency, while pride is the bursting inflation that flattens everything to the earth. Faith accomplishes the unnatural, establishes its natural course and portrays this.

THE ensuing period of my life had the laudable object of devotion to my friends, in which I included those whom we had recently discovered.

The representatives who had come with us had speedily ingratiated themselves into the good graces and society of our entire company; the three unmarried maidens were already the objects of much assiduous attention from as many zealous youths of our circle, and, as their attentions were by no means disagreeable apparently, the imminence of cemented union was noticeable, and auspiciously regarded.

The three masters of mechanical arts who had also accompanied us, had left their families behind. Now that they had accomplished sufficient to report an examination into affairs here, they yearned for a return to their loved ones (attachment to family being marked among these people, as, always, where virtue reigns; and as is perfectly natural, of course), but begged the privilege of returning with them and residing here, which we were glad to grant, feeling the honor of their choice and request.

Preparations were soon making for a return voyage to the land of our discovery. The merchant and his family, as well as the bridal couple referred to, were permanently ensconced among us. They were all very useful persons to us, of course, and added new life, encouragement and vigor to our institutions.

I had become a sort of annalist and political economist among them, for which purpose an "office" of this sort was created. In fact, I was what might, in civilized countries, be designated the editor and news publisher.

Of all the callings in the world, that of the "newspaper" appears to me the most important — the most valuable, as it is the most dangerous to the community. The finest tact; the most sensitive appreciation of honor and propriety; the calmest spirit of discrimination; yet, withal, the dauntless courage of true conviction, but tempered again with justice — the ancient Greeks would have created a special divinity for this, our modern, institution, and sainted, or semi-deified its successful votaries. The community is more at the mercy of this calling, than of any other, and its ready influence on the masses is its greatest aggravation. Where it caters to sordidness, and develops all the baseness in our characters, under the advertisement of ready means for its gratification, or parades the colors of vice, or, under the protection of licensed gossip, enters into the private affairs of individuals, the institution becomes one of iniquity and detriment to the community. A good "paper," in its merits, should be equaled by its patronage, being for undoubted good; engaged in the most public manner in the discussion of persons and their interests, what redress is adequate for a wrong, or a colorable misrepresentation from a newspaper?

But what a beautiful grand factor, within its legitimate objects, in the conduct of enlightened men! What special schooling could be too great for its votaries, schooled though they are largely in practical affairs and knowledge

of life. But if a special examination for fitness in any
calling or so-called profession is legally advisable, then
what could not be attributed to this, the noblest of all?
No less an adeptness is required for the presentation and
obtention of the matter, than the judicious and truthful
exposition and discussion of it.

God bless Hermes, or the bearer of tidings!

A crafty lawyer even would succumb to a righteous
newspaper; the public's "voice," when uttered by a truthful, eloquent mouthpiece, reliable for its known source and
resource, is unequivocal and certain; you can only pervert
the people by ignorance in the first instance. The avenue
of our enterprises! The throbs of the community's heart
are within its grasp.

We rigged up a primitive press, and henceforth the
statements and collections of recounted facts and occurrences were preserved in printed and bound form, and
copies thereof distributed for leisure perusal among the
individuals.

My first connected effort was the detailed narration of
our voyage and discoveries, and other incidental transactions and impressions connected therewith, and analogous
dissolution of illusions.

Every Friday evening found a "newsy" little sheet,
embellished by the thoughts of our cultivated, laborious
thinkers and writers, which presented all the happenings
of the week of a general consequence, and the speculations
and discussions of the matters and affairs before us.
A permanent chronicle, which, if there had been any
discreditable reflection on anyone, would have constituted
so much disparaging history for such individual, and, collectively, of all the individuals, for the community — thus,
what an essential for truth, as history above all should be
authentic. Such annals are intimate with the health and

prospects of the people — constitute and shape them for their history. Herein lies the sound that gives the tone, or a wide-spread dissonance will cause an overwhelming clangor. Food for reflection creates the action of feasible reform. There is no improvement save reform or liberalization.

The school-master was my efficient and enthusiastic collaborateur, and contributed many instructive, philosophical disquisitions, that had all the elements of unfailing progress.

The community was fast assuming a very different aspect of activity, and numerous investigations and experiments that were now being entered into gave thoughtfulness to the enthusiastic countenances. In ignorance there is no happiness; but when the thoughts and sights seek and obtain a true glimpse into the higher realms, then the reflected light is at once apparent in the glow of the thereby measured delight. Our whole disposition is to popular government by popular intelligence; and that carries with it virtue, companionship and mutual usefulness. Here it was principally a maintenance of such and the advantages of such an excellent foundation; beyond, the inculcation thereof. We knew its value; faith upheld it, undoubtedly.

All kinds of mechanical devices were essayed, at first with varying success, then with the inevitable result of development due to persistence and the suggestions and polish arising out of and from continued contact.

And this factory and that concern, together with the various productive interests for material in their manipulation, were making the hum of industry loud and almost unbroken; and true delight hailed each new achievement, as each novel article was employed with manifest pride. Labor is the principle of achievement and success of life.

Nor were the results eventually in any regard mean, but, from the books and my personal knowledge, besides the experience of our visitors, combined with the ever important personal genius of individuals, presented an excellent array adequate to our rather limited demands. We actually soon reveled in good living and in enjoyments, and had no reproaches to make ourselves therefor — the addition of our acquaintance with our new neighbors had wonderfully stimulated our joys and activity — at less cost to all of us because we did not curtail use, but, guided intelligence to general use, which left no time or room for abuse.

Towards the middle of the following summer another cruise, or rather a repeated visit to *our friends* was decided upon. All our visitors, excepting the merchant and his wife (his daughters, however, were going to visit their old home) were going on the voyage, but intended to return; the artisans with their families, besides the three attentive young men, were also to go, and Mr. and Mrs. Bertram, the former to resume his charge of the helm, and Mr. and Mrs. Mason, and several of the young folks of both sexes, and the school-master, the latter as the historian and chronicler of the trip. Mr. Mason stepped into the direction, young Betram resumed his post at the engine, and the others were necessarily distributed, such "veterans" only being retained as were requisite. We enabled as many as possible of those who remained behind before to participate for their edification. I assumed whatever charge there might be at home. The hold of the vessel was laden with the handicraft and produce of our last year and winter's productions and such evidences of our genius as might prove useful to our friends, as gifts to them.

We expected quite a colony to return with our vessel, and, to that end, had adopted suitable unanimous resolutions of invitation, couched in the most friendly terms. Our resources needed population for their development, and, too, we felt they could develop a population for their happiness and health here. The evening before witnessed a banquet, with song and speeches and happy joyous moods; and the morrow an early, glorious departure.

CHAPTER XXIX.

HIS LAST LECTURE.

A young, bright, able assistant attended to the schooling of the children, with great pride in his grand work and respectful attention from them.

I went on with my accustomed work of chronicling events, and in my best style of continuing the current history, which, besides being condensed in the weekly newspaper reports, was embodied in a printed publication, or a cyclopedia of history, as it progressed and transpired. I thus also supplied the school-master's vacancy, in his functions as regular chronicler. Literature was cultivated in all its fine elevating arts here, now, besides, at which I attempted to assist.

The reader can already mentally picture the changes wrought in affairs since my advent, embraced in my stay already of five years, but quite different ones from those spent previously alone. Will anyone doubt that the advantages should be attributed to my present stay over the previous solitude? "Ages" of time were not now constituted by wasting monotony! I began to delineate a plan for a city; but as a first proposition, not such a

compact mass of structures and habitations as I was
accustomed to in the olden times; the necessity of such
an arrangement was not in existence now, and would not
be; and the question of transportation, as well as communication was now more happily solved, with no discouragement for the future.

That I at least would be forever tainted with old ideas,
might be expected from early training; I was still at best
a "connecting link," that cannot be effectually eradicated;
but I hoped to lay sufficient foundation for whatever
progress might be possible in another, I believed, higher
way. Thus my city, while not a marvel or a "heavenly"
place, should at least embrace all the modern improvements for convenience and happiness and health with the
local ingenuities to be there suggested respectively in
addition. That the few "vipers" and "parasites" who
constantly infest our humanity, are to be regarded as an
expected detriment, if not met by precaution, must, unfortunately, always be taken cognizance of; nor do they
necessarily appear in rags, and are so easily distinguishable.

In the first place, the residences were arranged in
spacious groups on high grounds, and extended over continuing, not circumscribed space to space, each in garden
or park of nature and art's embellishments — for mental
and physical discipline, at least; then, therewith, the connections of all sorts of the devices of communication and
transportation.

The places of the heavy industries were more assigned
to the low lying grounds, with spacious and airy surroundings, and adjacent, as nearly as possible, and widely distributed to their several points of respective advantages.
I also made a skeleton suggestion, by which in due regulation these conditions of affairs should be preserved, and, in
the case of necessary change, how the same should be

adjusted.   At the beginning such regulations are practical and easily understood and observed thereafter.

Hence, in plan, every conducement to facility and pleasurable occupation were observed, congruous to the locality, its topography and opportunities.

The spreading out had further practical purposes for the territory, making no particular spot *unnaturally* valuable, but giving everyone a choice, with no marked superior advantages in that regard; still intimate friends and relatives could commune together, but no other combination of interests found encouragement from me, esteeming, as I do, the universal brotherhood of all well-intentioned mankind.   Even the family connection should be based solely upon its natural affections and seek no sordid interest beyond that.

In my opinion people err more from ignorance than deliberate intention; they learn a lesson well as is evidenced by the manifest difficulty of changing old ways. So that the present mode and idea of building and maintaining cities in their compact form are the institutions of times when such order was for mutual protection, and the value of land not in scarcity but in the labor of covering it.   Now, although the *reasons* have long since been overcome or abolished, see how *reasonable* we are; we perpetuate all the inconveniences — from force of habit and inculcation.   Hereby is manifested the potency of proper inculcation and habits of thought; advantageous changes must occur, from time to time, and as a tribute to humanity, it must be said they keep their precepts well — only, too long.

Beautiful villas would string far out into the country and connect, blend the farming lands, leaving no ridiculous distinctions to create caste or conditions even between communities.

In vocation there is no practical or honorable difference; labor is alike and dependent on the same laws. All are duties and callings and only one would I term a profession — the practice of law.

A plain necessity must be regarded until it can be removed; then, at least, the cause should be ridiculed into intolerance.

The industrial arrangement, or the government, receives the next attention.

To erect these abodes and habitations, and to adduce and maintain the means of access and communication, as well as to devise further agencies and improvements, owing to ever-recurring conditions, industry must be required, and that, too, in diverse form and variously distributed. And this is based on and maintained by individual intelligence! The individual concerns, then the common address, and finally the support of those necessarily employed to perform what can only be done by part, while the rest supply the means of support.

The original family relation explains these themes and their mutual respect and importance.

First, how to be agreeable to the minds of all; second, to satisfy them with the enforced arrangements; and third, in what respect to limit or enlarge on the provinces of some.

We must presume upon the proposition, that where you add you must, first, take away somewhere; this must be followed by the statement, that when you take away it should be, only, from surplus and added to dearth — unless in times of general calamity, which *naturally* are very infrequent. The balance must be preserved to maintain equilibrium and contentment.

> Man may be on the pinnacle of vision,
> Thence to survey the glory far and near,

Or earthly doom, distress, or happiness.
If, thereupon, he grovels in their midst,
These earthly worms of pilgrimage will hold
Him to their sight of limited, small range.
Within their dust his dull sight is not strange.

Everything sounds well done in whole mission, even monotonous thump or rumble, which, however, may be shaded. Sound comes first, declaration next, then perusal. The natural tendency of man is to music, speech and art, literature, the last culminating his culture as the first arouses his elevating impulses to find full development in their full, deliberate, reflective discussion and impression. Literature is their repeated dwelling in all elegance and repeated partaking. Some day the spiritual development will take place with the many other invisible, potent factors, in force but now repelled by the penetrable wall of misty gloom. Only the weak and doubtful are affrighted hereby; but properly illumined there will be a shadowy fleeing of this unstable thing of its own advancing object.

That a wise man, a good one has undue or unbalanced power, all the bankruptcies attendant upon one absorbing creditor, requires a readjustment of the practical fact. In an incipient plan collective power must be tolerated for universal good. We are *naturally* the best organization of individuals; yet we contrive individual organizations to debar the weak, sick, decrepit, the useless to those who shame the appeal to humane, good nature lingering in every constitution despite any vicissitude. The brotherly love the world has learned to vaunt is narrowed down to worse than a selfish policy — even a grasping one. All mere associations tie knots in the universe.

The unobstructed universe is required to facilitate its constituents. If a neighbor is clearly shown to be self-sacrificing then every obstacle should be zealously removed for such a noble cause —that is, your co-operation should develop for the general benefit. No organization is necessary except to embrace all. To what extent the differences can be adjusted remains to the power of the All-governing; we can only approach it by agreement and that by education. We unitedly are not enough in the world to adduce all our benefits therein, but must by understanding even have a higher Faith and these in all events involve our collective force. Man is his own beauty.

But in what plight are we—our strengths, efforts and industries are decimated and worse; piles are made out of reach, over-production in the hollow calamity exists by the depths of despair.

Where the pleasures of enlightened ingenuity and distribution, the fruits of love, have borne out the enjoyment of the promise, not surfeited by a few moments' handiwork, the relish lies in further desert. "Everything has its enemy," except man, when he becomes his own to make up the seeming natural law.

Well, I spent all my spare time in deciphering these details and placing the results on record in outlined drawings and markings. I embodied the few simple creeds of government. My most elegant structure, there where all hearts and minds and hands and geniuses could unite in one grand cause — no preacher was necessary but merely as the servant of God, and man —no individual elegance — was the edifice to knowledge, the Temple, where God was devoted to with His manifestations of Mercy for Faith. Oh, that truth, ever, makes the ignorant more ignorant, and—but, light makes the remaining gloom darker!

Now my meaning may appear deceptive. It is the

knowledge of the suppression of evil, that I have reference
to — that makes the room for and brings the enlightment
of good — which is as clearly a result of Mercy, as that
those tall structures do not topple onto us beneath, as long
as held by the law of stability; but, as does occur, when
that law no longer is manifest or controls, then the fatal
denouement follows.

The American institutions, in their youthful vigor and
healthy birth and rearing approach this principle.

Let that be the palace of the World, as it is the Temple
of God, where is the Public School of information and
worship, the establishment of equality, the elevation of
united energy, and the common dissolution of foisted
mysteries, which will then also destroy most of the miseries — no longer the mysteriously preserved walls for their
not-to-be-understood contents, and protections where there
is no danger to righteousness, but all is unrestrainedly
imparted — where evil, in all its forms, is shown by shun-
ning it; where the humble Grace of personal significance,
for universal application, is inspired, as it then will be.

One year, with its seasons of storm and sunshine, blight,
dearth, regeneration and recurring harvest (I felt as
though I were nearing my ripening-time) had passed over
the resting-place of my unforgotten love; and I dedicated
the productions of my inspirations to pure love, at its
place of abidance.

> Ah, harvest, thou prepar'st the annual feast —
> Oh, man, but thou enslav'st thy fellow-man ! —
> Thyself thy slave!

The ensuing Fall brought our ship "returned," with a
large cargo of substantial well-wishes, and airy products of
the wealth of man, in raiment and provisions and articles
of *vertu*.

All our folks returned, save young Samuel Mason, who had there married one of the young ladies of that locality, the one referred to as the sister of the "bride;" Mason was an intelligent, quick-witted, excellent fellow, and we had selected him to represent us there, residently, as a sort of minister or consul in our behalf, and, as he was wonderfully well adapted, to further study those people as well as to disclose to them our advantages and disadvantages, in order that we both by complete knowledge of each other might prove of service, mutually; besides, his contemplated and, as stated, then consummated marital alliance made residence not so undesirable, gaining for him the greatest amount of influence and confidence there possible under the circumstances, and to us such esteem and advantage, by the practical demonstration of our good faith.

Their voyage had been tempestuous, but in nowise disastrous. The old poet, they said, regretted that I did not return, though, he added, he had felt such an admonition, and felt not a little grieved that he should thus never again behold me here, as he expressed himself. Had he the insight of prophecy? This he transmitted to me:

> "Tempests fly with raging toils,
> Sorrows steep themselves in foils;
> Oft the heart is sad and blast—
> Dominance cannot e'er last!
> Though you may esteem to trouble,
> Ignorance and shift are double.
> Though you may not ken the deeds,
> Sigh and pray for all your needs
> And your soul will never tremble —
> If you do not e'er dissemble.
> Ah, my friend, what griefs wear boots,
> Traveling do they take roots?
> Or when steaming have they boats?

Nay, and sink, each always gloats.
Let me say, all friends have inklings
Through reft space of sorrows' sprinklings,
Coursed by twinge to hearts' fond beats,
Passed by spirits' listing heats.
When you wish to fly a sore,   .
Open every other pore —
Steep contagion in a pest;
Then survive and fit the best.
'Tis no gladness makes my own;
Neither joy, at which I frown,
For I hate distressed concern,
Neither will I inwards burn.
But if ever you should prate,
Leaving out sore cause and hate,
I'd confound you with a stone,
Better than your flesh and bone. —
Now, my friend, hear one last sigh:
Shall we meet hence, by and by ?
Shall we travel where the souls
Purge their ever pungent roles,
Where the heart-aches cease to be —
And the blind can clearly see ?
Yes, yes, there we shall not sever,
There our souls will dwell, forever,
There no sadness will enshroud us,
Never turmoil be about us;
Hence, hence, far removed from hell,
Thither, thither — there we'll dwell !"

Ah! that man had divined my sorrow, had read my
fate! The seeming chasm, space itself is bridged by the
impulses, knowledge of the hearts and spirits.

I could imagine that weird attitude, in which,
with his strangely sounding voice, solemnly assumed, he
would have repeated these lines, and added to them their
worth, and in them I recognized an intended prophetic
forecast, perhaps aided by my own spiritual admonitions,
which may have communicated some intelligence to him

also of my speedy future dissolution — but happy spiritual realization. A large colony accompanied this return — splendid enthusiastic people.

Every comfort which we possessed was soon at their command (how we love to render up even our last possession to those who we know properly appreciate the service) and scarcely ten days had elapsed, before these personages, so industrious, willing and thrifty, were assigned, upon their requests, or had chosen their various vocations and were busily, contentedly engaged.

Our colony was still one large, loving, lovable family — and remains so until vice creeps in; and why should it not be thus of the whole world? Whose fault is it? Let those answer, who can distinguish. This is science.

Time swept by, and so it must have been doing all on earth; an annual voyage was made every summer to our neighbors, but I have not yet again participated — time seems so short for me; my health is broken a little, but the silent vigor of spirit reigns the same, though admonishing me to proceed at once — at once with my labors.

It had been suggested, that I deliver, orally, before the assemblage here, which had considerably augmented with this influx of "immigrants," a lecture upon the social cataclysm, and that, thereupon, the same should be published and transmitted to our friends. The world, now, is our friends!

The subject being "Caste and Castaways," and embracing the reflections and commentary history on the social conditions, into the sea of which we were about embarking, or had entered — whether a calm or a turbulent one would be of vital interest to consider at the outset for proper steering — I, as carefully as I could, prepared and delivered the following:

"God is our greatest servant, therefore absolute Ruler. 'A so-called ruler should be the best of servants,' which is true not only theoretically but practically. His elements of distinction by no means remove him from, but rather add zest to his immediate, direct contact with his brethren.

"That this requirement is so sadly overlooked in those who are selected, and entrusted with the administration of our affairs, accounts for many of our national troubles. From this fountain-head of oppression emanates the desire for pernicious inquiry into the minutest details and the most trivial of private affairs. What, for a time, successfully becomes the object of a course of conduct, soon has assumed the features of habit; and, where ignorance knows no other custom, having experienced no other contact, the pursuits are speedily under such circumstances a law unto themselves, the ways of common practice.

"With this introductory premise we recognize the fundamental principle of 'caste;' and, incidentally, resulted 'castaways.'

"A few intriguers, wielding with and through the ignorance of persons, who gladly unthinkingly hail such a leadership, a power of physical might, coerce the multitude. Then, thoroughly wrapt in their selfishness, and the masses warped into the desired intimidation and increasing ignorance the wheels, thereby, of tyranny are put in motion.

"First, a subversion of right through intrigue, then an ignorance or confusion of what is right, lastly a settled presumption, foisting slavery upon all those who cannot protect themselves — which, finally, resolves itself into but the very few, until all cause an upheaval. This, practically, embodies the results of perverse society.

"After we have cautiously threaded all the mazes of

life, the fortunes of our children, or their 'station' in 'society,' depend upon our success in having achieved for them a distinction in the power of wealth, or the influence of name or connections, which all others are bound to recognize through fear, rather, than respect.

"Their maintenances are, hence, their individual concerns. Another child begins under the circumstances of unfortunate surroundings, and the situation is reversed — it is considered profitable, that this one should be virtually a slave. These are the rough outlines of an unpleasant exterior.

"After a while, these lines jostle each other, as an upheaval takes place, and settle themselves back upon a somewhat altered plane; but the principles remain the same.

"Now, this is really unnecessary, and conduces to the good of no one, not even that of the favored classes; they would be happier, if everyone they met could be regarded by them as an equal, and not an inferior; for, to say the least, they would not have to dread on the other hand their 'superiors,' as, with our cherished rule of 'ups' and 'downs,' no one is without his or her superior. Thus, we are all slaves, and terrified!*

"If to the desire for riotous living, with individual indolence, is to be attributed, as it may, this rise of divided power and slavery, then, the conditions should be traced to their source, mistaking slavery for real service to themselves.

"My dear brethren, it is awfully true that our lamentations are more the result of disappointed expectations, than realization of the iniquity of the principle of prece-

---

*"*Gleich und Gleich gesellt sich gern*;" even the tendency, where development has not yet ensued, of similarity and elevation, in the mate to any person, or meet in any community, is zest and within the outward measure of happiness.

dence, and no more could be expected from us, as enlightened rulers, than industrious subjects.

"But the conditions are sad and mar an otherwise pleasant world, in the main; the natural evils here could be cheerfully borne, as all ought to be, anyway, with every zealous effort to remove them, were they not burdened additionally by human ingenuity in perversity. That real powerful evil spirits are forever among us, cannot escape our notice, nor that they are something over and beyond our control, until we thoroughly shield ourselves in humility with the saving and protecting grace of merciful intervention in our behalfs, by and through good spirits. This is, comprehensively, a scientifical, philosophical disclosure of the human system.

"The castes are precisely what we esteem them, a man's employment and another's service. The answer to this instigation gives its unmistakable evidence. If all acts are voluntarily rendered, likewise so endured, there is no cause for complaint, provided the restriction to personal liberty is not to these several avocations. In various capacities, each should be profitable for the whole, otherwise there is an irredeemable waste; and to make the services endure to mutual advantage they should be interchangeable, as they practically are. Where success is achieved in deceit, and not so designated and hence misleads by the false name, we may regard the appellation to serve the thing to destruction.

"Now, we come to the prime and fundamental feature of 'caste and castaway,' and that is ignorance.

"Fie upon institutions, which uphold the latter, and arrogate to themselves that right — in anything!

"Wherever tyranny has prevailed, and its preparation requires that step, there will be found a corresponding ignorance; not even flattery can always nor bribery, ever, assuage the wrongs against the knowing; and wherever mere dominance was sedulously aspired to and selfishly cherished, ignorance was fostered and maintained among the subjects; the devil's greatest wand is that wherewith he shrewdly stirs the ignorant slothful mass, but tenderly, that it may not awaken beyond his immediate use.

" Whether so-called religious rites or of statecraft, the gloom of uncertain, unenlightened designations of their ministrations by the controlling left the masses in overwhelming and conducted misery. The more resplendent in outward manifestations, therewith, hence the gaudiness in practice opposed to the proper simplicity of their teachings, the less could the uncomprehending unfortunates and dupes, who were furnishing their very marrows and blood for these revelries for a sad pageant of a glossy drill of their cruel deceptions, ever aspire beyond a dazzling superstition and false admiration. But when the knowledge of things, inevitable in such a pernicious course, and events dawned upon them, they burst the encircling manacles of slavery. Humble instruments have led these forces, galled by the emphasis of suffering themselves, the charge of the fearful union of such powers. The outcries of these sufferers are the piercing poignancy of truth, that effectively searches this earth. Knowledge and light are synonymous, they dispel ignorance and gloom.

" And ignorance and gloom go hand in hand. The happy light of joy cannot shine where half the world is kept in ignorance by the machinations of the other.

" No prevailing different degrees of society will exist in a friendly community hence the enemy need not be far sought for — and the one which is within striking distance is the one to be feared, despite any fervent protestations, that the removed, far in the rear, absent cause is the incentive to the danger. While history cannot justify its atrocities, misdeeds cannot rest their justifications on it.

"Where nobility or ruling classes by birth are recognized, or the power by similar means is in countries which do not vigilantly guard against this insidious influence, the unwholesome distinctions are entailed and embodie l which seek maintenance for their own interests and embrace the most pernicious evil. As a potent evidence of the right of universal equality among men, the unrestrained respect for the practical demonstration of popular institutions in my dear old country, the United States, even by scions in the inimical establishments, may itself serve as a criterion. Nobilities esteem their environments and inflict slavery and serfdom on others. Their aversion to American institutions by those who oppose them is written on the pages of antecedent history. Either they were tyrannical oppressors with their abettors, or viciously disregarded all law and order of right, and destroyed all human felicity.

"Man in all conditions loves to progress — he dislikes even to refrain from teaching a like condition in Heaven. But he too often deludes himself in the fact.

"Unfortunately he begins with *that* and ends with *that*, the same, merely his mystery. Hence any ignorance, which sometimes allows over-handed conditions to be fostered and does not embrace even their enlightened extensions for amelioration from the wielders of this overweening power, fortifies itself in grief and embodies the insatiable yet uncomfortable ill, from all kinds of excesses, which its powers allowed it in abuse. A gourmand which will even devour itself in its blind, passionate greed. This disease must be cured and burden lightened by progression back to original purity.

"Now, my dear brethren, what would it seem well for

you to avoid? In the first place, the different adverse
organizations: For they, if only engendering and carrying
on strife against themselves, eventually draw you into
their vortex, under the pretext of your eventual good,
which they pretend to hazard in your favor and be concerned about. And true, every result is embraced in your
eventuality and what earthly cause must not envelop you?

"The remotest points of the earth must be drawn to your
interests! You cannot escape any burden, that may reach
you, and, hence, no enjoyment can be, legitimately, denied
you, if you conduct yourself properly with regard to the
burdens.

"The elements of discords exist in diverse interests: As
long as the theory and practice prevail, to give as little as
will be received for as much as can be obtained, instead of
delivering as much as can be taken for the least requisition, the sole interest of individuals will be in grasping,
and injuries will arise from the struggling, the conduct
being wrong and unreasonable and causing more waste
than would be adequate for actual consumption by all.

"The worst fray is an indiscriminate tug — eventually
the destruction of the thing tugged at. An irreparable
loss; in this case of good principle. And good principle
gives rise to good interest. The destruction of the head,
or judgment, destroys the sight.

"You cannot disregard principle because a momentary
bliss seems to ignore it. It sometimes chances that a success is achieved by illegitimate means; but it is bound to
have its results of illegitimacy. If this were not so, law
and order would be as naught; but you cannot logically
express it in any other way, and the experienced or practical results demonstrate no other conclusion — unless you
reason or practice falsely, as against it, when it is opposed
to you. Then, small principles may be rife with good inter-

est rates, and, therefore, oppressive, but cannot carry good,
substantial interest. If you speculate, that is, if you prevent the natural, daily flow of the currents of daily life,
you stem its stream, for the time being, and may cause an
overflow, and how is your home on its banks to avoid the
inundation, or if only your foundations are weakened, have
you not incurred danger and injury? Or, if you stem the
stream to withhold the supply, for a time, from those lower
down or not possessing your advantages, and you cause a
desert there, will it not consume all with one, mighty, precipitate rush? With destruction on the way, the supply
not only more rapidly exhausted than accumulated but
disastrously so, and loosened on a rampage by its own
force from the unnatural restraint! You relinquish, but
the unnaturally created voracity below is not satiated —
nay, it is so hardened that the major portion of the flood
goes over in waste, but still leaving a torn and destroyed
surface by its very obstinacy to commemorate its history.
Where this accumulation has now been allowed to gather,
let the escape be by a gradual, continuous stream until the
equilibrium has again set in and nature is allowed to
course upon its smiling way. Good men are made by
happy vocations. When once the flood sets in you are
powerless to stop it, or to escape above from the stench
arising from the perished victims left below to vanish thus
in their last remnants from this earth. So lonely and
alone you are even unable to dispose of their sickening
corses and cannot escape their pestilence — which is destruction from God, therefore overwhelming.

"No powerful house arises except permitted through our
vices and fostered by our follies. The transaction may
thus far be legitimate as respects your conduct. You are
dissatisfied and your deal follows. You have a very poor,
unsteady hand.

"A little enjoyment bought you — of indolence. Shifting, you labor and the other takes ease. The advantage gained, your single is trebled by the other's double, for the ratio of advantage is unequal, bears harder on the downward, bounds higher from below and fairly on the swing increases with impetuosity by the slightest maintained incentive. Ah, learn how good is the comparatively stronger element in its tendency out of question to mere ratio! Would you it otherwise?

"Wealth is good — be careful the ratio is not against you. Strength in any progress disregards plain ratio. Once it has well taken up its role, over its well-provisioned, rapidly executed route it grows to great proportions, by its own weight packing its particles and adding the new closer to its body, until it really becomes hard and obdurate. With comparatively little perceptible addition it sweeps a comprehensive surface in its cumbersome way and consumes vaster quantities. Its mere maintenance soon becomes its sole necessity. It adds to its mass continually until all are destroyed, either by being embodied or crushed, when its own destruction inevitably sets in from want of further maintenance. Is the result to either its consumed or itself different?

"Even an opposing might to the one outlined could but result in their mutual stoppage and decay.

"Thus unhappiness is the fruit of mere desire; a prolonged abasement over an early course. Reasoning man may leave a little for the other. The composition is to be made, bound, borne in mind, first over the surface of the earth and then maintained thereon. In the tender solicitude it takes the scum and is amply cared for by the embodiment within.

"Unless the constant chipping from the whole, massing of independent quantities is avoided, the very fundamental principles will be frayed away only to vanish in a spiritual outcry of agony and remain such.

"A free intermingling of parts can only prevent the disintegration of any from dearth or withering hope, or prevent a vast accumulation of a selfish or restricted one from the whole to render destruction to itself feasible by the absorption of all its means from the proper sustenance of the rest.

"Reform is sometimes based on progress. But any abuse of good prepares the way for its destruction where it has piled itself.

"Where evil is wrought, in the first instance, a deep hole or chasm is made, wherein much traveling good must plunge to again make an even way to pass over. Thus reform and sacrifice make even ground.

"You plant a seed and it starts to grow: charm is or not the commonplace to your ordinary eyes. But, having begun with ardent desire, the wish grows ardency. Or, having enlightened your eyes with love, you find treasures and maintain them: the youth or the maiden is oppositely enchantment to the other. Your delusion will be a fond memory even when your judgment has awakened your abandoned apprehension.

"With embellishment you have two-thirds of art: grace draws its inspiration from the surroundings.

"Wealth is an anomaly. It is a natural sequence that all persons should be rich, a happy but none the less true allusion and realizable. A few exceptions may be the unfortunately perverse. The scriptural verification, or the philosophical doctrine of accretion to the strong and attractive from the weak and unretentive or not strongly relative is a disturbing force hard to dispose or eradicate from the unremunerative species.

"The proper enjoyment of anything constitutes wealth

itself for the time being; to secure these recurring times
and in as many instances as nature has provided constitutes the problem. Free intercourse, unrestricted trade
lay the foundation for this system — to favor a few and
restrain the others works its bane. What favors the few?
Your indulgence and the privileges you give them by curtailing yourselves. You should not only not countenance
the wrongful practices of the other, but you should scru-
pulously yourself eschew them and your community will
be rich and prosperous. Your nation, that will employ
all fruits properly wherever produced, will offer you the
satisfaction of the world, as well as the highest patronage,
and will profit thereby and enjoy a lucrative trade, in
equal compensation; but, restricted trade to home production or consumption cannot compel virtue nor prevent
abandon. Due precaution must meet any interference
with a natural right, whilst the observance of the latter
comports more nearly to any mutual compact. The
mutual consolidation of interests in the community life
has not as much relegated natural privileges as intended
to make them more rational. To this end not a restriction but a liberality is required. There are no restrictions
of compact, but there is practically the enlargement of
natural rights therein.

"Winds may blow and stir the things on and above the
surface and cast them down — yet may not move the human
ashes or break a cobweb; but something from within
must cause an upheaval. Should the prudent encroach
the whole domain? Why do rivers congeal deeper with
greater and continued cold? Questions contain their own
answers if philosophically framed.

"What then makes the rich and the poor man?
The former the latter and the latter himself; and the
latter the former. This intricate interlineation is a

perfectly traceable labyrinth with due threaded caution.

"Advantages, at this stage of the world, can only be obtained by overwhelming, mental diligence and characteristic deceit. And can only be accomplished over the weakly, the unwary and the indolent. The opposites to the development of power are harassing circumstances, as all power is beautiful and naturally beneficial; but the happy votary and successful prosecutor of the enlightened course so far should not forget him or herself, when the provisions for necessity have been wrested from this benighted opposition, as to forget the elements of mercy, which, after all, enable him, too, to succeed. Hopelessly irresponsible, individuals are afflicted by extraneous, natural causes over which we have little or no control and always merit the utmost compassion; and, in my old country, they have come the nearest, that I am aware of, to esteeming this a prime law.

"What develops, practically, overreaching power? The catering of all to it. In your lovely, comprehensive country here would you desire to purchase only of yourselves, and thus limit yourselves, with all the surrounding opportunities of no benefit to you; or only obtain from the others what you could not produce or did not, otherwise, possess? Power can wield itself only over necessities. This brings us to economy: Make everything you can yourself for yourself, and obtain from others only what you cannot make for what you can produce. But adduce this with a liberality that brings you the products of the world for your disposal.

"And add to that your products for the world, and Christianity is complete. This is common sense. Thus in order together: Mere economy, intelligent economy, Christian economy or endeavor.

" In a proper sense everything is a necessity, and nothing a luxury; yet, under certain conditions, for the time being anything may become a luxury. Thus, be not deluded by the canted division of necessities and luxuries, for who can presume to know my and your absolute needs, or can determine what is a deprivation and what is not, when the requirements of our constitutions are as diversified as there are principles and means to sustain them. Our ignorance of them is our greatest stumbling-block. To a Christian, these principles present no unenlightened announcements.

"Economy is the employment of all things to use. Ignorant discrimination is equal to willful abuse. Slavery may be a negative as well as an affirmative proposition. Restriction will naturally lead to abuse, to satisfy a certain quantity, while enlargement of provision must curtail single employment to meet the extent. Those who have selfish interests teach forbearance as economy, and absorb the greater portion, while the judicious have plenty in forbearance.

"Economy means to obtain what you reasonably can. It is not unreasonable to deal with the whole world, because your existence therein is not a fault. To limit yourself from useful possibilities is to limit the proper use of them. The space of the world is required to contain itself; the earth is probably not elastic although it may be hollow — in the latter event it will collapse. But it is all the ground you have. The different provisions are not as much for local uses as for interchange. Logically each part is for the support of the other parts, being unable to support itself. Whatever connections therefore contrive for themselves are merely incidental to such productions. Interchange is the rest and strength of the universe.

"When those supplicating for protection constitute the

affluent, and the intrinsic values of their possessions broach
to you their inherent inabilities, these circumstances should
arouse your apprehensions.   Who shall protect you in turn
from them ?   It is in vain to invoke the same power when
that power has sacrificed all in creating the iniquity.

"So-called local pride is a personal hauteur, bringing
but trouble and disappointment. A healthy prosperity
and tranquillity to the community is the affability of the
individuals to the world.

"Nations are not abnormal creatures nor their govern-
ments but man himself in the individual. You cannot
escape your fellow-man to increase your bounty, and certainty grows, beautiful, delightful, with its accumulations,
which is encompassed by range; and beauty comprises and
bounds the earth. Some malcontents would upset everything and create something else in the wind. These create
division in the multitude, then in the individual and are
self-seeking heads.

" You cannot practice economy from gaining nothing, nor
protect what you have not gained. From narrow principles you can gain but a small strip—and all cannot stand
upon it. In this event only the favored few will be
accommodated, of necessity. Establish all the room you
can get for a free engagement: do not imprison yourself
for the battle.

"Can you feed upon your intestines? If another can
produce cheaper or better than yourself, that is his enti-
tled opportunity: help him with your knowledge and support. You are not a natural imbecile : there is a field for
you because there remains so much more to do and your
neighbor has his employment. *He needs your productions
and that is his compensation.* The base of this principle
is broad enough, embracing the world, and affords its own
compensating mission.

"The principle of 'high protection' is wrong because it is a piercing projection, impaling friend or foe, who is forced to encounter it—therefore solely a marauder's implement.

"A protective tariff is the exclusion of the products of anyone, even is what would restrict local production, because on no trade basis with the world, therefore of easy local overproduction and stagnation in unhealthy 'pools'— for selfishness knows no bound save force. Your beautiful country will rapidly build up from and with outside aid; you will benefit them and they you. This is reciprocal free trade; the happy tendency, yet incomplete, must lead to the happy chamber, reached when the final step is taken. As is right, if universally applied free trade would thus evolve itself. The projectors of limited reciprocity contemplated no less and adopted it as an expediency even in their narrow, selfish views because of necessity. And complete reciprocity is the most happy interchange of life—but it is the freest trade possible, which guarantees and gauges benefits and not mere measures, mechanical in their hard sciences. Encouragement is the life of trade—and general trade is the life of man: encouragement must come from someone, first. He who oils the spindles of his running-gears, will have smooth-going vehicles.

"But, how about that nation, that will not exchange with you; or, can produce cheaper what you can, also, produce (that obstetricated *also* itself implies the want of the necessity of its product there, by those means being itself a producer in any direction; hence, note, again, a philosophical question) and will not, or, cannot, take as much from you as you from them—who will suffer most by this obstinacy or inability, or, if they do not admit your products, and you do theirs, who will be the wiser?

"What yields the most breaks the last, of otherwise equal strength against like force — and man is alike the world over.

"If you receive their goods, and they refuse yours, they must take their pay in something, or go without it, thus making you a present — in the latter event, of course, you would rightfully maintain, that you were the gainer by their obstinacy, by no fault of yours. But, they want their pay. *Do not give it to them by a provision, by means of which, they may, at any time, have you, completely, at their mercy: your provision of remuneration is what encourages their trade with you.*

"No medium of exchange is merely adequate, excepting the spiritual understanding by true values. Neither the object, nor worse, the vehicle, can bear it.

"The credit-system and open record, which all the enlightened world now practicably employs, in the main can accomplish the profitable ends of business with security against oppression. The trouble lies in the want of their completion — the worrying, diverting attentions to divergent aspects. This dead, barbaric usage of an insignificant article as a symbol and therefore as the most ready means of manipulation and oppression, requiring every faith to maintain it and yet is the saddest travesty upon credit itself, is the poorest evidence of man's intelligence this day and a burlesque on his supposed advance. The plight of uncertainty brings its own caprice — and uncertainty cannot create complaisance.

"This is not preaching an abstract morality, but is a true deduction. Popular government has proven itself the blessing, not the bane of the world, as is evidenced by my old country. Therefore by a popular interchange of values, based upon a greater credit than has been known before, the world over, with open record and transaction the dawn of prosperity in the welfare of mankind will first gleam in this progressive age, as by the same rule of extended enlightenment and faith the present progress may be traced back in whatever is good therein to such like incipient motions. Read history in pairs, it begets its usufruct, and solve the union with discretion!

"No foreign provision can bankrupt you.

"Rest assured, your industry produced and produces what they want from your natural and accomplished advantages — and if it is business you want, in every sense thereof, then you will find it only beneficially complete and happily unbroken, in meeting these charges on you at the best advantage.

"Imagine a farmer producing solely for his own living on and from his farm — what inducement, what incentive, which alternatives? And could the world permit this, for his and its own enlightenment?

"Yet, suppose, you become indebted to these others for their products, what will they have? Gold and silver and your lands and such products, which they cannot produce, or as well, and yet want — must want, in all reason, as already shown. It is folly in you to add to their values anything, which may bind you and no one else, excepting, again, that it be as a matter of mere industry, when, being compensated as such, you have the inevitable profit of labor; but, your fiat to a worthless article, makes a baby of a reeking rag or a cymbal of your sounding brass and ignorance — gold or silver move no degree, but, are a poorer solder than even lead!

"Why do we esteem vanity our highest glory, when it leaves such terrible heartaches in its stead? God places in nature the symbols of good and evil that daily may be read the living page of awful yet beautiful truths of life. Pointed maxims are dead creeds.

"But, you say, you do not wish to be confined to 'farming' and 'mining'—as though there were any difference, but, want to make 'pretty things,' too.

"Well, granting your whim, that the one vocation supersedes the other or is less a duty or labor, if conscientiously prosecuted or more 'respectable,' should everybody else be compelled to trade with you, in the first instance because you wish to follow a fancy with your friends; but is not your scheme one to compel these to purchase from you at your own terms, or better to have all other resources therefor cut off, to enrich yourself by the monopoly? Put yourself, mentally, in the place of a monopolist and reflect.

"Would you not, cheerfully, extend this monopoly over the whole world and accept from every government the protection for your goods as the sole ones to be sold, and cry, 'blessed protection'; is your love of country, in the abstract, more than your greed; and would anyone, other than yourselves and the few, comparatively, you would select and wield, be commensurately benefited?

"Two nationalities or races are to-day from divers sources and causes at the apex of practical life in its empty enjoyments. Without home or land, exiles in, but the product and possessors, in a measure of natural freedom of care, of the world, one enjoys life in the incipiency of dawn but in ignorance, the other is satiated to an abstract and abandoned endeavor. The first, the victim of mankind and original own folly, the other its own, while the former rises into light by the beaming grace of redemption, the latter might almost perceive this abandoning gloom still settling upon itself; but is the world to emanate from its humblest, and prophesy "—

CHAPTER XXX.

TIME HAS FLOWN.

A QUARTER of a century ago (this twenty-fifth anniversary observance of the event reminding us forcibly of the occurrence) Penrod Hilbuck was discovered at his desk, serene and quiet and complacent in death; a contented aspect of features marked his restful repose. The shock to the community can be better imagined than described, as the sad intelligence coursed like lightning to its heart; consonantly to his teachings, it would not have been to respect him, not to believe that he had gone to his peaceful rest, and all utterances by one accord so beautifully interwove his departure with that, preceding by less than five years, of his beloved unforgotten Kathleen, that the pathway o'er which he had trod, seemed enveloped with such a bliss of roses that scarcely a sigh could be suppressed to pass over a similar one.

The solemn purpose of a cherished joy, in purity, is, ever, the disillusioned penetration of gloom.

Resting, in their silent chambers, side by side, the earthy bond connects them, as it disunited them: by the walls of the grave. But, annually, those graves are strewn with flowers by an admiring people, thankful that these had lived to show their love of beauty and the beauty of love, for his instructions and services to them, coming alone, would have been a service; and, he loved her and they loved each other, and she bore with her his reward, as her distinction the object of true devotion.

Annually, the seasons have wept and joyed again over

their resting-places; and the tributes of flowers and tears to the dead are a token of the withering from which springs new hopes of joy. In the language of the old school-master, when he returned from his first voyage: "The earth is one surprise; it overhangs all its shadows!"

But he too has passed away, from surprise and shadows both, to the beyond, and the elderly ones, of the early stirring times, from which this present prosperity immediately dates, are alive only in their works which will never die, in loving memories and in art, the earthly thing, which has striven to maintain their earthly figurements, by stone, paint and *threads*. We gaze with wonderment upon these delineations; new agencies are at work among us and in their places, yet they preceded them and gave the impetus and are the foundation!

Young Penrod Hilbuck Mason has arisen to the greatest prominence of affairs, to the utmost commensurate with his youth and age; his abilities are of the highest order, and his integrity and morality, as though it were possible for his great namesake, in addition, to have shed "his mantle" upon him, are an illumination to mankind. He could barely remember the elder Penrod's devoted attentions to him, as little more than an infant; how he directed even his amusements to intelligence, and made the pursuit of early knowledge the pleasure of or a pastime to him. But although early and suddenly bereft of the attention, that would have fostered his every good attribute, he never forewent the inclinations which were so kindly indicated by this master of the human arts and mind.

Thus, his connection with the newspaper office, which is handled by an able, honorable, conscientious faculty, gives him that distinction, which nature, at some times and in certain places, allows to a subject: he is looked upon, by nature and acquirements and perseverance, as the center of embellishment, from which all could radiate with becoming credit to themselves, for, he is inherently modest and pure.

Are there qualities, strictly earthly, which nature may, through its spiritual connections and flights throughout the universe, transmit to their following, or leave behind to constitute a following? Young Penrod must have delighted his illustrious sponsor. While the latter's spirit, in the nature of things, being in his craved rest and happy union, could not imbue him, yet the spirit that moved the former as a result of or from the latter, was the one he left behind; the living spirit of his faith, in his work; that he could transmit, and that solely be now available to the former, because that spirit alone remained connected with the deed.

Dead are all the spirits gone, dead to this world —
Their work was done, and fusing to a higher point,
Their vapors cannot fall in clarified reform,
But lingering form the ether of the beauteous sky.
The falling is from that twixt heaven and earth,
The vain outreaching; thus their efforts fail,
Since all of earth no choice can them avail.
A manifestation, seemingly from yon bourn,
Is by we creatures' efforts not here born,
But what may come is sent by that Yored Power,
Which sends here that which will endure fore'er.
'Tis vain to hope that earthly things can help,
And hopelessly for earth its spirits t' envel'pe;
Nor do the spirits supplicate the Lord —
The Lord implies and they know but His Word.
With too much early striving, hence, therefore,
He took his reason; whither was it borne?

Things are great to us, compared with that to which we were previously accustomed; thus in panegyrizing the achievements, in this community, for its quarter of a century it is only a comparison, and the completion is still far off.

———

CHAPTER XXXI.

HILBUCK.

A beauteous state ; a charming city this jeweled Hilbuck,
It built its fountains in the rocky sides,
And with its pinions formed the sturdy flights,
Which swept the air through storm and clouds and lights,
Nor when the gloom was close with its black mantle's shroud,
That e'er it faltered ; but green its e'er refreshened base,
And with the course as meetly to its, *lightning*, mate.

GENIUS is unfolded by grand opportunities; and opportunities are unfolded by meek genius.

Hilbuck has become a glorious, a delightful city, or rather circumference; one of the capital spots of the world — but, they are all that, now — no, no, in fact, they have become one, one city — one world, with parks and lakes and oceans, and grand mountains and grottos and canons, and beautiful streams, all by way of general embellishments, and uses; for, lightning has drawn all together — melted into one glowing mass — the warm impulse of the heart, and its correlative, the dashing fluid, as its visible steed. Its work is never a slow progress, though sometimes its uncompleted circulation will leave a momentous unfinished or partial wreck.

Penrod Hilbuck never saw his beloved United States again; the old poet (together they are where he predicted) had a Heaven-sent premonition of his friend's early departure, whither he himself followed soon. Hilbuck had felt impressed, that his beautiful, typical American

state of Ohio — its feet laved in the "Beautiful River,"
resting the rear one on the "Old Dominion" and stepping
speedily on the bright, velvety carpet of "Blue Grass;"
"Gemmed" at the "Wolverine" (voracious) capped brow,
between the "Keystone" of its fortunes and "Hoosier
State," rotund, shining, fecund "Buckeye," poisonous to
be devoured; "freedom" and "union" at its base, a
"beautiful outlook" at its head, "virtue, liberty and
independence" at its heart and the mighty right of earth's
fruitful industry, an "empire" in the world — should
never see him again. But he lies in ignorance of the
developing changes that have been wrought in his
beloved domain.

> We love the old, all-failing things of Past,
> The useless traps that call their memories dear —
> To clean our hearts in moments from our days,

and could he now comprehend the intelligence that a new
state, a young unsophisticated thing, had to build the new
foundation of a worldly progress, while old states were
crumbling, but so benighted in their gloomy structures
that they could perceive nothing but their most immediate
surroundings, he would have lamented the failings of old
age and experience, and, while glorying that his own
country was the fountain-head of refreshment to the
world, must have, pityingly, followed the old orders to
their graves. Make a habit of success of undertakings;
but make the undertakings proper, too. Avoid prejudice;
eschew cant, and taste a little of the bitterness of woe, to
tone you up, that you may sympathize with the afflicted.

What land may prosper by sudden convulsions? Though
the filth may be covered thereby, it takes much righteousness to do it.

No greater monument could exist to him, to the public

and private unselfish and enlightened efforts of Penrod Hilbuck, than the practical demonstration and realization of his tenets. But a grand work of art, nevertheless, such as the annals of the world do not, to our comprehension, disclose a parallel, has been erected to his memory by an appreciative populace. Artistic genius had received a wonderful stimulus from his doctrines, everybody obtained such unbroken employment by his enlightenment, which made them a part of the science of life, that it is not to be wondered at, that it exhausted itself by jubilance, for the time being, to his remembrance.

A huge edifice of gray polished and ornamentally chiseled granite forms the body of the building (co-temporaneous, detailed records will give you facts and figures, while ready facilities to give the sight will not allow you to forego the pleasure of a personal inspection, well to be rewarded for beholding the untrammeled and delightful genius of man), then follows the interweaving of science and art, almost identical as they are, blending into pleasant shades, the results of discovery and invention, production and application, that not a metal, nor a pictorial device, is forgotten in the embellishment and durability of the mausoleum.

How he loved the fellowship of mankind and so taught its indispensable benefits here, the gentle passions, the yearnings, the doubts, tribulations and fears, and the impatience, which sometimes mars human tranquillity, all have their resemblances, in the graceful delineations of shade and material, in their suggestive, exquisite outlines.

The building rests on an eminence, which overlooks the surrounding country and upon the immediate entrance of the harbor, the open portals of the world, created so by nature herself, and this principal entrance of the stately portal as though typical of the next earthly discoveries is directly on the north, and the principal portal itself looks that way. A broad avenue leads up the incline, over which pass the elevating cars on almost invisible tracks, seeming to come into existence when required and then they disappear. As the whole memorial is a speaking paragon, this may be likened to the course of mental discipline upon proper instruction, by which the smooth aspect of the way itself is a shielding light of reflection.

This course is daily cleaned by a flood of clear water over it discharged by an electrical clock-work.

The cars themselves are marvels of human delight, which transport the passengers to the portals above, moving noiselessly by power transmitted from beneath invisibly, and constructed wholly of bright polished metals and glass, in which enter all the fantasies of color as though to bear study in the waiting expectations into all the realms of bliss. The exterior walls are adjustably removable, leaving a strong railing of clearest, crystal glass, making protection in that regard even an invisible obstacle. Mechanically moving fans waft fresh breezes into the compartments, which may be created by readily placed partition of, also, glass. Isolation is not accompanied by concealment, and is really only employed by those requiring a secluded atmosphere for the time being from physical need.

On either side of this avenue grand pillars arise, typical of historical facts; on either side, respectively, the noble figures of Adam and Eve stand in the entrance to the way, heroic size, of gold, but so refined and administered as to intimately resemble the texture and coloring of the human skin, which together with the speaking attitudes of the figures make them very realistic and even awful, so little removed from our ideas of the visible angel, that we are glad that they are only our own productions and that we know it, especially as at night their countenances are electrically illuminated and a halo of glory surrounds their heads, which we have placed there, however; thus, they present the beginning. At times sadly intoned, musical renditions sweetly, softly emanate between their outlined lips, and when the blending, great harmony of all the figures produce a wave, or ocean of charmed execution, of hope, at stated periods, the world's delights seem to be wafted, giving rise to entrancing reflections; this is a popular resort.

As space would be too brief, there need be no attempt at describing the marvels of suggestive possibilities, demonstrated in metals and mould and by hammer, that are portrayed here — the grand figures, which represent the various struggles, ever upwards against the deepening gloom to light.

A punishment on the way of progress and elevation, until shortly before the last era the greatest hopelessness is depicted, easily described as the age of philosophical transcription. A little dawn becomes perceptible — the tendency upwards, the gloom forever serene.

But so realistic and fiery is every flash of light, and so demoniacal is every burst of passion, as betrayed here by man's skillful counterfeits, to honor the man who suggested their existence and removal, as to be lesson, unmistakably, in their artistical expressions; and a solemn music, in tender tones, recites the incidents of woe, in thrilling heart-rending inflections, yet sweetly counseling peace to the troubled heart, through faith and perseverance to the certain glory beyond.

Man's mechanics, through his latest accessory, or his arrival into the present age, almost hold the throbs of the universe in his hands, and could communicate, from a common center, the impulses of his joys and terrors — for the removal of the latter.

Arrived at the top, a broad expanse of granite flooring, roofed over with a labyrinth of beauty in blending of threads, all *strings* of glowing electrical lighting, and the hues and shades of metallic coloring, lofty arched vaults, with the brilliance of the lights in cut glasses, vari-hued globes, on the wires, like veritable arteries — all is a burst of glory, all the more remarkable, as superseding all the wondrous things below.

Weeping figures, in mankind's size and of its distressed attitudes, are distributed all over in the places prepared therefor, and represent miseries of the devotees of this world in their various aspects, a contrast, in the neighborhood of this tomb, to its well-earned, exquisite rest.

The abnormal aspect of lamentation for the peaceably departed cannot detract from the latter's glory, except by the mere appearance. There is too much hope beyond!

What a touching scene, at a glance, of what suffering may have wrought upon this enjoyable earth; here disease, there lamentation, supplication, slavery, the restlessness and brutality of passion, the worn, abashed regard of vice or indolence, or timidity its utter hopelessness, frustrated purposes, vain ambitions, the frenzy of abandon, and last, but not least, the loss of reason — all ignorance so susceptible to computation — so that this portal presents the entrance at grief, which is gladly passed to the silence within the chamber of death, where all the ingenuity of man is expended in its marvels, the works to embellish, the ideas and reality of this last resting-place, reveling in the most gorgeous devices, an overwhelming finale of fitting plaisance, with still a tender pathos of regard for the depths of a profound solitude. As life-like productions of the human are here presented, as to so nearly produce them, to require conviction of the counterfeits, the elements of motion and the articulations of speech are omitted, as the productions of man, because their addition would make the spectacle truly gruesome — whereas, now it beautifully embodies its true idea and fascinates the beholder.

Death they paint you, and alone they see you thus!

The artist must exhaust himself in rendering the beauties of the human figure. Kathleen sits, in this portrayal, demurely beautiful, pensive as in life, in a fitting robe of white; her regard is to the circumscribed distance; at her feet sits the master, Hilbuck, gazing radiantly up into her countenance; a feeling of inexpressible peace pervades the view — no illusion, but a stationary figure. They appear in the mere semblance, grand enough though, of their own human forms and figures, and speak, as likenesses, out of their Past in this blissful quiet and inseparation of the Present — no attempts at idealization, and the lesson is that purity accomplishes its surroundings; love is an accomplishment to purity; but a serene temperament and a calm devotion portray the unmistakable developments of joy.

The spiritual world is represented, and as fittingly at this point, in its surroundings, about and above, as to tread equally as mazily this realm as our best suppositions may describe in it; such an easy, vapory, yielding disposition, that never vanishes entirely, but gleams with the faces here and there which we forever conjecture to our aids, which we truly invoke by their strong, pure considerations; but our fancies are measured by their earthly origins.

Gloriously this temple towers, a beacon-light, far out to sea.

The city or rather the environments of Hilbuck extend, many miles from this point, in every direction, and the relative abodes, until another practicable center, of the machinery of general distribution and for substitution, is reached, embraces all around beyond; electrical contrivances noiselessly, swiftly, in ornamental exhibitions, or invisibly, contrive a decided net-work, or arterial system of communication and all kinds of transportation; the whole country, the entire world, in fact, can be one continuation of illumination, for wherever foot of man can or did tread, there, with his *united* might, nothing can withstay his construction, and no expense is considerable. Floods of harmony may swell over the earth, and can be garnered and preserved for future use, or the visual reflections of the most distant friends or personages can be transmitted to view while any conversation may, at the same time, ensue between them — in fact, localities and distances but serve any individual convenience, or desire, as they are intended, always, to do; no unusual occurrence is to hear millions of good-nights exchanged where good-mornings are simultaneously answered.

The electrical age of purveyance and conveyance has carried with it the electrical current of human hearts to feel and express tender, communicated regards. It is no wonder that one is tempted to believe that God works in graduated progression; but such a fallacy is self-apparent in the fact that those before us were not merely the stepping-stones of our existence. But we are their revelations, out of their ruins, by our reform.

God has created eternity for the good and the wicked, with no fascination to delude an interchange or exchange hereafter between them.

Abiding no further, if we use every facility in our ingenuity, for proper device, we do more than those who accomplish a sort of happiness for themselves and are astonished thereat.

CHAPTER XXXII.

A TYPICAL MEETING.

AN annual meeting of representative men delegated from the several circles is held at a different place each time, at which the occurrences and statistics of the past year are discussed. The general welfare and progress are the themes about which the sole concern centers and the few, simple remedies of legislation are easily adjusted. Law is man's obedience solely by his intelligence, which regulates its necessity as well.

No complicated order of government, in the world nor at these meetings, is involved. A thorough daily report of our affairs, an analysis of the same and the quick and ready transmission kept up over the rapid and easy communications enable everyone to be informed and make the items of our lives a scientifical calculation. Mere chance and every effort at mystification have strenuously been banished. The world is to be an open book.

It is customary to select an eminent personage to preside at each meeting — this year the choice fittingly fell upon Penrod Hilbuck Mason, representing the circle of Hilbuck. This profound scholar is the embodiment of unselfish and exalted nature.

The meeting this year was held in New York circle, the large hall being on the former site of Wall street, but extending from which the cleared and beautified stretches are acres of charming lawn and shrubbery and trees, nature having been allowed to exert its pleasant and invigorating but cultivated self. This structure, with its grounds, dimensions and embellishments is the beautiful realization of man's better desires and is sweetly marvelous. Yet, the times are rife with such enterprises and surprises upon surprises.

The simple government, involving but few functionaries, gives no room for bickerings of honor, or the adjustable means give no choice of iniquity in its ministration. The various officers are those of the present inquiry, while the affairs practically carry on themselves in the natural, unswayed course of man. It is not likely the world progresses by the elevation of a few. As man is elevated to the higher recognition of his order he remains with charity in the fit enforcements of his intelligence and discretion. The natural law is obedience to simple compunctions.

Thus, developments have broadened the base on which mankind mutually stands in consideration. The less is the regard to and power of the individual over the mass.

Mr. Mason had an admirable audience to address. Everyone in the world might be his auditor by the system of telephone, and every eye view him by the system perfected to that aspect. What with the preservation of his words to be identically rendered in sound again a thousand times, at will, cogitated upon, recorded in or against his behalf, if the latter were his charge, the precaution of the speaker of to-day to his vast audience, to whom he is visible as well everywhere, and yet perceives but a few with his eyes, his responsibility, all tends to test a man of integrity. Mr. Mason is profoundly identical with the times—the knowledge from the Past is his glimpse into the Future, yet his hope. In no voluminous expression he spoke:

"We feel overjoyed at our temporal aggrandizement and personal liberty brought about by universal freedom from the tyranny of man. How long shall we enjoy them? The ghostly apparitions answer out of all days, 'Until we enslave ourselves again; until we abuse them. Until idleness, by supplanting enthusiasm, burdens again the few with the welfare of all, when the patience and strength of the former will not endure, and the latter are overwhelmed with the precipitated load. When the few absorb the substances of the many and all miserably perish, the former from surfeit, the latter effeit. Faults are interchangeable and give rise to new eras.'

"Since at the present the world has become ours, wrested from the tyrants whose semblance was not man, we are no longer divided. Our ports are opened and all are freely accessible. Why? Because we have so much trade with one another.

"No longer need we tremble at the unsophisticated touch of various parts. Great schools flourish over the world, where every principle is taught as humanity may unfold it.

"Now a personage may discourse to all the world by his lips and in his presence, from the north-pole or other extreme, the east, the west or the equator, and all others be simultaneously attentive and appreciative. And the mother at the cradle imbibe the knowledge and impart it with its impressions fresh and unobliterative in her endearings to her instructed darlings. The happy mechanic is at his bench and his shop is at his home, with the assistance of his family and his guide and instruction to them. Know that old land-marks have vanished. We have come into the presence of *Heaven-blessed science*, and man is not man's master, but is acquiring the knowledge to be his own, if possible.

"Now when the concerts of the world render the old masters and the new in union, under some master director at now this now that point and each musician, unnumbered, discourses his notes and part into the ready transmission of sound everywhere, what a rendition of sound — one band the world over and one audience! Such entrancing sounds literally, and the charmed sights which accompany every hour, are they not the value of life? Love is the value of a laborious day. Labor is the cost of love and its produce the price of exhaustless destruction of vice. Such are a few realities, to which we now refer.

"What we have produced is manifest in the higher intellectuality and material welfare of man.

"Now since the old walls of fortification have crumbled, even though their departure long afterdates the absence of savage warfare; now that whole streets have lost their rental values and fortunes, thereby raised their scions into equality with man, that is, the hard-hearted existence of monopolists has yielded to the sway of progress and humanity, the sigh is that of emancipation and an air of self-relief. It seems marvelous to us how conditions could so long remain contrary to the intelligence of mankind; how sordid motives even could so long sway all destinies.

"What is traffic? When it is extended to the home for its affairs and transactions and the family is the coadjutor with the master in charge and responsibility, then our wonderful citizenship, our endeared manhood and womanhood is appreciated. When these homes extend to and within the bounds and bounties of surrounding nature and the vigor and delights and healths of the community are understood, the benign blessing of God is comprehended, untrammeled by the artifice of man. These beautiful features are the undoubted progress of ourselves. But, God forbid, can we sink to the level of beasts again, when we denied ourselves our blessings and harbored ourselves worse than they who must yield before us?

"In these beautiful endeavors, that have reached into all the universe, see we not the beckoning reach of art, of science, of knowledge, of truth? Surely there is a balm to be sought with confidence and universal fellowship.

"When we behold in our midst, in this renovated and beautified, reclaimed field, the circle in which we are now discoursing, the grand structure and monument, erected to that benign genius of mankind, whose efforts have cast light and speed, sound and sight into this comprehensive universe, then may we not rejoice at the groveling edifices that have been removed to make place for it? The fire of electricity, that first taught the mind to strive for comprehension!

"To engender in a man's own industry his concentrated efforts is to elevate his character.

"As in former times the rule of one man power, or monarchical government, gave way to confidence in the real knowledge of the elevation of responsible man, so in industrial enterprises have we discovered his individual integrity. Accomplished after the knowledge of business men and the so-called respectable people was reared beyond their mere routines and after their moralities were cleansed.

"Thus we have arrived at the threshold of prosperity; the light of day has dawned upon our beaming minds."

A great burst of acclamation greeted this admirable effort and man.

It is true this day has advanced far beyond even the expectations of former times, but thanks to their progressive thinkers and principally doers we are in enjoyment of fellowship and that humanity that enables one to realize something more than the theoretical eminence of man in the creation of things.

Nothing is more conspicuous than that eminent structure, referred to by Mr. Mason, erected in New York circle to that eminent genius of light who flourished there and led the course practically to our emancipation, first by means, then in thought and deed. But elsewhere, and scattered o'er are the tributes in such art and wonders as man seems scarcely then to have dreamed to the memories of many great personages, who have realized the destiny of man in his higher and highest order and opened the way.

At the conclusion of this session a grand exhibition was given, as illustrative of the many features, which have now arisen to give still greater hope for the future. As may be apprehended the basis laid of our progress and prosperity is *knowledge and freedom from the dominion of man in the realms of reason and force.* How unchimerical this is in practice we have in our results. Popular government proven the truth, abrogated government in interference of the whole and responsibility of man acquired as the service to the union of mankind; while those ties are abolished, depriving man of his natural responsibilities and depraving him. Such sweet regulation as accompanies civilization is the destiny of elevation. The exhibition referred to was a magnificent drill and parade of school children over the immense floor of the hall solidly laid with gold. *Their feet trod the mammon of former times.* No greater monument, in this physical development of representation produced, could have been erected to the originator of the " Rays of Light," than this sublime perpetuation of his unique but divine ideas, though grand works of art commemorate otherwise, too, this noble, benign old seer.

Where the old business blocks have given their place of monopoly to bright and natural scenes; when following upon the periods of depression the same means that had caused them were organized, and had caused them for this purpose, to benefit by the depreciations thereof, but mankind had developed a new insight, aided by the disclosures of honest, able men; aided by the electrical currents of physics and the human heart, and spread the concerns in the hands of the individuals all over the world, there upon one such cleared spot commends a huge, electrical buckeye the philosopher Hilbuck on the site of his birthplace—and as an emblem of protection against "internal disease." Protection must come from without; and the trouble is of living alone—be it in selfishness, state or society.

ADDENDA.

ADDENDA.

"That distinguished citizen's" (an ex-president) "humble carriage, to-day, insures, furthermore, as the most potent worth of its rulers, the perpetuation of this Republic." — *A diplomat.*

"A patron of education."

He paused not where the scions said
To lift, there, an imperial head;
But, humbly followed with his clan —
Arm side by arm, man with the man!

Not cared he, that he should be known:
The cause was honored by what was shown
To meet the approval of his heart
In pleased procession as his part.

Such dignity never bends to harm;
This simple pride gives the alarm
To scheming breakers of the state;
The simple mind is wisdom's mate.

The gait, which so unfaltering stepped,
Was the calm pace where sages wept:
To find the like had saved great realms;
Ah! with such minds at statecrafts' helms!

With what awed feeling viewed the throng
This man, so plain, forever strong;
For, naught will blemish his pure shield,
Which he has shown how, well, to wield.

A simple act lives thousand's long;
Pride must crush that where it among
To gain distinction tramples right;
Thus, fares extinction by its might.

In word the deed, a servant's meed
Is his distinction by his creed;
That, which he follows, is his word;
That, as he goes, his deed, his lord.

Therewith you judge him, without fear,
This is, your fellow-man's career —
Therewith you honor him for time,
Forever and fore'er the same.

And, on that day, *he* served that cause
Beyond all oratory, laws —
He preached no sermon — yet, there lives
In history, its, which he there gives.

With blessings such a man goes hence,
With blessings there received, and whence
The spirit of his last act and ways
Will make immortal — virtuous Hayes.

DEDICATED TO THE MEMORY

—— OF ——

CHRISTOPHER COLUMBUS.

1894.

COLUMBUS.

(Dedicated to the Duke of Veragua.)

Whence blew the fearful storm-wind of your sorrow —
 And let you hope, when others would have quailed;
Whence was it that your Faith could ever borrow,
 Hence thus you found where others would have failed.

When storms blew hard, no less dissension's voice,
 Your ever tried and stilled tongue spoke, Peace;
Nor did you quail, when scarcely an earth's choice
 Gave you upon its domain any ease.

As flight of bird is, for conjecture, course,
 So, are the likely comments of most men;
Nor most, for hope, who have the greatest source,
 The least may drivel to their utmost ken. ·

Ah, with what sorrow must, e'er, ignorant cant
 Roam in the light of future, illumed days!
The bliss of knowledge is, then, no more scant,
 Than when sequences do not heed their ways.

We feel your weight of woe, now, that we know
 How right were your endeavors and your creed,
In substance, though, what little depth did show,
 Your brethren did retard your wisdom's speed.

Whence sped that wisdom, to your meagre range,
 And caused your faithful soul to glow therewith?
And whither flew it, when all thoughts were strange,
 To stay, abidance, for the ever myth?

And oft you paced a painless deck at night,
 In sweet communication with your certain hope —
Oft, there was solace which another's fright
 Had turned to gall and bitter wormwood's scope.

Why did you not concern yourself for power —
   Why were not worldly glories *all* your ends?
You sped o'er seas, that troubled every hour —
   You caused your sighs to offer all amends.

Ah! faintless — had your heart not known its store,
   'Tis doubtful, that one thought or deed had fostered —
There were the creeds, which left you, all the more,
   By which your every solemn creed was pestered.

'Twas less the object of discovered land,
   Than that your Faith had learned its plenteous creed —
An independent creed — from God's demand.
   Alone, a solemn version of "God-speed!"

No church nor state or dominance of man
   Could ever quell such outburst of the soul —
Nor did it owe, thus, even, its brief span! —
   Betrayed it would have lost its complex whole.

When thou hast fought and, falling, hast sworn true,
   Up sped the incense of a virtuous vow
And you were worthy of no name ; but, through
   The speeding sense of Imminence Art Thou!

Your Master may not speak in thunderous tones
   Nor hush His silent Breath in speechless vows;
It is not imminence, alone, atones
   Nor fallacy, by speeding, that allows.

In what a prayer is uttered, so, it speeds —
   It passes over every thought and range
Nor is delayed, detained, whate'er, its needs,
   Is fostered over every list and mange.

A prayer is true, because it finds the truth
   And, ever, is fulfilled for every wish —
Constrained and sadly, never lost, forsooth,
   It finds its solace, then its ends' finish.

In recollecting, now, your deeds and fame,
   It is no less, that we ascribe them true;
In having seen, with us, who bear your name,
   We cherish that, which was but simply due.

That gentle maid, that youth, who saw *our* might,
　With which it was our "grace" to entertain —
But saw reflected what may come of right;
　This principle we ask them to maintain.

Maintain their ancestor's benignant Faith —
　Recall, no "nobleman" was, greatly. he,
When all the world became in aftermath
　His pure admirers from a people's see.

As self-styled gentry, trust a people's vows,
　Who have not catered to a cringing lot —
Found, for the world, here, are no empty shows —
　Here is devised his own, his sole, pure plot.

Learned from sublimest lesson of this life :
　An ancestor's desire and his fray ;
Seen, when the scene of all his thoughts were rife —
　What thought, what right, that you should hence delay ?

But, being noble, of this Country, sole —
　What other title such estate as this ?
There leaves you but one stake for honor's role
　To cast all other ranks aside, amiss.

And, with these people, feel your honors grow —
　As, by the people, thus, he glorys, hence —
And for all people let yourselves bestow,
　Then this your land will serve your virtuous sense.

Democracy is truth and truth untorn :
　Nobility is wrath and that, too, steeped ;
When realms have passed with scions, there, forlorn,
　Perceive *all* kings where each has not o'erleaped.

No staid reward can fit Columbus' blood,
　Than such, that would not, save for people's good ;
Himself aspiring, let us place your spud
　With all aspirants for, here, hardihood.